A funny, irreverent novel which could serve as a primer on how to make a classy stag film, *Blue Movie* is not for the squeamish. Anyone who expects it to be another of Terry Southern's maniacal, absurd, kinky pieces of naughtiness will not be disappointed . . .

'Terry Southern is vastly talented, a master of macabre humour, well ahead of his literary competitors . . . and bold enough to be banned in Denmark!'
SAN FRANCISCO CHRONICLE

'Makes *Candy* look prudish'
BOSTON GLOBE

Also by Terry Southern in Panther Books

Red-Dirt Marijuana and other tastes
Flash and Filigree

Terry Southern

Blue Movie

Panther

Granada Publishing Limited
Special overseas edition published in 1974 by
Panther Books Ltd
Frogmore, St Albans, Herts AL2 2NF
Reprinted 1974
This edition published in 1975

First published in Great Britain by
Calder and Boyars Ltd 1973
Copyright © Terry Southern 1970
Made and printed in Great Britain by
Hazell Watson & Viney Ltd
Aylesbury, Bucks
Set in Monotype Times Roman

For the great Stanley K.

Poetry is not an expression of
personality, it is an escape
from personality; it is not an
outpouring of emotion, it
is a suppression of emotion –
but, of course, only those who have
personality and emotions can
ever know what it means
to want to get away from those
things.

T. S. Eliot
The Sacred Wood

ONE

'...now dig this...'

1

'Then *she* says, now dig this, *she* says . . .' and he broke up laughing, a strange, rasping laugh, for maybe the fourth time since he started what was shaping up as an interminable story, '. . . *she* says: "Listen, who do I have to fuck to get *off* this picture?!?" ' And he began his final laugh, his boss laugh, the kind that quickly, smoothly, turns into a monstro *cough*. The way some people always laugh till they cry, he would always laugh till he coughed. In many respects though, he was considered quite a grand guy, tops in his field, etcetera, etcetera—and about seven people listening to the story either laughed or coughed along with him. Actually, what he was was a curious kind of opportunistic film-producer—Sid Krassman his name, a hairy, chunklike man —at ease in every B-phase of the medium, from *Girls of the Night* to *Tamerlaine*, 'just so long as it puts some flour in the barrel,' as he was a bit too fond of saying. 'Put *this* in the barrel, you crooked cocksucker!' was an occasional riposte on the part of certain outrageously deceived participants in his projects, as they delivered a terrific straight right to his mouth, followed by a whirlwind flurry of chopping blows to the head and shoulders.

'*Hurt* me?' Sid would reply with a sly grin when queried later about the quality of the attack. 'Sure it hurt me—ha, ha, I cried all the way to the bank!'

Among those who took advantage of the terminal-type cough to steal away to a more active, and less demanding, corner of the part was Les Harrison—handsome, forty-

9

three-year-old vice-prez of Metropolitan pix, whose father more or less owned the studio. Les, or as he was more often called, 'the Rat-Prick' (tonal emphasis being on the word 'Rat'—so that it was pronounced '*Rat* Prick'), had had quite enough of this 'compulsive loser,' and simply shook the loose ice cubes in his glass as he stood to indicate, *noblesse oblige*, that he needed a refill.

Sid stared after him, almost wistfully, as though he felt he'd really blown it, since in his heart of hearts he had hoped to show Les that a certain Sid Krassman possessed some kind of secret knowledge, something that could hold seven people spellbound, or at least speechless, for seven minutes. By analogy and extension, this could apply to a seven-million-dollar picture, which Les was capable of springing for. So Sid was somewhat brought down by the departure.

Among those who remained, however—less out of volition than lethargy and a supremely invulnerable detachment— was Boris. 'Boris,' 'B.,' 'King B.,' as he was variously known, was a film director, and he was the best in the biz. Of his last ten films, seven had won the Golden Lion at Cannes, the Golden Palm at Venice, and whatever other festive and critical acclaim one might think of. Besides this they were all smash at the box. The genius, beauty (and hard-ticket appeal) of his work was so striking and undeniable that it had finally penetrated even the bone bugbrow of Hollywood itself. So that his two most recent pictures had copped the coveted Oscar—and, in short, he was swinging. Except that by now he was very tired. He had seen too much, though he was only thirty-four, and yet he had not seen what he was looking for. He had made twenty pictures—all of them dealing with the three things no one understood. Each of the films was completely different, and yet, to him, they were somehow all the same—like chapters in a fantastic soap opera that can never be finished because the end has not been written. The films were concerned with (what in his interviews he occasionally referred to as) the 'Big Three,' or in lighter moments, the 'Wig Tree': *Death . . . Infinity . . .*

and the *Origin of Time*. These posed interesting questions all right—though his ceaseless inquiry had often earned him nothing more than the dubious sobriquet of 'dirty creep,' 'Commie fag,' and especially from the panicked Hollywood contingent, 'crazy ass-hole,' but, much worse still, the ineffectualness (in his own mind) of the films had exhausted him. He felt that his delving, his probes, had come to nothing —a glimpse here, a glimmer there, a startling 600-millimeter shot into a fathomless crevice of absurd wonder—but nothing to go ape about, although he was surrounded by people who did just that. And now, for the last two years, he had been profoundly idle—not even reading books, much less anything from the deluge of scripts that arrived daily at an office he never visited.

Although he was thought of as a 'director,' he was really a *film-maker*—in the tradition of Chaplin, Bergman, Fellini— an artist whose responsibility for his work was total, and his control of it complete. In certain instances, however, despite his acclaim, his films had met interference. Movie houses had been closed in Des Moines, in Albuquerque, in Temple, Texas . . . and in the staunch little Catholic town of Chabriolet, France, there was a warrant out for his arrest. 'Obscene,' 'indecent,' 'immoral,' 'pornographic' were the charges. The studio chuckled, of course—what did they care about a handful of red-neck religious-nut hunkies ('They're whackin' off to it, fer Chrissake!') in the general world market—but it gave the B. curious pause. In the idleness of his past two years he had sat still for the showing of several so-called stag-films, and had found them so pathetically disgusting, so wholly lacking in either eroticism or conscious humour that now he occasionally wondered if this wasn't, in a deeper sense, true of his own work. He was thinking of this at the moment, not hearing Sid Krassman, whose stories he already knew too well, when their hostess, the incredible Teeny Marie, beckoned him with an elaborate wink and a lascivious smile, followed by rounding her glistening lips, inserting two fingers and pumping them

11

vigorously in and out with great slurping sounds, while allowing her eyes to roll back wildly in a monstrous simulation of ecstasy. The sheer grotesquerie and unexpectedness of this vignette caused the cute starlet who was talking to Les Harrison nearby to drop her mouth agape and turn away. 'What in God's name was that?' she whispered in urgent alarm. But Les only chuckled. 'Why that's our delightful hostess,' he said, taking the nifty by the arm. 'Come on, we'll get her to drop on you.'

'Huh?' she said, going all wide-eyed and suspicious. A pretty girl had to be very careful at one of these Malibu bashes.

Teeny Marie. Actually her name was *Tina* Marie, but this had gradually altered into the endearing diminutive, mainly because of her childish, indeed almost birdlike, delicacy. A scant seventy-eight pounds she weighed, and a reedy four feet nine she stood—when standing, which was not too often, since she mostly seemed to crouch, to spring, to slither . . . to move with a weird crippled-animal grace, which may seem all the more remarkable, or perhaps even understandable, when considered against her infirmities. For truth to tell, she was a rather artificial person; inventory-wise, from tip to toe, and in rough chronology, it was like this: severe malaria as a child had made her totally hairless; carcinoma had taken her breasts; and finally she had lost a leg, her left, in an auto crash outside Villefranche-sur-Mer, and an eye, her right, during an incredible 'dart-fight' in a Soho pub. What was one hundred percent true, pure, and all her, however, was her *mouth*. And her mouth was boss beauty; her lips were like young Rita Hayworth's—a composite of Hayley Mills and Muhammad Ali; and her teeth were the ones used in the 'Plus White' commercials—perfect. Small wonder then that Teeny Marie, in over-comp for real and imagined inadequacies, should develop an oral orientation and a vivaciousness, which was, in combination with her one fantastic eye ablaze, quite astonishing to behold.

B. managed a smile of genuine, if somewhat wan

bemusement. On an occasion several years ago, in a moment of morbid curiosity he had actually gone to bed with Teeny Marie, to observe her in disassembly. Now the image returned: she hobbling wildly around the room, scrambling about like an eccentrically wounded creature, tiny bald head glistening, child's scrawny chest, a flat surface of scar tissue, her detached limb held outthrust in front of her to simulate an outlandish phallus, teeth blazing in a surrealistic grimace of hilarity, and shrieking at the top of her voice: '*Put the wood to me, B!*'

Now, as she jostled her way through the guests, administering a goose here and a pinch there, Les Harrison attempted to intercept her and introduce her to the cutie-pie starlet. 'Teeny!' he shouted twisting his face into the same mocking nightmare mask of ecstasy as her own, 'for Christ's fucking sake you've simply *got* to meet my Miss Pilgrim! She's *very* keen to give you some head!'

Miss Pilgrim blushed terrifically and turned her wide eyes up in exasperation and annoyance. 'Oh *really*, Lester!'

'All right, Teeny,' he continued impatiently, ignoring the nifty, 'come on now, *show her your thing!*'

But there was no delaying Teeny Marie; she darted past them toward B., only pausing to throw one frozen smile of exaggerated insanity at the couple, demanding gaily: 'My thing? *Which one ?!?*'

She reached the cluster around B. and Sid Krassman just as the latter was concluding another studio story of questionable taste—this time detailing the persistent theft of panties, dance belts, leotards, body stockings, etcetera, from the dressing room of a certain celebrated beauty—the precious garments then being returned with the reinforced and highly absorbent crotch crudely torn out. After all manner of security measures had been thwarted ('obviously an *inside job*' quipped Sid with coughing guffaw), the girl was persuaded to let the all-important section of the articles be tinctured with strychnine—the end result being that a complicated Crowd-and-Crane sequence was suddenly

13

disrupted when an obscure electrician, known simply as 'Al, the Pal,' plummeted headlong from a sixty-foot catwalk above the set, crashing in the midst of it, his face purple with poison-seizure, his coarse member stout and spurting—a bit of beige and scalloped Danskin panel still protruding from foaming blue-black lips.

'Well, anyway,' the actress had remarked (according to Sid), while dabbing at her great tear-filled eyes, 'at least he wasn't no lousy *fruit*! Which is more than I can say for *some* of the creeps around here!' adding this last with a cross and narrow look at her own leading man—he whom the public regarded as a Don Juan of exceptional prowess.

As Sid completed his anecdote, Teeny Marie cavorted on the periphery of the small group, repeating her frantic suck-simulation and grimacing madly—to the distraction of one or two persons who didn't quite know where she was at, simply thinking of her as their gracious hostess—a bit eccentric perhaps, but a very important member of the Malibu film colony.

'*Soirée cinématique!*' she screeched at B. '*Soirée du film bleu!*' And she gestured with elaborate urgency toward the part of the house where the projection room was.

'Hey, that's great, huh, B.?' said Sid, nudging Boris and grinning absurdly. 'I ain't had a hard-on in two weeks!'

Boris nodded. 'Terrific,' he said, almost inaudibly.

The *soirée cinématique* was a series of typically nowhere, dumbbell stag-films—each about ten minutes long, with no plot, no sound, no credits, nothing. Ugly people in harsh, flat lighting, dominated by the same rear master-shot or 'monster-shot' as Sid kept shouting ('Hey, here comes the monster-shot! Pass the tissues!'), of some cretin's buttocks thrusting half heartedly into a dopey girl's black-stockinged honey-pot —except somehow it looked more like a cesspool. The last one, however, was a cut above the others; it featured a well-known Texas stripper and was in full, if somewhat washed-

14

out, color. The setting was a Beverley Hills swimming pool and there was even a vague attempt at plot—the subtitles beginning: She (cheerfully): 'Say, how about a dip?' He (suggestively): 'I wouldn't mind dipping into *you*, baby!' Then cut to the water where they are swimming nude. Quick cut to him sitting on the edge of the pool, and her, still in the water, head half emerged, closed-eyed, avidly sucking him.

'Hey, the water sure looks cold!' shouted Sid with a raucous belch.

He (smiling): 'We're going to have some fun, sister—now that I know how you like it!' Cut to the bedroom where he's throwing it to her in the same old dumbbell master-shot.

B. was annoyed at the waste. 'How is it possible to make an attractive girl look that bad?' Sid pretended not to understand. 'Attractive? You want that broad, you got her. Hey, Eddie!' Shouting for his real or imaginary assistant, who presumably would arrange for immediate transport, head, etcetera. Teeny, sensing malaise, rushed over, beckoning Boris and Sid to follow.

Of the twelve accessible bedrooms in the house (two more were locked) six had mirrors on the ceiling above the bed, and on the walls alongside it, and four others contained video-tape cameras, concealed in the walls at strategic positions. The two rooms which did *not* have hidden cameras had a compensating feature: the mirrors alongside the bed were Duolite glass, which can be seen through from the outside—the outside in this case being the two rooms that were locked. And it was to one of these rooms that the perfect hostess led them—herself in front, absurdly wide-eyed, a finger to her lips in exaggerated caution and stealth, tiptoeing, exactly like a little girl stealing down a corridor toward the pre-dawn Christmas tree.

She carefully unlocked the door and ushered them in, gesturing silence all the while, and bade them sit in Eames chairs facing a wall-size panel of glass, which proved to be the reverse side of a two-way mirror, against the bed in the adjacent room. Next, she unlocked a control-box, and flicked a switch inside it. There, at first like a mural, then as on a Panavision screen, with deep romantic back-lighting, were Les Harrison and two identical teeny-boppers, blond, sixteen, and cute as two buttons—in a posture of lovemaking perhaps better diagrammed than described. Les himself was lying flat on his back while the two girls sat facing each other astride him—one, with vage covering his member, the other with vage covering his mouth—while the girls themselves, sitting upright, were locked in what appeared to be a very passionate embrace, bodies and mouths fastened together like suction-cups. A curious tableau, almost a still-life, for at the moment they scarcely moved, just sitting there, as in some kind of extraordinary exotic tea ceremony. But then, still entwined in a deep, deep, closed-eyed kiss, two blond heads as one, they slowly began to writhe ... languorously, caressing each other, hands delicately tracing the contour of the face, neck, shoulders, breast, waist, stomach, thighs, of each, simultaneously. Because of their incredible resemblance, it was as though a girl were fondling her only image in a three-dimensional mirror. Narcissism at its nadir—and Les Harrison followed it closely in the glass ... the same glass through which *he* was being observed by the fun trio on the opposite side. This gave rise to a weird countenance on his part, because in order to observe, and yet not falter in his tongue-in-vage work, he was obliged to case his eyes sideways in a manner which seemed both eccentric and grotesque.

In addition to the real, live visual image before them, there was also sound amplification of what was taking place in the room ... an amplification with such gain that the slightest move, sigh, or breath could not only be *heard*, but came across as a veritable scream of anguish or delight. One of the microphones was placed, in a unidirectional manner, at the foot and exact center of the bed, so that the actual viscosity of the thrust, the wet membrane friction of penis going in and out of mucous vage, could be heard in a way never heard before—at first even unrecognizable, but then of course, being in perfect sync and all, becoming quite un-mistakable.

'Hey, that's some *pickup*,' said Sid, never adverse to dropping a bit of expertise, 'what is it, a Nigra Special?'

'Probably an A-R seventy,' said Boris, 'with a booster.'

Sid nodded. 'Jesus, *listen* to it! The sound of teeny-bopper pussy! There's no other sound like it!'

Meanwhile, Teeny Marie, for her part, was far from idle. She flounced about the room, skirt raised to her waist, kicking in can-can style.

'Who wants a taste of my lamb-pit?!?' she screeched. 'Who wants to dip into my fabulous honey-pot?!?'

Not getting any takers, she dropped to her knees in front of Sid, and began roughly grappling at his fly.

'Aw fer Chrissake!' he growled, pushing her away. 'Lemme watch the show!'

She cleverly channeled her sideways momentum into a crotch-lunge for B.

'You're a real doll,' he said gently, 'but I think I'll have to pass, too.'

'What a couple of wet-blanket creeps!' cried Teeny crossly, scrambling to her feet and executing a little dance of wrath. Then she seized a microphone from a wall bracket, flicked the bottom, and wheeling toward the glass tableau, screamed at the top of her voice: 'Sock it to 'em, Les! you rat-prick fruit!'

The volume of this transmission must have been stupen-dous. It had the effect of a tidal wave, literally knocking the three revelers off the bed into a tangled heap on the floor. But then Les was on his feet in a trice, hopping mad and shouting furiously:

'You crazy freak-bitch! We were *coming* I tell you! *We were all coming!*'

Presumably he knew that his tormentor was behind the mirror, because he stared in that direction—but he was staring at the wrong part of it, so the impression of being unobserved persisted.

17

'We won't listen to that kind of talk!' shrieked Teeny, and turned off the amplification on their side, while Les covered his ears against the new blast, then began to shout (silently, for he could no longer be heard) and race about the room looking for something to hurl against the glass—but apparently the room had been designed with such contingencies in mind, for although lavishly appointed, there were literally no movable furnishings; everything was either built-in or secured to the floor. Finally he was reduced to snatching up his own shoes and flinging them ineffectually, at the wrong section of the mirror.

'Missed us, you great ninny!' Teeny cackled. 'It wasn't even close!'

By now the two nifties had gotten it slightly together and were sitting up on the floor on the far side of the bed, only their blond heads and bare shoulders visible, their lips moving at Les in some indecipherable remonstrance or perhaps simple inquiry as to what was happening.

His reply, if any, was not audible, of course, as he slumped down on the bed, a total collapse of defeat and dejection.

This seemed to tear Teeny apart.

'Oh my God,' she moaned, 'what have we done to him?'

She began ripping off her clothes. 'I'm coming, Les!' she cried, 'I'm coming, my darling!' Then she flipped the switch on the two-way mirror, twisted the lock, and rushed madly out of the room, still tearing her garments from her and dropping them in flight.

Boris and Sid sat looking at the dark panel for a moment.

'Well, that seems to be that,' said B.

Sid grunted, and lumbered to his feet. 'You know, I wouldn't mind some of that teeny head.'

B. was thinking of something else, walked silently, while Sid continued to muse: 'Wonder where the hell he found them . . . Christ, they sure are shicksa . . . probably *Swedes* . . . I hate the fucking Swedes. Except for Bergman, natch,' he added, hoping to amuse B.—who acknowledged the effort with scarcely more than a grunt.

18

Sid looked at him, undisturbed by his preoccupation. One thing in particular was locked in his mind concerning Boris; it was a conversation they had after the premiere of one of his movies, a movie on which Sid had been executive producer—a simple, poignant, tender, love story . . . a film which received the highest acclaim, and which was distinguished for, among other things, a poetic and rather daring (for its day) bedroom two-shot. In this brief scene, the lovers, entwined in bare embrace, are visible only from the waist up. The man is lying on top, gently kissing the girl's face, her throat, her shoulders . . . as his head moves slowly down between her breasts, the camera remains stationary, and his head gradually slides out of the frame and, presumably, down to her honey-pot, whereupon the camera moves up to her closed-eyed face and holds on her expression of mounting rapture.

Naturally, the film had been interfered with in various quarters of hinterland—including New York City. Petitions were rife, and vigilante groups active, to get 'that monstrous cunnilingus episode' (as the DAR described it) out of the film.

There were abortive attempts to delete the major portion of the scene . . . with the projectionist, under union instruction, or management bribe, causing the film to jump the sprocket at the crucial point, and then rethreading several frames (two hundred feet actually) afterward.

Responsible critics, of course, were quick to seize ready cudgel in the film's defense. The scene was lauded by the editors of *Cahiers du Cinéma* as a '*tour de force érotique*' unique in the history of contemporary film. It was described by *Sight and Sound* as 'masterfully aesthetic . . . sheer poetry, and in the best possible taste.'

The critic's use of the word 'taste' in this instance had caused B. to smile. 'How can he talk about *taste*?' he asked Sid (putting him on a bit), '. . . with the camera on the girl's *face*, who knows *how* it tasted! Right, Sid?'

Understandably this had elicited the coarsest sort of

19

rejoinder from Sid. 'Huh?' not quite getting it at first, but then nodding violently, laughing, coughing, spitting, slapping his leg, urgently scratching his crotch: 'Yeah, yeah, I know, *you'd* even like to show the guy *after*—pickin' cunt-hair outta his teeth, huh? Haw, haw, haw!'

'Not necessarily,' said B., gentle and very earnest, 'I would like to have followed his head, though ... when it went down, out of the frame. I should have done that. It was a cop-out not to.'

Sid realized he was serious. 'What ... you mean, show him suckin' her *cunt*, for Chrissake?!? Whatta you, *nuts*?'

Of course this had been several years ago, six in all, and was now a part of forgotten history. In a subsequent film, *Enough Rope*, during a scene in which the voyeur-antagonist fastens his eye to a crack in the wall, while in the next room the heroine disrobes against the terrible heat of a Mexican summer afternoon, the camera (voyeur's POV) finds occasion to linger, in a desultory, almost caressing fashion on her pubis. In commercial film prior to this, other than documentaries on nudism, a view of the pubic region—the 'beaver shot' it was called—occurred only as a brief glimpse, a seven- or eight-frame cut, never in close-up, and, above all, never integrated as part of a 'romantic,' or a deliberately erotic, sequence. Naturally, the studio was quick to snap its wig.

'Good Lord, man,' Les Harrison had wailed, 'you're sabotaging you whole career! And you're taking a lot of good guys down the drain with you,' adding this last a bit piously, voice faltering, '. . . guys who were counting on this picture to get into general distribution ... guys with families ... kids ... toddlers ...'

Changed his tune, of course, when attendance pressure moved the film from the Little Carnegie to Loew's big circuit, breaking all prev.

But last time out had been the big one: *male genitalia*. Somewhat flaccid, granted, but still there it was, right up there on the silver screen, bigger than life you might say.

That was a bit too much—even for those who had cheered him past previous milestones of cinema history. 'Well,' they muttered, 'this time he's gone *too far!*'

But Boris, of course, knew better. No erection, and no penetration—how to explain that little oversight to the muse of creative romance?

From his point of view, the stag movies they had just seen were more relevant, albeit unwittingly, to the crucial aesthetic issues and problems presented by the film of today, than were those of the master film-makers, including himself. He was aware that the freedom of expression and development in cinema had always lagged behind that of literature, as, until recent years, it had lagged behind that of the theater as well. Eroticism of the most aesthetic and creatively effective nature abounded in every form of contemporary prose—why had it not been achieved, or even seriously attempted, on film? Was there something inherently alien to eroticism in the medium of film? Something too personal to share with an audience? Perhaps the only approach would be from the opposite side.

'Listen, Sid,' Boris was asking now, 'those films we were looking at—do you think they could be improved?'

'Huh? "Improved?" Are you *kiddin'*?' Understatement always seemed to antagonize Sid. 'Christ, I seen better cunt at a senior-citizen trailer camp! Jeez, half the time I didn't know I was watchin'' a *stag film* or a *dog-show*, for Chrissake! Ha, you bet your sweet ass they could be improved! Get some halfway decent cunt in there for openers!'

'Okay, what else?'

'Huh? Whatta you mean "what else"? What else is there?'

'Well, that's what I'm talking about,' said Boris, 'the *totality* of it, not just how the *girl* looks—that's only one aspect . . . besides, the redhead wasn't bad, you know, she could have been very effective; she was wasted, totally wasted.'

Sid could bear it no longer—he flung his cigarette over the

21

balcony, and struck his fist against his palm in a gesture of complete and bitter defeat. '*Jesus fucking Christ, B.!*' he said between clenched teeth, 'here you are with everything in the *world* going for you, and you worrying about making some dumb broad hooker look good in a dirty movie! Whatta you, *nuts?!?*'

That's how frustrated and impatient he had become with Boris. During the past two years he had approached him with any number of lucrative, if not exactly original, film properties and ideas—ideas which seemed uniquely suited to the genius and prestige of the master ... without whom, forget it. One of his so-called '*boss* projects,' for instance, had been a monumental 'fictional documentary,' entitled *Whores of the World*—a twenty-hour, ten-part film, to be shot in every capital and metropolis in both hemispheres. 'Talk about your everlovin' audience-appeal,' Sid had exclaimed repeatedly, 'this baby's got it *all! Sex, travel, human interest!* Christ, we'll give 'em so much fuckin' human interest, it'll be comin' out of their ass-hole!' He claimed to have researched the project thoroughly, '... at considerable personal expense,' he would always add, paving the way for a handsome reimbursement out of the first front money that might come to hand. The way he envisioned it, the entire series of ten feature-length flicks would take two years to shoot. 'Now get this,' he said softly, with a dark glance around the room, as though he were about to divulge the World War III invasion date, 'by the time we get into release, each of the hooker scenes will have changed—new broads, new prices, etcetera—and we can start all over again! Like the old "Follies" pix! *Whores of the World—1968! Whores of the World—1969!* It'll become a fuckin' *institution*, for Chrissake!'

And for a while the notion had actually seemed to interest B., but when finally pressed by a desperate overextended Sid ('I got 'im, I got 'im, I got the King B.!' he had told the studio with tremendous glee and what proved to be typical exaggeration), he declined. 'I don't think whores interest me very much,' he had to admit, almost wistfully, 'I don't think I understand them.'

'So we'll go for the *pathos*,' pleaded Sid urgently, 'Christ, we'll have the fuckin' pathos comin' out of their ass-holes!'

But B. shook his head. 'I have a hunch that whores are all alike,' he said, with a little smile that seemed especially for Sid, and momentarily depressed him no end. But Sid was nothing if not boss resilient, so he was quick to bounce back with additional 'winners.'

But as yet they hadn't been for B.; he was after something else, something more . . . *ambitious*, if that was the word— and tonight he thought he'd found out what it was.

'You know what I'd like to do?' he said with studied deliberation, while he and Sid lolled, smoking pot, on the moon-washed, wave-lapping terrace of Teeny Marie's monstro hacienda, and through the candlelight and the fragrance of pine and gardenia, the chicks floated or flounced by, in minis and micros, in leopard leotards, in bikinis and bell-bottom peek-a-boos—all looking to get discovered, or otherwise straight, if only for the moment. 'I'd like to make one of those.' He nodded toward the projection room. 'One of those stag films.'

Sid stared at him for a moment, then looked at the cold roach of cigarette between his fingers. 'This pot is better than I thought,' he said, flipping it away. 'You wantta make one of those, huh?'

Boris nodded.

'Yeah, well, that figures,' said Sid with painful irony, 'the best director in the world wants to make a stag film. That's great. Yeah, that's very amusing. I mean that's really hilarious, ain't it? Hah-hah-hah . . .' converting his forced laugh into a sound of sick retching.

Boris simply stared ahead, expressionless, into the endless Pacific night of stars and dark waters, his head somewhere else.

'I ran into Joey Schwartzman today,' said Sid, with what now sounded like cold hatred, '. . . he told me how you blew

23

the Metro deal.' A deal, it should be noted, which Sid himself had proposed and would have participated in.

From a farther room, and drifting past, came the incredible wailing lament of the extraordinary *Plastic Ono*. Boris said nothing, didn't appear to have heard, nodded benignly in time to the sound.

'Okay,' said Sid, emboldened by drug to self-expression, 'okay, okay, you're a *saint!* You're a motherfuckin', insane *saint!* You turn down a *ten-million-dollar picture—Dante's Inferno*, and that's one helluva property, you know that, don't you?—you turned it down, and the next day you're talking about making a *stag film!* That's very amusing, that's very cute. Another chapter in the legend . . . *The Legend of King B.!*—could be a title, right?'

Through drug and adrenaline, Sid had worked himself into a state of vehemently righteous indignation. He coughed, searched his pockets for a cigarette, tamped it with great vigor against the onyx tabletop between them, cleared his throat, and was about to speak again, but was circumvented by the sudden appearance of their gay hostess, cavorting right up to their faces, swirling the raised skirts of her new costume—featuring several crinoline petticoats—in haughty can-can fashion, flashing black lace panties and one spoke-like stretch of ivory thigh, screeching: 'Anyone for *box lunch?!?*'

Sid chortled lustily: 'Whatta you got in it—*dried shrimp?* Haw-haw-haw!' slapping his leg, coughing and spitting, while she flounced on and away in her mad dervish.

'I've got to find out,' B. said, having barely noticed her flashing pass, 'how *far* you can take the aesthetically erotic—at what point, if any, it gets to be such a personal thing that it becomes meaningless.'

'I got news for you,' said Sid, firm and terse, 'they been doing it for years—"*underground movies*" they're called, ever hear of 'em? Andy Warhol? They show *everything*—beaver, cock, the whole store! It's a fucking *industry*, for Chrissake!'

Boris sighed, shaking his head. 'They don't show

24

anything,' he said softly, even sadly, 'that's what I'm trying to tell you. They haven't *started* to show anything. No *erection*, no *penetration* . . . *nothing*. And besides that, they're *Mickey Mouse* . . . *amateurish*, just like the stuff we were looking at tonight—bad acting, bad lighting, bad camera, bad everything. At least in the stag films you actually see them *fucking* . . . in the underground movies, it's only *represented*, *suggested*—erection and penetration are never shown. So the underground films don't even count. But what I want to know is, why are the other ones—the stag films—always so ridiculous? Why isn't it possible to make one that's really *good*—you know, one that's genuinely erotic and beautiful.' This said with an ingenuousness not to be denied.

Despite the pot, Sid's years as a yes-man had given him a quick automatic nod in certain serious circumstances, which he now recognized as prevailing. 'Yeah, yeah,' he said expectantly, but obviously confounded.

'I mean,' said Boris, 'suppose the film were made under *studio* conditions—feature-length, color, beautiful actors, great lighting, strong plot . . . how would it look then?'

'Christ, I can't imagine,' admitted Sid.

'Neither can I,' said Boris, and after a pause, 'I just wonder if it's possible.'

Sid, now taking it all as a perfectly absurd joke on himself —the joke of Life—didn't care much anymore. 'Possible? Sure. You gotta camera? You can start shooting tomorrow. You can use, uh, let's see . . . you can use Teeny as the lead, and you can use *me* . . . we'll both work on deferment, hawhaw . . .' He laid his head down laughing—crying really, morosely, thinking about the waste of it, B.'s turning down the Metro deal, '. . . you've really gone round the fuckin' bend this time, you know that?' Saying this through a hairy-arm-covered sob as Teeny arrived with Les's previous miniskirt starlet in tow.

'Gotta live one for you, boys,' she screamed. 'Last one out is a hole in the ass!' And she began grappling at Sid's fly.

'Aw for Chrissake,' he said in mock anger, feigning

karate chops at her hand, 'lemme work it up first!'

'But she likes you simply for what you *are*, Sid,' explained Teeny with an extravagant expression of outraged innocence, 'a short, fat, hairy, simpleminded . . . *kike creep!*'

Sid closed his eyes, in a gesture of exasperated, weary tolerance. 'Oh, that's great,' he said, 'that's all I need right now, some kind of racial . . . racial *allusion*—is that what you call it, "*racial allusion*"?'

'Actually,' Teeny went on, glittering toward B., 'she's really interested in Mr. King Fruit here,' pressing the cutie-pie starlet into him, 'she said she'd be pleased to suck his thing. Correct, Miss Pilgrim?'

'Oh Teeny, really!' the darling girl gushed, 'you're just too awful!'

'Well, anyway,' said Teeny, suddenly bored, 'here she is— Miss Penny Pilgrim, if you can believe that. And she wants to be in the movies. So go ahead boys—*fuck her brains out!*' She cackled and gave the girl a playful—not entirely playful— push into their midst, then flounced away.

Sid made elaborate motions of brushing spilled drink and ash off his front. 'Jesus Christ, I'm sopping!' he said.

'Oh, I'm so sorry,' said the girl, trying to help him, leaning over in such a way that her extremely brief mini revealed the back of bare brown legs and a precious, perfectly rounded derrière, gift-wrapped, as it were, in panties of ice-blue trimmed with white. Boris fingered the edge of lace then patted her bottom. The girl didn't change her position immediately, just turned her head toward him and smiled sweetly.

'You have a very cute bottom,' said B.

'Why thank you, sir.' And she straightened, turning to him, and did a little girl's curtsy. She looked about sixteen, all dimples, thighs, and pert little breasts, with short, fluffy honey-colored hair and a very sweet smile.

'Yeah, how'd you like to be in a stag film?' said Sid gruffly.

'I'd like to be in one of Mister Boris Adrian's films, she

26

said, still looking at B. with something close to adoration, 'I'd like that more than anything in the world.'

Boris smiled and took her hand.

'You're very pretty, darling. What's your name?'

'Penny. Penny Pilgrim. I've seen every single one of your pictures, and I think you're the greatest director in the world.'

'Wait'll you see his new stag film,' said Sid, 'with Taylor and Burton. Terrific. We got a little distribution problem though—the projector won't fit in the sewer.'

'How did you like the movies?' Boris asked, gently pulling her down into a chair beside them, where she sat now, properly, all little-girl goodness, feet and knees together, hands clutched in her lap, just at the hem of her upper-thigh mini. She made a cute but definite expression of distaste. 'Gosh, I thought they were just *awful*. I couldn't take it after the first two—I went outside. I think most of the girls did . . . except for, you know, a few,' adding this in sotto voce with an uneasy look around the terrace, since Teeny had been cackling and whistling throughout, shouting 'Sock it to me, baby!'

'Yeah,' said Sid dryly, 'well, you see, that's what *we're* up against in this new project of ours—*instant audience alienation*. It's sort of a new gimmick. Something like what was in the mind of the kamikazes.'

Neither Boris nor the girl paid any attention to Sid's remark.

'Was there *any* scene,' asked B., 'that, you know, *interested* you?'

The obvious sincerity of his question, along with her avid desire to please, made the girl take it very seriously. She thought about it for a moment, her brow crinkling cutely as she did.

'No,' she finally admitted, 'there honestly wasn't—unless it was when she was making up . . . in the first one, when she was sitting at the mirror, putting on her lipstick . . . just before, well, just before what happened . . . happened.'

She said it with exactly the right combination of coyness

27

and a self-deprecating smile, as though to acknowledge an awareness of the possibility, in their eyes, of her own provincial ignorance—though preferably innocence, natch.

'I don't think that coon had a real cock,' said Sid, 'I think it was a strap-on.'

They both continued to ignore him.

'Have you *ever* seen anything in a movie,' Boris pursued it, 'that sort of turned you on?'

Now the girl, wanting more than anything simply to be liked, and yet not be thought of as just another 'dumb little broad,' was really pressed.

'Well, I don't know,' she said, still smiling, of course, but her smile nervous now. 'I mean, gosh, I *love* love scenes, I mean, you know, in the movies, but these were just so . . . *awful*.'

'Yes, but what if they were beautiful?'

'Huh?' Her great fawn eyes widened a little more.

'What if the film were done with good actors, beautiful costumes? All very romantic. What if it were the work . . . of an artist?'

'He means maniac,' explained Sid.

'And had a three-million-dollar budget?' Boris continued. 'How do you think it would look then?' he insisted of the girl.

She glanced from one to the other, wondering if they weren't surely putting her on.

'Well, gosh, I don't know,' she admitted. '. . . I mean, you'd actually show . . . you know, show his thing—I mean, going in and out and everything, like in the ones we saw?'

'Yes, do you think that could be beautiful?'

The darling girl seemed to gulp slightly. 'Well, gosh, I . . . I really . . .'

'Or to put it another way,' interjected gross Sid, 'would *you* be interested in the role?'

'Wait a minute, Sid,' said Boris, 'I'm not saying that you can't use inserts there—I mean, in the close-ups, on the . . .

on the cock, where you show, uh, *penetration* . . . I'm not saying you can't use doubles there. I mean, it's something I haven't thought through yet.'

The girl, obviously sympathetic to anything either of them might suggest, was troubled. 'But how could you get the film . . . well, you know, how could you get it *shown* anywhere . . . I mean, it's against the law, isn't it, a film like that?'

'Aw well, you're missing the point, baby,' said Sid brusquely, 'I mean that's the whole idea. to spend three million dollars on a film and then never show it. Don't you think that's sort of cute?'

'Well, gosh . . .'

She was at a loss to continue, but reprieve came with the lurching arrival of matinee idol Rex McGuire, whacked out of his skull. He was half crying and half laughing; and while it is unlikely that he was actually wearing makeup at this hour, his face was so strangely tan that the two separate streams of tears seemed to be etching furrows down each cheek. In any case, it was a grand job of weeping, thespwise.

'Hi guys,' he said in the sepulchral tones of the New York stage; there was almost no discernible connection between his drunkenness and his voice control as he stumbled slightly then leaned over to support himself on one arm against the rail of the terrace.

'Hey, you know what that bastard Rat Prick Harrison just said? Go on, guess what he just said.'

'That you were pissed?' hazarded Sid.

Penny Pilgrim twittered nervously, thinking what a daring thing to say to Rex McGuire, but the latter was quite impervious. 'Well, you know this thing we're doing, it was *supposed* to be a *three-way co-production*—I mean, *me* and *him* and *the director* were *supposed* to have an *equal say* about *everything*. Democratic, right? Handshake deal, right? Good faith, right? Right. Okay, so Rat Prick Les has got this little cunt he wants to use in the picture—tests her, she's lousy, he

29

still wants to use her. So we argue back and forth, *I* don't want her, *Allen* don't want her, but *he* still wants her. Finally we say to him, "Sorry, Les, but, well, it looks like the vote is *two to one* against you." And he just smiles and shakes his head. "No, boys," he says, "it isn't *two to one* . . . it's *one to nothing*." So now we're going to use this lousy little cunt, and it's going to fuck up the whole picture! How do you like that for a dirty rat-price trick?!?'

Sid shook his head solemnly. 'Gower Street is paved with the bones of guys who thought it was two to one against the Rat Prick.'

'What's the girl's name,' Penny wanted to know, 'the girl who *did* get the part?'

'*Name?*' Rex howled like a wounded Lear. 'She *has* no name! Her *name* is Lousy Little Cunt, *that*'s her name! That is *actually her name!* Incredible, isn't it? I mean how is *that* going to look in lights?' He turned, facing the rest of the terrace, and moved his outstretched arm in a dramatic sweep to define an imaginary marquee. '*Night Song*,' he intoned gravely, 'starring Rex McGuire and Lousy Little Cunt!'

'Maybe she'll get top billing,' said Sid.

'That's right!' yelled Rex with hysterical glee, 'that's right!'

'Or you could make it the title,' suggested Sid.

'*Perfect!*' shrieked Rex, and began shouting at the top of his voice, à la Olivier: '*Lousy Little Cunt! Lousy Little Cunt! That's* the name of our picture!'

People nearby looked around, startled not so much by the sentiment expressed as by its sheer volume and rage-like intensity. It seemed to herald violence of some sort; and he did actually wheel about then, and fling his empty glass in the general direction of Les Harrison—bad aim though, and it shattered explosively against a driftwood candelabra. 'LOUSY LITTLE CUNT!' he bellowed.

'Did someone call?' asked Teeny Marie shrilly, with a devastatingly sweet smile as she scurried up out of nowhere.

Rex, who was prepared for a stout kick in the groin, or at least a reprimand, was not prepared for this—or perhaps was especially prepared for it—and dropped to his knees, grasping Teeny about the legs. 'Oh, Teeny, Teeny,' he sobbed, 'why must everything in the world be governed by such total shits?' Then he collapsed at her feet, a quivering heap of Man-tanned muscle.

Boris had regarded the entire vignette with an expression of bemused interest. He tended to think of most things in terms of pans, angles, close-ups . . .

'Dig that,' he said, raising the thumb and forefinger of his left hand, boxed by his right into a rectangular semblance of a view-finder, focused on the curious image of the internationally famous film star crumpled at the feet of this crippled boss freak.

'Forget it,' said Sid, 'he ain't gonna sign no release.'

'Gosh, do you think he's all right?' gasped Penny.

'Sure,' said Sid, 'nothing that a kick in the gourd won't fix,' and he raised his foot to deliver a simulated stomp on the face of the fallen Rex.

'Oh, my God,' screamed Penny, bursting into tears, 'don't, *please don't!*' Not realizing, of course, that iron-in-the-soul Sid couldn't care less, and, in fact, wouldn't hurt a fly—especially a fly.

Boris had to comfort the girl, drawing her close, smiling, whispering: 'It's okay, it's okay—just a little Freudian equation being worked out.'

And, natch, Sid didn't really kick him, just pretended to, and Teeny fell on top of him, cradling his Man-tan head in her arms, closed-eyed and murmuring, 'Oh my baby, my baby, my precious motherfucking baby.'

Then his agent, Bat Orkin, arrived, all loyal efficiency to Rex but hip enough to be slightly embarrassed in the presence of Boris and Sid. 'I'll take care of him, I'll take care of him,' he kept saying, hoping for Christ's fucking sake there were no photographers present, giving a sly wink to B. and Sid as he began to hoist and drag Rex off the terrace.

Penny was still upset—not really too upset perhaps, but did recognize the chance of expressing a bit of emotional sensitivity, and also, of course, not adverse to her cute sobbing being calmed and soothed away by boss B., and she sat down in his lap to be cuddled.

'That loony fruit,' muttered Sid, 'he's as crazy as you are, B.—except *he's* working. Excuse me, I gotta get a drink,' and he got up and trudged toward the bar.

'I'll take you home,' said Boris, very gently to the girl. 'Where do you live?'

'The Studio Club,' she said, dabbing at her eyes. She couldn't cry as well as Rex, but somehow it was more engaging.

2

She didn't really smoke pot, but she was afraid to admit it— so, after they were there, at Boris's place, on a terrace over-looking the dark-blue twinkling lights of Hollywood (each light, natch, fraught with promise), and he, not really caring much one way or the other, lit a joint, took a couple of drags, and handed it to her, she had just enough presence of mind to accept it and say, 'oh, *groovy*,' yet could scarcely repress surprise when, after passing it back (as she knew one was supposed to), he just smiled, and didn't take it. Suddenly she was very much in the wrong—now he would think of her as some sort of dopey flower-person, and not a serious actress at all. 'But I thought *you* . . .' she began, holding the smoldering stick helplessly between them, '. . . well, I mean, *I* don't really . . . that is, I've never actually . . .' She stammered, holding it at a distance now, as though it were a hateful thing which had surely destroyed their future.

'Don't worry about it,' he said, taking it from her, 'it isn't important.' And he took a few deep pokes and sat it on the ashtray. 'You know . . . the thing that *really* attracted me to you,' he began quietly, as though thinking aloud to himself, 'the thing I find really . . . *beautiful*, maybe even *uniquely beautiful* in you, at least for today—and I say this with all humility and respect, because I know you must have other qualities, and I recognize that it may be some kind of weakness in myself—not weakness exactly, but still not the sort of thing I'd like to be able to say, the sort of thing I imagine you'd like to hear . . . but the thing that makes you really . . . *exceptional*—well, I mean to me, anyway . . . is your ass.'

He said it with such patent, introspective, almost childish sincerity that the girl was unable to take offense. It was as though two art dealers were discussing the qualities of a Dresden mantelpiece. In her loss for a reaction, she reached out and picked up the cigarette. 'Well,' she began uneasily, but then channeled that into the motion of relighting it.

'I've been thinking about it,' said B., 'I've been trying to figure it out—I mean, in the aesthetic sense. I've seen a lot of great, marvelous asses.' Saying this in an objective, clinical way, and proceeding then to give as examples a bevy of famous nifties, about whom his familiarity with their derrières could not be questioned. 'Is there such a thing as the "perfect ass"—and if so—what does it mean?' Then he turned to Penny, looking at her very directly, almost as if he had suddenly remembered she was there. 'I don't think it's homosexual,' he said, and she just stared at him and nodded dumbly. 'I mean I don't care about *making love* to a girl in the ass . . . you know, fucking her in the ass—it isn't that. I'm not sure *what* it is. I mean, why should a girl's ass be so aesthetically erotic? Maybe it's just something to hold on to . . . an extension of her thing, you know, her cooze.'

He reached over and took the dead cigarette from her.

'Oh sorry,' she said, a little flustered, having forgotten it entirely.

33

He relit it, inhaled deeply, and stared out at the blinking world, his world, below.

But Penny was the kind who couldn't stand silence—perhaps a subconscious cultural memory of the 'no dead-air' radio concept. 'Well,' she said, 'I just hope that, uh . . .'

He handed the joint back to her.

'Take *you*, for example,' he said, 'I mean, what was it about . . . your *bottom* that was so attractive? You leaned over, right?'

She nodded.

'But I'm sure you weren't doing it deliberately to provoke.'

'Oh no, I . . .'

He retrieved the joint.

'I don't mean to say you may not have been *vaguely aware* of what was happening. I don't mean you're *insensitive*, or *imperceptive*, or anything like that, I just mean that you weren't really thinking of it as your *best shot*. Right?'

'Oh right, yes, right.'

'And yet . . . it was.' He sighed as though at a loss with himself to understand the vagaries of human nature, mostly his own. 'Maybe it was . . .'—he searched for the answer, one hand to contemplative brow—'. . . maybe it was the underwear, maybe it was something completely superficial. Here, let's do it again. Now, how was I sitting? Yes, I was sitting like this, and you were . . . yes, you stand here, and . . .'

The girl, under his direction, obeyed like someone in hypnosis. She took her place as though adroitly 'hitting her mark' for the big production number in *My Fair Lady*.

'Yes, that's it,' said B. 'Perfect. Now bend forward. Not too fast,' he reminded her, 'not too fast. Easy does it . . .'

3

When the phone rang at one-thirty the next day, he was already half-awake, and he knew it had to be important. His instructions with the service were never to ring through unless it was a call from one of his children—four, six, and eight. He reached for the instrument which, by chance, was still draped with the tiny, ice-blue, white-trimmed panties, just as they had fallen, and he didn't bother to unveil it when he spoke—nor yet fail to consider the irony of talking to the eight-year-old boy (who, being the eldest, always initiated the calls) with the filmy sheen and scent of Arpège against his cheek. As it happened however, it was the gross Sid, who through the ruse of mimicking the child's voice, had out-maneuvered the vigilant service.

'I *got* it,' said Sid with an excitement that trembled, 'I mean, this time I *really got it*—and this is no fucking shit, B., I swear to Christ!'

Boris closed his eyes again, waited about five seconds just breathing Arpège through blue sheen, then said: 'Uh, *what* is it you've got, Sid?'

'The *picture!* The *three-million-dollar dirty picture* we were talking about last night! I got the *money*, baby, I tell you, I got the *money!*'

Boris didn't reply, nor hang up. Eyes still closed, he reached his free hand behind him over to the other side of the bed—where it came to rest, as with a homing instinct, on the girl's perfect bottom, she lying on her stomach, her marvelous tush perked out, round and all golden down, the resilience of two rubber balls inflated to exactly the right pressure.

'Uh-huh,' said B. slowly, 'that's swell, Sid.'

'Listen,' said Sid, 'I'll be right over.'

'Uh, don't do that, Sid.'

Sid was becoming frantic. 'Oh Christ, Christ, Christ, you gotta believe me! You gotta believe me!'

Boris gently replaced the phone, then took it off the hook and laid it on the night table—but all the while he could hear Sid shouting—and in a tone he had never heard Sid use before: '*You got final cut, baby! You got final fuckin' cut!*'

4

They met at six that evening at the Polo Lounge, at a table on the side which, through an arrangement with the maître d', was permanently reserved for Sid at this hour. The arrangement, incidentally, was that Sid would lay starlet cooze on the maître d' by letting him come to the studio on his day off and introducing him to the girl at hand as an Italian film director 'who will probably use you if he gets to know you better,' lascivious wink, 'know what I mean? One hand washes the other. Hee-hee-hee.' By the same token he had run up a bar bill of about five hundred dollars.

Sid was already there, drinking a Ramos gin fizz ('keeps my weight up'), when Boris arrived. They were both wearing shades, which made B. look even more weary and brooding than usual, and big Sid, in his white linen suit and green silk shirt, just plain sinister.

'Two questions,' he said tersely, 'one: What do you know about Liechtenstein?'

'Roy Lichtenstein?' asked B. absently, nodding to acknowledge a greeting from across the room.

Sid grimaced in pain. 'No, *mishugenah*, the *country* for Chrissake! *Liechtenstein!*'

Boris shrugged. 'I drove through it once, if that's what you mean—I don't recall stopping for anything.'

'So you didn't *stop*,' said Sid, 'big deal—it's still a *country*, right?'

'It's a country,' Boris agreed. 'Actually it's a principality. It's run by a prince. I met him once, as a matter of fact—at the Cannes Film Festival.'

'Right, right, right,' said Sid, 'it's a *sovereign principality*. Now let me give you a little run-down on the *sovereign principality* of Liechtenstein: situated in the colorful Alps Mountains, between Switzerland and Austria, occupying an area of sixty-four square miles, population of seventeen thou—one half-hour by twin jet from Paris, Rome, Berlin, Vienna, you name it—'

'What the hell are you talking about?' Boris interrupted.

'Will you please just this once listen to your own Sid Krassman,' he pleaded, but was momentarily distracted by a passing miniskirt. 'Hey, I forgot to ask, did you get into that little chickie's pants last night?'

Boris sighed. 'Yes, yes, yes,' as though it were all too futile.

'How was it?'

'What do you mean "how was it"? Haven't you ever been laid, for Chrissake?'

'She give good head?'

'Not especially.'

Sid nodded agreement. 'Young kids like that never seem to give good head. What was she, about eighteen?'

'Seventeen.'

'Seventeen, huh? She had a great ass.'

Boris nodded. 'Yeah, a great ass.'

'You suck her pussy?'

'Ha. That would be kiss-and-tell, wouldn't it?'

'Aw come on, fer Chrissake, did you suck her pussy or didn't you?'

'No. Well, not much anyway, just sort of at the beginning.'

'How many times did you fuck her?'

'Uh, let's see . . . four.'

'*Four?!?* Jeez, she must've been great ass! You fucked her *four times*, for Chrissake?'

'Yeah, well, you know, twice when we went to bed, and twice when we woke up.'

Sid seemed greatly relieved. 'Oh, when you *woke up*. I thought you meant *four times in a row*, for Chrissake! Did she come?'

Boris shrugged. 'Yeah, I guess so. She said she did.'

'Couldn't you *tell*, for Chrissake?'

'Yeah, she came.'

'What, every time?'

'Christ, I don't know if she came every time.' He regarded Sid curiously. 'Have you gone nuts or something? What was all that goofy talk about Liechtenstein?'

'I said I'd ask two questions, right? Okay, second question: You know Al Weintraub? He's Joey Schwartzman's cousin, right? Strictly legit. Now, are you ready for this? Al Weintraub is a *very close friend of the Minister of Finance in Liechtenstein*.'

'Uh-huh,' said B. He looked like he was about to fall asleep.

'Al knows *everything* about that country. We were up all night, we got a call in right now to his friend, the minister . . .'

'Listen, Sid,' Boris began, glancing at his watch, but Sid implored him, 'please, B., just this once listen to Sid Krassman.'

'Well, I don't know what the hell you're talking about.'

'Listen, B., before I go any further, can you let me take a thou until Thursday?'

'What?'

'A thousand bucks—just until Thursday.'

'Sure, I guess so.'

'You'll never regret it, B., believe you me!'

38

5

Liechtenstein, as it turned out, had the lowest per-capita income of any country in Western Europe. Although of Alpine splendor scenic-wise, its relatively inaccessible location had simply not put it on the map, so to speak. The tourists—who, for generations, the country had tried desperately to attract—never came. And yet it had the requisites: inns (picturesque), saline baths (piping hot), ski slopes (mediocre), casino and opera house (closed). It seemed there was something missing—something perhaps even intangible, but a trifle more conveniently at hand . . . in St. Moritz, Klosters, Kitzbühel, Innsbruck, etc.

The plan devised by Sid and Al Weintraub (friend of the Liechtenstein Minister of Finance) was simplicity itself— the movie would be financed by the government of Liechtenstein, in return for which it would be *filmed* in Liechtenstein, and *exhibited there exclusively*. People from London, Paris, Rome, Vienna, Geneva, Zurich, anywhere, would jet in on special charter flights—to the only place where they could see the latest film by the world's greatest director. They would stay overnight, perhaps longer, at the picturesque inns, with eiderdown *pouffe* and the cozy hearth; they would go to the opera, the casino, the ski slopes, the health baths, and the shops, both quaint and smart; they would revel in the scenic Alpine beauty of the place. Perhaps they would fall in love with Liechtenstein—its simple charm, its majestic grandeur—it might even become a *habit*.

6

'They want a ten-year exclusive on the picture,' Sid was saying, about a week later.

Boris nodded. He didn't care where the picture was shown, he just wanted to make it.

'And let me tell you something else,' Sid added slyly. 'Know who I was talking to today?—Abe Becker. Bet you don't know who Abe Becker is, right?'

'That film cutter at Metro?' suggested B.

'*Abe Becker*,' said Sid, almost tersely, 'is the brother-in-law of Nicky Hilton. Know what he said? He said if this goes through, Connie will put up a *Liechten-Hilton* like that!' Sharp snap of fingers. 'Shops too, the whole arcade bit. They'll clean up—and Abe *knows* it, believe you me!' Adding this last with a note of resentment, as if he felt they should cut him in for a piece of the action.

The waitress arrived, and Sid was momentarily distracted by the fact that she was topless. They were having a late lunch—about four P.M.—at a restaurant on the Strip called the Shangri-la Tropicana, whose specialty was spareribs and barbecued chicken, and waitresses with names like Honey Pot, Fancy Box, Charity Ball, etc. Sid went there often, and it was no news to him that they were topless, but it was a sometime source of distraction nonetheless.

'Hey,' he said to the girl—a rather heavy Scandinavian type, who maintained a steady frown of suspicious consternation—'you met my friend, the internationally famous film director, Mr. Boris Adrian? I been telling him about you.'

'Boris Adrian?' She was impressed, but then her brow

40

clouded a bit more. 'Oh yeah? Listen, I know *you're* in the show business, Mr. Kratzman, I checked that out already, but some of these guys you bring in, what do I know, maybe they're creeps or something. I mean, that's some sense of humor you got there, Mr. Kratzman.'

'Yeah, well, the thing is,' said Sid, 'we're doing these commercials, and I been telling Mr. Adrian here you might be just the girl for the job. What we've got to be sure of though is *nipple distention*.'

'Huh?'

'There's going to be a very tight close-shot, you see, and we've got to make sure that the line is just right. It's a public-service spot for CBS, it's for, uh, let's see, yeah, *it's for breast feeding of infants*, you know, to encourage breast feeding among young mothers. Some very harmful additives have recently been discovered in the, uh, you know, formula mixtures. It's a thirty-second spot—wouldn't show your face, of course, just the line of the, uh, bosom. Pays seven-fifty.'

'Seven-fifty? Seven hundred and fifty?'

'Give or take a few bucks—union dues, that kind of thing.'

The girl looked from one to the other. 'Thirty seconds, seven hundred and fifty dollars? Wow.'

'Uh, yes, well, the thing is,' said Sid gravely, 'we have to be sure about the *line*. Just step over here, will you, dear.'

'Huh?' said the girl, obeying immediately, '*what* line?'

'The nipple,' he said, 'is a very important part of the breast line. Now just relax.' He put one hand on her right hip, placed his other over her bare (left) breast and fingered it gingerly. 'Now, let's just see . . .'

'Hey, wait a minute,' said the girl, glancing about anxiously.

'No, it's all right,' Sid reassured her, releasing the nipple but still holding her hip. 'Here, this is better,' and he took a half-melted ice cube from his drink and began massaging the nipple with it.

41

The girl tried to draw away, discreetly but somewhat wildly, looking right and left. 'Listen, the manager will flip if he sees this!'

Sid ignored her remark, turned to Boris. 'Yes, you see, Mr. Adrian, there's quite a satisfactory distention there, don't you agree?' And even the girl then looked down in curiosity at the nipple, which was perking out like a tiny top hat. And a number of nearby guests, ordinarily blasé, were shooting uneasy looks at the odd spectacle.

'Okay,' said Sid, 'let's try the other one.'

'Hey, listen,' she said, really quite apprehensive now, 'can't we do this later?'

'Okay,' said Sid abruptly, and returned his attention to the menu at once. 'How's your deep-dish Beaver Pie today?'

'Huh?' She stared at him dumbly for a moment, mouth half-open. 'Say, that's some sense of humor you got there, Mrs. Kratzman, you know that?'

Boris sighed and smiled sadly. 'Oh, he knows that all right. Yes indeed.'

In a town and an industry where the tasteless quip is rife and men of *mauvaise foi* are legion—even here was Sid Krassman notorious for his obsessively aggressive wit and chicanery, always with a slight compulsion toward the grotesquely banal. Getting into a cab, for example, he would sometimes wait for the driver to ask 'Where to?' and he would reply, 'What the hell, let's go to *your* place!' And guffaw raucously. Or, stepping into a crowded elevator, he might intone with tremendous authority: 'I suppose you're all wondering why I've called you together.'

'Okay, King, are you ready for this?' he asked now, still at the Shangri-la Tropicana, opening an attaché case which he had taken from beneath his chair. He extracted a large white folio, untied its ribbon, and began passing eleven by fourteen color prints across the table to Boris. Most of the photographs were of places, rather than persons, and featured town squares, cobblestone streets, country lanes, meadows, forest glades, streams, lakes, cottages, churches, castles—all of obvious European motif, and most against an overwhelming backdrop of snow-covered mountains. Boris went through them in silence, with a slightly bemused smile.

'Well, there's our locations, baby!' exclaimed Sid, with a glee he prayed would be contagious.

'Where'd you get these?' asked Boris, turning one over to look at the back. On it was stamped: 'Property of Krassman Enterprises, Ltd.—Unauthorized Reproduction Strictly Prohibited.'

Sid flicked his cigar, caught the waitress's eye and signaled for another cognac.

'Flew Morty Kanowitz over to scout it,' he said easily.

Boris returned his attention to the photographs. 'Didn't you tell me the other night you were *broke*?'

Sid coughed and glanced about the room uneasily, tried a diversionary tactic: 'Say, I think I just saw Dick Zanuck, going into the other room—'

Boris smiled wearily and continued to look at the pictures. 'My thou, huh?'

Sid was greatly relieved that the deception was finally out in the open, and that Boris did not seem too bugged by it. He leaned back in his chair, rolled the cigar from one side of his mouth to the other. 'Well, B.,' he said with a grin, 'it *takes* money to *make* money—am I right?'

'Nice pictures,' said Boris, handing them back.

'*Perfect* locations, am I right?'

'Locations for what? I don't even have a story yet.'

'But that'll *come* to you, B. baby,' Sid reassured in his most imploring tones, 'that'll *come* to you—from the Blue Fairy of Inspiration!'

It was common knowledge that his last two winners had been shot from 'scripts' about as substantial as a couple of matchcovers.

'And the money?' asked B. dryly. 'Blue Fairy too?'

Sid reached into his breast pocket, and produced with a

flourish what appeared to be a folded cablegram. 'Three big ones, baby! *And* final cut!'

'Three million? You're kidding.'

'Nope,' he shook his head solemnly, 'talked to Al last night—he's done one helluva promo-job on this, you know—told him to get me a cable confirmation of the deal. Here it is.' He held the cable up in front of his face, gesturing with it as he spoke.

'Well, that's terrific, Sid,' said Boris, and reached out for it.

'One thing, B.,' said Sid, not relinquishing it, 'one thing I want to explain—a technicality, you'll see it yourself in the cable, but I wanted to tell you about it first, so it don't take the edge off. Know what I mean?'

Boris, whose hand was still extended for the cable, gazed at Sid without expression, and slowly lowered his hand. 'Nope,' he said softly, 'I'm afraid not.'

'The government of Liechtenstein,' Sid proclaimed in serious measured tones, 'is prepared to advance us—in the form of both credit and cash—up to the amount of *three million dollars . . .*'

Here his voice faltered, and Boris reached out impatiently and snatched the cable from him. Unfolding it, he began to read, muttering the words half aloud, almost verbatim as Sid had described, until near the end, reading this part, quite distinctly: '. . . "in combined accreditation and national currency, to a maximum equivalent of three, repeat three, million dollars (U.S.)—providing that such an amount as to be agreed upon is duly and equally matched by an investor or investors of the second party. Stop. Letter detailing proposal follows. Regards, Max von Dankin, Minister of Finance, Liechtenstein." '

Boris carefully folded the cable and placed it on the table. 'Where's my thou?'

'Now wait a minute, B.,' said Sid with real earnestness. 'I *swear* to you I know how to get the match money. Just *please* give me the chance to explain.'

Boris sighed. 'Go,' he said.

'Well, let's get out of here first,' said Sid. 'I don't want anybody to know about this.' He looked anxiously around the room. 'Place is crawling with fuckin' lip-readers.'

Boris laughed at this, Sid's feigned or real paranoia, and they started for the door.

Things seemed to be going Sid's way again, and his spirits were rising. In the foyer they encountered their waitress.

'What's the matter, darling,' asked Sid in concern, 'do you have a cold?'

'A cold?' said the girl, frowning in surprise. 'What made you think *that*, Mr. Kratzman?'

'Oh, I don't know,' said Sid ingenuously, 'your *chest* looks all swollen.' And he reached out to proffer comfort to the afflicted area, guffawing raucously.

7

Beneath the great oil portrait of big Dad Harrison, chairman of the board and chief stockholder of Metropolitan Pictures, sat young Les—sitting at his mammoth desk, slumped almost racing style, as if the desk were some extraordinary vehicle, capable of tremendous power and speed—sitting as though he had been fitted into it, while arrayed about him, like a fantastic dashboard, were the various controls he operated so masterfully—telephones, intercoms, casette-recorders, tiny TV sets, video playbacks, and a miniature air conditioner (Braun of West Germany) that blasted right into his face, giving him an odd, windblown-hair look, and the illusion of actual motion. And, in fact, there *were* vibrations of power, speed, and above all, weird road-holding maneuverability emanating from this desk, for it was here Les

Harrison wheeled and dealed—and that, indeed, was the name of his game.

'I've got news for you, my friend,' he was saying quietly into the phone. 'Patriotism is in the shithouse these days. Too controversial. Nope, not even *dancers*—not if they're under contract to *this* studio, they don't. *Nobody who works for this studio goes to Vietnam.* Some of that shit might rub off on them, and who needs it? Right? Right? Talk to you later, Marty.'

He hung up, and in a simultaneous move with the other hand, flicked the switch of the outer office intercom.

'Okay, baby,' he said in his deceptively sleepy voice, 'let them come in now.'

He leaned forward, elbows on the desk, hands clasped, fingers intertwined, so that his nose rested on top of the locked hands, and his chin on the two extended thumbs below—Caligula style. The door opened, and a brace of William Morris agents entered, with, to be sure, a somewhat affected saunter. When talent agents arrive in tandem, it means one of two things: an old agent is breaking in a young one; or, the agency considers the meeting critical enough, ten-percentwise, to double-team the adversary. The latter is done almost exactly the way cops do it—in counterpoint, with one playing reasonable, soft-hearted ('Let's give Les a break, Al'), while the other ('I say we take it to Paramount') dons the antagonistic mask of the impulsive bad guy and ass-hole.

The grace and subtlety of such tactics would go for naught, of course, against the Rat Prick, and were not employed by those who knew him. It wasn't that he was oblivious to ruse, nor even unappreciative of it well-wrought, but because he was dealing from such a monstro power position it was difficult for him to assign relevance to ruse and the like.

The studio had eleven features in production at the moment. Three were shooting in Europe, one in Mexico, and one in New York. This left six shooting on the lot; of these

46

six, one was a Western, one a beach movie, one sci-fi, and one an art-house version of a two-character off-Broadway play. These pictures were budgeted at about a million each, and as a conglomerate, or individually, were referred to as 'the garbage'. Their multi-nefarious function ranged from cross-collateralization (i.e., juggling production costs and profits between winner flicks and loser flicks), to renting studio space and facilities (to themselves) at exorbitant rates (paid by the stockholders), and finally, making a token fulfillment of actor, director, and producer commitments—or, in short, grooving with the proverbial tax write-offs, and keeping the gargantuan archaic machine in motion.

This accounted for four of the six pictures, leaving two— and these were boss and monstro. One was the nine-million-dollar vehicle for Rex McGuire, *Hi There, Heartbreak*, and the other a hefty sixteen-point-five, *Until She Screams*, starring Angela Sterling, the highest-paid darling of the silver screen—nailing, as she did, a cool one and a quarter big ones per pic, plus ten percent of the boxoroonie, going in.

In any case, these last two were the sort of projects which interested Les—and he was highly doubtful that the Morris agents who had just come in would have anything of that caliber in mind—so it was rather laconically that he returned their 'Hey Les baby' big hellos.

'Saw you at the Factory the other night,' said the older, heavier one, flopping down on the couch with an exaggerated show of relaxation.

Les looked at him momentarily, raised his brows in a quizzical indication of 'So what?' and said, 'Oh?'

'Yeah, you were with Liz and Dickie—I didn't come over, I figured you might be, ha ha,' a sly wink to his partner, '*talking business.*'

Les continued to regard him without expression, then returned the wink, 'I see what you mean—ha ha,' adding the laugh very dryly indeed.

'I was there with Janie,' the agent went on hurriedly,

somewhat rattled, 'Janie Fonda and Vadim. Whatta gal! Having that kid didn't affect her figure one bit—she's still a knockout!'

Les nodded silently.

'Say, Les,' said the second agent brightly, pointing at a small painting on the wall, 'isn't that a new one?'—his purpose in this being twofold: first, to impress on his colleague how familiar he was with Les Harrison's office; and second, that Les himself might be somewhat touched by his interest. He was aware that the latter was extremely remote, because he was just bright enough to know that Les knew (and knew that *he* knew that *Les* knew) that this sort of thing—memorizing personal details of other people's lives, the names of their wives, their children, their tastes, their infirmities—this relentless effort to ingratiate, was the talent agent's bag.

Les looked up to see which picture he was talking about. Aside from the portrait of his father, there were six other paintings in the room—three on each of two walls, the third wall being an expanse of window, and the fourth, behind the desk, occupied by big Dad exclusively.

'I believe you're right,' he said. It was a blue and white Picasso, of the 'Girls of Avignon' series. 'Do you like it?' he turned back to the agent, smiling.

'Terrific,' said the agent, shaking his head in admiration, '*fabulous!* Jeez, could that guy ever paint!'

'I'll tell Kelly you like it,' said Les, jotting something on a pad, 'or at least that you noticed the change.'

Kelly, as she was called, was his personal assistant, or Gal Friday—if one may receive $1,200 a week and still be considered as such; in any case, among her responsibilities was the occasional rearrangement of the office decor, including the choice of paintings—which she selected from the family collection. She regarded this duty less a privilege than a necessity, because Les Harrison—suffering from an affliction that is curiously, even notoriously, prevalent on the executive level in Hollywood—was totally *color-blind*. So he

48

would tabulate remarks about his office furnishings in much the same way he would study the opinion cards filled out at film previews . . . quite objectively.

'Say, tell me something,' he said, looking from one agent to the other. 'The last time you guys were in here—weren't *you* wearing shades,' pointing to the younger one, who was *not* wearing them, 'and *you*,' pointing to the other, who was, 'weren't. Right?'

The two exchanged looks; the older, heavier one gave a low whistle, shaking his head.

'*Wow*,' said the younger one softly.

'Talk about *sharp*,' said the heavy. 'Jeez, that must've been . . . two, three months ago, for Chrissake.'

'How come?' asked Les.

'Huh?' The young one seemed surprised, then slightly chagrined. 'Oh yeah, well, it's . . . it's kind of silly, I guess. I mean, it's the old man,' referring to the head of their agency, 'he said we shouldn't both wear them at the same time—said it's a bad image. Looks *spooky*, he said.' He shrugged, smiling sheepishly, gestured toward the other agent. 'So today it's *his* turn.'

Les nodded thoughtfully, head resting on one hand. As he gazed at each in turn, the young agent shifted about uneasily, while the one wearing the glasses had removed them and was polishing them with his tie, chuckling and muttering, 'Jeez, Les, that's some *memory* you got, for Chrissake!'

Les appeared to be considering it, and it seemed to please him in a vague and absent way—as though this facility might, in some degree, compensate for his being colorblind.

He cleared his throat, and started to speak, but the intercom buzzed, and he hit the switch impatiently.

'Yeah, Kelly?'

'Eddie Rhinebeck on two.'

'I'm in a meeting, Kelly.'

'It's important.'

'Shit,' he said, flicking off the intercom, and picking up the phone. 'Bad news, bad news, I can *smell* it. Yeah, Eddie?'

He listened intently, the frown on his brow growing darker.

'You gotta be kidding,' he said finally, with a remarkable lack of conviction. He closed his eyes, and listened some more.

'The *cunt*,' he said then softly, through clenched teeth, 'the *stupid* . . . *irresponsible* . . . *vicious* . . . *cocksucking little cunt!*' Sigh. 'I just don't believe it. Wait a minute, Eddie.'

He covered the mouthpiece and looked up at the agents.

'I'm sorry, fellas,' he said, gesturing with his hand, his cool having undergone a Jekyll-Hyde collapse, 'it's *disasterville*—I'll have to talk to you later.'

They rose almost as one, with smiles of perfect understanding. 'No biz like show biz, right, Les?' quipped the older agent, winking broadly. 'Talk to you later, Les,' said the other, and with several waves of camaraderie, they went out the door.

Les uncovered the mouthpiece. 'Okay, Eddie, now what the hell happened?'

Eddie Rhinebeck was the studio's head of publicity. For the past two months his exclusive concern had been Angela Sterling and their sixteen-point-five biggie, *Until She Screams*, promotion of which he was handling personally. And to this end he had recently engineered what promised to be a PR coup of the very first magnitude. Through an elaborate process of fête and cajolery, he had managed to persuade a state senator and a rear admiral to allow, even insist, that the men and officers who were to serve aboard the newly commissioned battleship *California* 'elect' the lady who would christen their ship. The choice, to be determined by popular vote, was between: (1) Dr. Rose Harkness, most recent American female Nobel Prize winner, (2) Mrs. Hannah Bove, bereaved 'Gold Star Mother of the Year,' who lost three sons in Vietnam, (3) Storm Rogers, attractive wife

50

of the governor of California, and (4) the perfect Angela Sterling.

Studio heads (including Dad Harrison) were apprehensive about the possible outcome. ('Why take the chance —who needs it?'), but Eddie was adamant, and Les went along.

'The prestige bit can't hurt us,' he said, 'should be good for a *Life* cover story.'

'Yeah?' asked Dad, 'so what if she loses?'

'Aw, come on, Dad, Eddie's got the vote in his pocket, for Chrissake, he knows where it's at.'

The old man sighed, shook his head, whistled softly: 'So what if Eddie's wrong?'

Les smiled, faint and knowing. 'Eddie's not wrong, Dad— not when his head is on the line.'

Still, there had been a certain tension, a certain malaise, while they awaited the outcome—and ample relief when it was announced that Angela had won by a veritable landslide, garnering more votes than the other three ladies combined.

Naturally this was a boss feather in Eddie's proverbial cap, vis-à-vis Les—as likewise it was for Les, vis-à-vis Dad and the New York office. So there had been an abundance of backpatting all around in anticipation of the great day— which was finally at hand, on San Francisco's big Pier 97, with the 6,000 men and officers of the *California* standing at attention in full parade regalia, while on the pier itself, seated in a festively draped grandstand, not far from the beribboned bottle of bubbly, a host of notables—including three admirals, the mayor of San Francisco, the governor of the state, and the Secretary of the Navy. Ranged about them, as in ambush, was an army of newsmen and photographers, and on the periphery sat three TV camera trucks.

In order to fully exploit the event, Les had shut down production on *Until She Screams* for the entire day, at, needless to say, considerable expense to the studio. It would be difficult then, to exaggerate his pique in learning that Miss

Sterling, the fabulous object of all these arrangements, had, in fact, failed to show.

After waiting for more than an hour, there was no alternative to getting on with it, so a substitute was chosen. Trying to replace the boss beauty simply with an everyday run-of-the-mill beauty would have been folly. Instead they chose, and quite wisely, a very pretty little girl of seven, with a pink ribbon in her hair.

This substitution might have proved satisfactory, though far from ideal, granted, had not the girl, in her inexperience, and nervousness, missed with the ribboned bottle, and worse, was carried forward by her own momentum, lost her footing, and fell from the pier and into the water below, very nearly drowning before she was pulled out. All in all, the christening and the launching had been a fiasco—the worst, according to some, in naval history.

'I'll *kill* her,' Les said to Eddie, 'as God is my witness, I will *kill* her!' Then, very softly, he began to weep. 'It's not *fair*, Eddie,' he said, 'it's just not *fair* . . . and even worse, it's . . . it's *insulting*'—he glanced at the large portrait—'. . . especially to Dad. After all he's done for her, the cunt. I swear to God, Eddie, if we weren't eight weeks into the picture, and her in every goddamn shot, I'd fire her ass! Right off the picture! I don't dare *how* much she's worth at the box office! Right off the picture! I swear to God!'

He paused, touching at his eyes with a Kleenex, shaking his head slowly, like an old man in unspeakable grief, listening to Eddie.

'Yes, Eddie, I know, I know,' he said quietly. 'She's got us by the nuts. The cunt.'

8

11777 Sunset Boulevard, a gigantic stucco edifice of lavender and antique gold, surrounded by a spiked twelve-foot wall and an actual moat, was the home of Angela Sterling— beloved sex-goddess of silver screen and living color— whose last three times out had each grossed more than previous all-time champ at the box, big *GWTW*.

So incredible was her public appeal that it was literally not possible to open a magazine or newspaper without being confronted by yet another elaborately footnoted chapter of her rather imaginary life—imaginary in the sense that it was almost totally fabricated by the studio publicity department. And a grand job they did, too; her 'page-count-index,' by which such matters are judged, was twice as high as that of Jackie Kennedy during the latter's climax exposure-wise.

Approaching the house was like approaching a major studio: *Impasseville* at the gate. Unless you were expected, the big iron doors of the wall simply remained shut come what might. If and when they did open, it was necessary to pass a gatehouse occupied by two uniformed and armed attendants, who, after ascertaining the guest's identity, would cause the drawbridge over the moat to lower. It was generally believed that the natural security afforded by the moat was augmented by the fact that its dark waters were seething with flesh-eating piranha fish—but this was just more 'studio bullshit,' as it was sometimes called by the two men with the guns, resenting as they did the implication that they alone were not enough to protect their movieland princess, 'without a bunch of goddamn fish stinking up the joint!'

It was through these portals, and past this boss-freak' vigilance, that Boris and Sid had made their way, two hours earlier. And at almost precisely the moment when the perfect Miss Sterling should have been launching a battleship, she was delightedly signing a letter of agreement to play 'one of the romantic leads,' as Sid had described it, 'in a film, as yet untitled and unscripted, to be directed by Boris Adrian, and to be shot in and around Vaduz, Liechtenstein, principal photography to commence within three weeks of this agreement, dated May 2, 1970.'

Boris had also signed, and then Sid had been quick to add, with a flourish, his own signature following 'witnessed by . . .'

'Gosh,' said the girl, all smiling radiance, clasping her hands and raising them to her throat as though to trap the ecstasy before it could flutter out and away, bluebird of happiness style, 'I just never thought it could happen! I still can't believe it!'

Sid was beaming fanatically as he folded the paper and put it in his pocket. 'Oh, it's happened all right,' he said, nodding, 'yessiree bob!'

'Well,' she said breathlessly, 'let's have some champagne or something!' And she rang for the maid.

If it was curious that Angela's pleasure about these un-expected developments was equal even to gross Sid's, it was also understandable. Despite her monstro wealth, her incredible (boss) beauty, her outlandish power—or, by way of summary, her fantastic 'success'—she was truly a girl bereft. Two years previous she had undergone a fast and furious affair with a New York writer who had turned her on to certain phenomena *variés*, existence of which she had not previously suspected. It was nothing spectacular, just the standard below-Fourteenth-Street primer, or bag o' tricks as some called it: *I Ching*, Living Theatre, Lenny Bruce, *The Realist*, Fugs, Grateful Dead, and so on, including the voguish notion that movies should or could be 'good.'

Next, of course, she had found herself at Actors Workshop—not as a member (they wouldn't accept her) but as 'a distinguished visitor from the film capital,' auditing, four hours a week. It was there she learned she knew nothing whatever about her profession, and it gave her pause.

The studio (Metropolitan Pictures) flipped—first, because she was even interested in such a crackpot thing as a New York acting school, and second, and more important, because her being rejected had made the morning papers.

Her agent, Abe 'Lynx' Letterman, was nonplussed. 'Look, baby,' he gently chided, 'we're walking away with one million fucking dollars a picture—is that *spit*?'

'It isn't that, Abe,' she tried to explain, 'it's just that, well, there are more important things in life than . . . money.'

'Say, that really grabs me, that does,' Abe fumed, 'so whatta you *do* with them—cut 'em up and put 'em in the *freezer*?'

Angela Sterling, née Helen Brown, in the Oak Cliff section of Amarillo, Texas; age fourteen, cute-as-a-button drum majorette at James Bowie High; age sixteen, voted Most Beautiful Girl in the Senior Class; age seventeen, Miss Texas; and later that same year, in Atlantic City, she received the uniquely fun-laurels of Miss America.

And now she was twenty-four, veteran trooper of the silver screen and highest paid thesp in the history of cinema. But, here, the crux: although she had appeared in seventeen pictures, starring in the last twelve, not only had she never been nominated for *any* award, she had scarcely received a single decent notice. Granted, one or two kindly reviewers would occasionally refer to a 'certain natural ability'— comparing her in this, and other ('natural') regards, to the late Marilyn Monroe—but her only real accolades came in the form of several thousand fan letters a week . . . exclusively in the language of the adolescent, the moron, and the sex-nut. Thus, to Angela Sterling, at this critical point in her life and career, the prospect of working with the King B. Boris was salvation itself.

'Tell you what, Angie,' big Sid cautioned, 'let's just keep

55

this on the q.t. for the time being, okay? That way, the studio, Lynx, Les Harrison . . . they don't know, they don't worry—then the time is ripe, we spring it—you know, with a lot of classy PR, the real thing. Okay?'

'Sure thing,' gushed Angie, and beamed from one to the other, 'whatever you say.'

TWO

The Magic of the Lens

1

The spires, towers, turrets, and snow-capped peaks which compose the storybook skyline of Vaduz, Liechtenstein, also belie its essential fifteenth-century character. *Heidi-time* . . . Heidi-time in Heidiville. The nearest town of consequence is Zurich, seventy miles to the west—seventy miles, that is, as the 707 flies, except there are no airports in Liechtenstein, so that the trip from Zurich to Vaduz, meandering over mountain passes by train and bus, takes three hours. Therefore the first order of business on the part of Krassman Enterprises, Ltd., was to build an airstrip. This was accomplished by capable Production Manager Morty Kanovitz and his advance unit, who bribed and otherwise cajoled a local construction firm into working round the clock, in all weathers, to complete a 3,000-foot asphalt airstrip in forty-eight hours.

'How 'bout that?' said Sid, not without a trace of pride, as their chartered twin-Cessna touched town smoothly on the virgin strip. 'Old Morty's right on the ball, huh?' Saying this with a nudge and wink at B., to suggest that it was, in truth, he, Sid Krassman who was on the ball in having accomplished this important step in their operation.

'Is it long enough for a jet?' asked Boris, peering out dubiously.

'Are you kidding?' demanded Sid with great indignation, albeit somewhat nervous, 'do you think I'd make a goof like that, fer Chrissake?'

Boris shrugged. 'Looks short to me.'

Sid deprecated the judgment with a wave of his hand. 'Ah,

59

well, you're talking about the *Concorde*, one of those *big* mothers—'

'No, man, I'm talking about a DC-Nine. I'm talking about five thousand feet.'

Sid scrutinized the strip with a frown as the plane turned and taxied over to where a gigantic Mercedes 600 waited, with three men standing beside it—able Morty Kanovitz and his trusty assistant, Lips Malone, the third party being dapper Art Director Nicky Sanchez.

The Mercedes 600 is the largest car in the world; an exaggerated limousine, about twenty-seven feet long, it looked oddly disproportionate against the miniature airstrip.

Giant hellos were exchanged all around, and Boris and Sid were flourished into the front-facing back seat to sit opposite Morty and the art director, while Lips slipped in alongside the driver—this being the present pecking order within the tiny hierarchy.

'Ya looking *beautiful*,' Morty was saying, with a playful slap to Sid's knee, 'both you guys are looking *beautiful*, for Chrissake!'

Morty, a short, fat sort of professional Bronx type, had complemented his smart Cardin combo with regional headgear—a tight-brim Tyrolean featuring two colorful feathers —as, of course, had his front-seat shadow, Lips Malone.

'I'm telling you,' Morty went on, 'you guys are going to *love* it here!' He shook his head, rolling his eyes up, Eddie Cantor style, to indicate his hat. 'Look, we gone native awready!'

Sid stared morosely at the short runway, then turned to scowl at Morty.

'Get rid of that freaky hat, will ya,' he growled. 'Makes you look like a goddamn fruit!'

2

The production office had been set up on the top floor of the Imperial Hotel—a squat, four-story brown brick building in the middle of town.

'Come on,' said Morty, with a slightly nervous laugh, as he led Boris, somber in dark glasses, and Sid, mopping his perspiring brow, down a half-lit hotel hallway, 'I'll show you around the lot.'

An old-line production manager who knew where his bread was buttered, so to speak—or, in other words, a sort of sycophantic ass-hole—fat Mort had already fixed their names, in raised cardboard letters, painted gold, on the doors which they passed now in succession:

.

SIDNEY H. KRASSMAN
Executive Producer

.

BORIS ADRIAN
Director

.

MORTON L. KANOVITZ
Production Manager

.

ART DEPARTMENT
Nicholas Sanchez

.

WARDROBE
Helen Vrobel

.

ACCOUNTING
Nathan A. Malone

61

All the rooms were the same—ordinary hotel rooms, except that a desk and three telephones had been installed, and a large couch instead of a bed. Another unusual feature of each was a young, but not-too-nifty, miniskirted girl sitting behind a typewriter, smiling up eagerly when introduced as 'Gretel,' 'Gretchen,' 'Gertrude,' 'Hildegarde,' etc.

'Where'd you get those broads?' asked Sid, scowling. 'I don't know whether I'm at a whorehouse or a dog show!'

'Believe me, Sid,' Morty explained, 'I could of gotten some ravers, but it was hard enough finding broads that could unnerstan' English, let alone *type*, fer Chrissake! So I thought to myself, "what the hell, the picture comes first!" Am I right?' He cast a beseeching look around to the others.

'Whad'ya say the name of mine was?' Sid wanted to know.

'*Grunhilde!*' said Morty, with a vaudeville leer and wink. 'Takes twenty-seven words a minute and gives the best head in the city!'

Sid guffawed, and Morty, thus encouraged, tried to follow it up, grinning crazily:

'*Swallows* it too, Sid—just the way you like it, huh?'

Sid, in grand good humor now, and wanting to infect the silent Boris with it, gave a snort of mock derision: ' "Best head in the city"! *What* fuckin' city? This tank?' He looked at Boris in hopes of an appreciative take, but the latter seemed not to have heard, and Sid thought he might have said the wrong thing. 'Not that we can't make a whale of a movie in a *tank*-town!' he added, then nudged Boris, desperate enough now to insist. '*Get* it, King? "*Whale?*" "*Tank?*" Haw-haw!'

Morty, of course, joined in the laugh—but too heartily, considering the way the shaded B. looked at them now—one to the other, with a sort of deadpan compassion—so he choked it off abruptly.

'Yeah, I get it, Sid,' said Boris then with a faint smile. ' "Whale," "tank." Terrific. I guess I was thinking of something else.'

Both men nodded with vigorous understanding and a show of relief, but when Boris turned away again, Morty whispered urgently to Sid: 'What's the matter with *him*? He's not on the *stuff*, is he?'

'He's *thinkin'*, fer Chrissake!' snapped Sid. 'Ain't you never seen nobody *think*?!?'

But this display of irate impatience was not very convincing, so that a certain mild concern was evident in both their faces as they followed Boris through the door marked 'SIDNEY H. KRASSMAN, Executive Producer.'

This room, like such offices the world over, wherever films are being made, was intended to function as the nerve center of the production; instead of three telephones on the desk, there were five; against one wall was a combination bar and refrigerator; and against the other, a stereo and two TV sets; the oversize couch was covered with what invitingly appeared to be some kind of white fur and several soft-looking pillows of the same fabric in different colors. On the desk, along with the five telephones, digital-clock, and the rest of the usual stuff, was a small framed photograph of Sid's wife.

'Where the hell did you get *this*?' he asked, picking it up, frowning at it.

Morty beamed. 'Had it blown up from a snap I took at the beach one time we were all out at the beach—remember, out at Ed Weiner's place? Old Colony Road?'

Sid replaced it carefully on the desk. 'Christ, I haven't *seen* that cunt in two years,' he muttered, then to Morty: 'Still, it was a nice thought, Morty. Thanks.'

'My pleasure, Sid.'

Both their voices seemed to quaver for an instant in near-tearful camaraderie, or similar—a short-lived absurdity, however, as they turned to join Boris, who was staring at the most salient feature of the room: the big, wooden shooting board, which dominated one entire wall.

'Well, there she is,' said Sid, with a heavy sigh, and he and Morty gazed at it reverently, while Boris walked to the window.

63

The purpose of the board was to forecast the shooting schedule, day by day, and then to reflect its progress—all done with gaily colored plaques, pegs, and disks, to be fitted snugly into slots and holes against a dazzling white, like an elaborate children's game. Since there was as yet no schedule (in fact, no script), the board, still smelling of fresh paint, was empty—its red, blue, yellow, and green counters neatly grouped in readiness below the blank white rows, numbered one to one hundred, representing days to come, unfitted and unfulfilled. But this quality of freshness made the board seem innocent, virgin, and most important of all, optimistic.

'Where you going to put up the principals?' asked Sid.

'Sid,' said smug Mort, 'we also got the two floors below this—one for the actors, one for the crew.'

Sid was irately astonished. 'You're gonna put up the actors and the apes in the same hotel?!? Are you outta your nut!?!'

It is classic Hollywood protocol that the actors be quartered separately from the technicians ('apes' or 'gorillas,' as they are affectionately called)—allegedly in apprehension of the leading lady being gang-banged to death by a raving horde of drunken grips and gaffers, thus seriously jeopardizing the pic's all-important completion date.

'Yes sir, boy,' Sid stormed on, 'you must really be outta your fucking nut!'

'Have a heart, Sid,' Morty pleaded, 'it's the only hotel in town, fer Chrissake!'

'Whatta you mean "the *only* hotel in town"? It *can't* be the only hotel in town, fer Chrissake!'

'Awright, awright, there's two more,' Morty admitted mournfully, 'but they're complete *flea bags*, Sid! Believe me, we try to put the apes in one of them, they'll go absolutely ... well, it would be a disaster, the union would kill us.'

'Okay, okay,' said Sid, pacing about, gesturing, making the most of the film's first production problem. 'We'll work it out, it ain't the end of the world, right?'

'Right, Sid.'

Sid pointed to the phones on the desk and spoke sternly: 'Just you find someplace else for the apes to stay, Morty. Got it?'

'Got it, Sid.' He went straight to the desk, picked up the nearest phone, and started trying to locate Lips Malone.

Sid joined Boris at the window, rubbed his hands together gleefully, then put at arm around his shoulder.

'Well, B., we're off and running! Right?'

Boris looked at him absently for a moment. 'It'll never happen,' he said.

'Huh?'

'We can't make a film working out of a place like this. There's no way.'

Sid looked around the room as though he must surely have missed something.

'Well, I admit it ain't exactly the *Thalberg* Building, but Jeez . . .'

'That's the trouble,' said B. sadly, 'it *is* the Thalberg Building. Can't you feel it?' He indicated something unseen with a slow arc of his hand. 'Death—there's a lot of death here, man. I expect Joe Pasternak to crawl through that door any minute.'

Sid shot a quick glance at the door, as though it might actually be possible; then he looked back at Boris, and an expression of panic moved into his eyes. 'Listen . . .' he faltered, 'listen, B. . . .'

At the desk Morty suddenly began talking in a loud furious voice into the phone: 'Where the hell you been, Lips?!? We're tryin' to make a *picture* here, fer Chrissake! Now get your ass over here pronto, we got a problem!'

'Will you shut the fuck up!' Sid bellowed at him, then turned back to Boris. 'B. . . .' he pleaded, one arm outstretched, the other touching his heart, 'whatta you *doing* to me?'

Boris nodded toward the window and beyond. 'Look at that tower, Sid.'

'*What?*' Sid peered out wildly, '*what* tower?'

'There,' said Boris, pointing with childlike excitement, 'isn't that *fantastic?!?*'

In the distance, just beyond the edge of the town, rose a dark turret—apparently the remains of a castle.

'A *Gothic tower*, Sid—*that's* where the production office should be. Beautiful!' He turned again to gaze out the window, a soft smile of rapture on his face.

Sid stared at him morosely. Behind them Morty was still on the phone talking in a low voice. Sid sighed and slowly turned.

'Morty, would you please get your ass over here, we got a problem.'

'Don't move, Lips,' said Morty tersely into the phone. 'Be back to you in five.' He hung up and bounded over, assuming a jovial mien.

'Kanovitz reporting! No job too big or too small.'

'Uh-huh, well whatta you know about that pile of rock over there?' He pointed to the tower.

'Whatta I know? I know *all* about it. We scouted it for locations awready.'

'Never mind location, would you believe it as a production office?'

'Are you *kiddin'?* It's a *ruin*, fer Chrissake!'

Sid nodded, satisfied, turned toward Boris.

'It's a ruin, B.'

'Beautiful,' said B.

Sid and Morty exchanged quizzical looks, and Sid gave Morty the nod. Morty cleared his throat: 'Uh, you don't seem to understand, B., there ain't any, well, you know, *electricity*, things like that.'

'Get a generator,' said Boris.

'There's no *water*.'

'We'll drink Perrier, it's good for you.'

'B. ...' said Sid, with the maniacal calm of someone trying to prove that the earth is not flat, and at last comes up with the clincher, 'B., *there are no telephones.*'

66

'And if you knew what we went through to get these phones,' exclaimed Morty frantically, 'I mean, there's a *six-month waiting list* for phones. We had to go to the minister hisself—'

'We'll use field phones.'

Both their mouths fell agape with total incredulity, and they spoke almost at once:

'*To talk to the Coast?!?*'

Boris turned to look at them for the first time, removed his shades, breathed on the lenses, and began rubbing them against his shirt.

'There's *nine hours difference* between here and the Coast,' he slowly explained, 'and any talking we do will be done from the *hotel*, at *night*—when it's *night here*, and *day there*. Got it? Now why don't you just use your fucking heads?'

He put his glasses back on and turned to the window again, leaving Sid and Morty face to face in defeat. Sid shrugged. 'So give him his tower.'

3

When Tony Sanders, the hot-shot writer from New York, arrived, the first item on the agenda was to get him laid . . . or so gross Sid had reasoned, because in order to entice the writer away from his novel and onto yet another amorphous screenplay, halfway around the world, Sid's inducements— aside from the usual cajolery, flattery, appeals to loyalty, friendship, art, and seventy-five hundred a week—had also included the blatant fiction that 'it's a swinging scene, baby!' And to this end, he had contrived to engage an ambulance to meet his plane, and inside the vehicle, two panty-and-bra nifties, who had been given a hundred each with instructions to 'do him up right' on the way from the airstrip to the tower. There had been a last-minute hitch in the scheme, however, in that the ambulance, the only one in town, was pressed into some local emergency use, and the single other suitable vehicle to be found was a hearse.

Sid was at first somewhat disturbed by the necessary substitution, remarking gravely that he didn't 'wantta show no disrespect,' but was reassured when Boris broke up laughing. 'Well, that's show biz for you, Sid,' he said when he was able to speak.

In any case, Tony Sanders stepped from the extraordinary vehicle, in fine form and fettle, looking completely relaxed after his long journey. He sauntered into the room where Boris and Sid were waiting, champagne in three buckets sitting on the desk. They were already drinking.

'*News*,' Tony said, still holding his bag, 'I got the *title*.'

'Beautiful,' said Boris, handing him a glass of the bubbly, 'how about the *story*?'

'Story can wait—' he gulped down the drink. 'Are you ready for *this*? Dig ...' He raised the empty glass and moved it across an imaginary marquee:

The Faces of Love

He scrutinized Boris's face for the almost indiscernible take, as the latter, head to one side, slightly quizzical, stared back at him, waiting for more. 'Yeah?' he finally asked.

The writer, still carrying the bag, walked about the room, gesturing with the empty glass, and talking rapidly:

'*Episodic*, right? Stories about the different kinds of love. Five, six, seven kinds of love—*Idyllic ... Profane ... Lesbian ... Incestuous*, like brother-sister, father-daughter, mother-son ... *Sadism ... Masochism ... Nymphomania* ... are you with me?'

By now Boris was ahead of him, and turned to Sid. 'Angela Sterling,' he said, 'we'll use Angela Sterling as the nympho,' then back to Tony, 'beautiful blond American heiress from Georgia ... no, from Virginia ... *tobacco* heiress, an only child ... she's uptight because she thinks Daddy wanted a boy instead of a girl ... Daddy's a very distinguished *southern gentleman*, mint juleps on the veranda, watching the happy darkies bring in the crop—"Yessuh, ah can tell a *field* nigra from a *house* nigra as fah as ah can see him!" Daughter flips out, goes to Morocco, fucks every spade in sight.'

'Beautiful,' said Tony, 'beautiful.' He dropped his bag abruptly and collapsed on the couch. 'Man, those chicks wiped me out. ... Gimme some Scotch, will you, Sidney ... whatta town—*wow*.'

Big Sid beamed as he moved to the bar, on tiptoe, almost clucking like a mother hen protective of the brood—because now it was happening, the magic had started, the weird creative thing, the Great Mystery ... one minute, no story—the next, a smash-fucking-hit! God was in his heaven and all was right in Sid Krassman's world.

4

Working straight through three days and nights—aided by the judicious use of vitamin B-12 injections, stoutly laced with speedy amphetamine—Boris and Tony were able to come up with a script, or at least enough of one to show to the departments concerned: Art (for the sets and the props), Wardrobe (for the costumes), and Casting (for the extras), and for them, in turn, to submit an estimate of the cost. In this way, eventually, would the film's above-the-line budget be determined—'above-the-line' meaning the cost not counting the actors.

The budget breakdown and a rough schedule were most important to Sid, because he was still wheeling and dealing in getting the money together—although with Angela Sterling committed to the picture, this was largely academic, simply a matter of accepting the best proposition. He was 'talking to the Coast' about ten times a day—very often with Les Harrison, whose overwhelming anxiety these days was an imminent meeting with Dad and the New York Stock-holders, at which time he would have to divulge the fact that their principal asset, Angela Sterling, was making a film in which they had no participation—especially awkward since the chairmanship had been virtually *given* to him as a result of his 'absolute personal assurance' to the board that Metropolitan Pictures had her exclusively.

'Well, for Chrissake, Sid,' he kept shouting on the phone, 'at least tell me what the picture's *about!* I can't ask for a million and a half if I don't know what the picture's about! What the hell's it *about*, Sid!?!'

'Well, I'll tell you, Les,' said Sid, sounding very serious, 'I'd say it's about . . . oh, let's see, I'd say it's about, er, uh, *ninety minutes!* Haw-haw-haw! How does that grab you, Les?'

'You son of a bitch! Have you forgotten that Dad gave you your *first goddamn job?!?*'

This caused Sid to go wide-eyed with indignation. He began pounding the desk and shouting. 'Job!?! Job!?! You mean he gave me the *first shit-end of the stick* I ever got, *that's* the job he gave me! He beat me for *two-and-a-half points of gross*, that's what he did! The old bastard is *still* making money off Sid Krassman!' Having put this last notion actually into words seemed to give it a reality it might not otherwise have had, and Sid was overcome by the sheer monstrosity of it. 'He's . . . he's a *criminal*,' he stammered, then recovered, shouting again, 'and you can both go fuck yourself!' And he slammed down the phone, just as Boris came in. 'Can you imagine the nerve of that rat prick Les?' he demanded, pointing at the phone, 'telling me old man Harrison give me my first job! When the fact is he *stole* my two and a half percent of the gross!'

70

Boris lay down on the couch. 'Poor Sid,' he sighed, 'always living in the past.'

'I told him to go fuck himself, B., I swear to God I did.'

Boris rested the back of one hand over his closed eyes. 'You did, huh?'

'*Beach Ball*,' Sid reminisced, 'cost four-ten, grossed six million. I'd be a rich man if it weren't for that old cocksucker.'

'I want to use Arabella for the lez,' said Boris. 'Can you get her?'

'Huh?'

'The *picture*, Sidney,' Boris explained without opening his eyes, 'remember the *picture*? Remember the *lesbian* sequence?'

Sid brightened. 'Arabella for the lez sequence! Terrific, B.! Now you're talking *marquee!*'

Arabella was a celebrated French actress of great talent, and spectacular beauty—only slightly fading at thirty-seven. She and Boris were close friends and had worked together on several films, at least two of which had won them both many awards. She was an extremely serious artist; she was also notoriously lesbian, having publicly so proclaimed, and moreover, had lived quite openly for many years with a series of equally beautiful, but successively younger, girls.

Sid was amused at that aspect of it, and guffawed coarsely. 'Boy, is that ever *type*-casting! I'll tell her we'll get her a gold-plated dildo! Haw-haw! When do you want her?'

'Find out when she's available—we may want to go with that sequence first, if Nicky can't finish his casbah in time.'

5

For their sound stages, Morty Kanovitz had leased a huge derelict building, formerly a button factory, on the opposite side of town from the airstrip. It was here that Nicky Sanchez would conceive and build whatever interior sets they could not locate in or near the town.

Raphael Nicholas Sanchez. Born in the smoke-black slums of Pittsburgh in 1934, the youngest of seven boys and a girl. It was a family with two preoccupations, steel mills and baseball—neither of which seemed to grab the young Raphael, he who showed a marked preference for playing dolls, jacks, and hopscotch with his sister and her girl friends, and a little later, in trying on their clothes.

Now, at thirty-five, he was considered one of the world's top art directors, or 'production designers,' as he called it, and had worked with Boris on several of his best films. Throughout the years he had continued to determinedly favor women's clothes over men's—though he did manage to limit his expression of this, in public at least, to an endless variety of cashmeres in powdery pastels, sandals, and skin-tight pocketless slacks with zippers anywhere but in the front. His manner, perhaps in overcomp for the extreme sordidness of his Pittsburgh childhood and the subproletarian level of his education, was exaggeratedly effete—even to the point of occasionally swooning. He adored Boris, was jealous of Tony Sanders, and loathed Sid beyond imagining.

Fastidiously picking his way through the maze of cables and carpentry in progress, he now escorted the three of them around the half-finished Casbah set—only occasionally pausing to compliment one of the younger laborers on his work: '*Beautiful,* darling, just beautiful!'

They entered what was obviously going to be the heiress's boudoir, and stood before the monumental, ornately canopied four-poster bed in the center of the room.

'Well,' said Nicky with an elaborate sigh, 'I suppose *this* is where a lot of the, pardon the expression, "action," will take place. Like it?'

'Wow,' said Tony, genuinely impressed.

It was, indeed, an extremely rich and impressive room, a saga of ebony and gold—the bed, a luxurious expanse of gleaming black satin, its four posts regal with huge carved golden serpents, supporting a fantastic canopy of rose-tinted mirror.

'A fun *set,* Nicky,' quipped Sid, 'but will it *dress?* Haw-haw!'

'Oh dear God,' murmured Nicky, closing his eyes in exasperation, and then very crisply: 'You can go back now, Sid—they've finished cleaning your cage.'

Boris was meanwhile moving slowly around the bed at different distances from it.

'These two are wild,' explained Nicky, indicating where two of the walls would break away to give the camera a longer shot.

Boris nodded. 'It's great, Nicky, just great.'

'Perfect,' Tony agreed.

'*Terrif,* Nicky,' said Sid, '*terrif!*'

Nicky was about to express a bit of blushing pleasure at their praise, when Sid's face clouded over, and he pointed to an opening in the set.

'Is that a *window,* for Chrissake? That's going to give us trouble, Nicky.'

He was referring to a wide empty space opposite one side of the bed—which at present looked out on an assortment of struts and guy wires securing that side of the set.

'Yeah, we better get rid of the window,' said Boris. 'I

don't want to use any back projection. What was going to be outside it anyway?'

Nicky became wide-eyed with apprehension. 'Oh, the *lights*, darling! The twinkling lights and music of the Casbah! The *romance* of the Casbah! Oh, we've just *got* to have the window!'

He looked beseechingly from Boris to Tony for some sign of support, but Tony only shrugged. 'With all that *fucking* going on, Nick, we won't be shooting much out the window.'

'But maybe you *will* need some place to cut away to!' Nicky exclaimed, '... if only for the sake of *taste!*' He turned haughtily from Tony, and pleaded with Boris: 'Listen, I'll make the mat myself! It'll be *perfect*, B., I promise you!'

Boris considered it, doubtfully. 'You can try it, Nick, but it can't be hokey. In fact, you better make up *two* walls— one with the window, and one without—so if the mat turns out Mickey Mouse, we can use the other wall.' He turned to Sid. 'Okay, Sid?'

'Got it, King,' said Sid, making a note of it in a little black book.

'Thank you, B.,' said Nicky, his voice soft with gratitude.

'It's a great set, Nicky,' Boris assured him, putting one hand on his shoulder as they all started to leave. Then he suddenly stopped, and turned back toward the set with a frown. 'Wait a minute, there's something wrong ...' He stared at the bed for a moment. 'Those *sheets* won't work. We'll be shooting *black cock* against *black sheets*—we'll lose all definition.'

'Hey, you're right,' said Tony.

'Good heavens,' said Nicky, 'who would have thought of that?'

'Too bad,' Boris mused. 'I sort of liked the *sinister* quality of it. Black satin.'

'The *come* would of looked good on black,' said Sid, and watched Nicky shudder.

Tony shrugged. 'Why don't we go the *pristine* route? White satin sheets, with a nice white crucifix above the bed. Same thing as sinister, same effect.'

Nicky was shocked. 'The *same?* What on earth do you mean?!?'

Sid was also disturbed. 'Oh, fer Chrissake, *not a crucifix!*'

'Well, I don't know about the crucifix,' said Boris, 'but *white*'s no good. Too stark. And with white you always blow some of the *blond* quality. How about *pink* satin? We'll get a good definition on both of them with pink, and,' he pointed to the canopy, 'it'll go with that mirror.' He looked at Tony and smiled. 'Might even work in a line about "*la vie en rose*," right, Tony?'

Tony laughed. 'Beautiful. Give the scene a little prestige— something for the critics to get their teeth into.'

Sid greedily made a note of it in his book. 'Now you guys are talking *box office!*' he said with glee, then implored, 'but for Chrissake, let's lose that fucking crucifix!'

6

A sunny June morning, with the splendor of pine and snow-capped peaks all around them. Boris and Sid sat in the monstro Merk, parked alongside the airstrip, waiting for the plane to arrive from Paris with Arabella. Boris slouched in one corner of the huge seat, perusing an old German racing form he'd found in a drawer in his hotel room, while Sid, beset by his chronic nervousness at the approach of the great or near-great, leaned forward, forehead perspiring as he fidgeted, loosening then tightening the red silk scarf at his throat, and lit another cigarette.

'You really think she'll do it, huh?'

Boris folded the paper, glanced out the window, then back, unfolding the paper and shaking his head. 'It's weird,' he muttered, 'you think you know something pretty well—like *German*,' he indicated the paper, 'then you come across it in a different aspect, one you've never seen before, and you realize you don't know it at all. I can't understand a fucking word of this.' He folded the paper again, dropped it on the floor, and stared out the window. 'I guess it always happens when you get into areas of specialization.'

'Yeah, yeah,' said Sid, pulling at his scarf again. 'Listen, you really think she'll do it—Arabella, I mean.'

Boris regarded him curiously. 'Why not? She's a very serious actress.'

'Yeah, I know, I know,' said Sid, shifting about on the seat, rubbing a hand across his forehead, 'that's what I mean.'

Boris continued to look at him for a moment, then smiled. '*Art*, my boy,' saying it lightly and looking out the window again, 'she'll do anything for art—the perfect darling.'

Sid was greatly relieved by Boris's tone, and began pulling himself together. 'Yeah, right. Well, listen, what's she like anyway? I never met her, you know.'

Boris shrugged. 'She's a groovy lady.'

'Yeah?' Sid's somewhat guarded lasciviousness began to ooze out in the form of a half-twinkling smile, or leer. 'Guess you and her are, uh, pretty *close*, huh?'

Boris continued to gaze out the window. 'Closest,' he murmured.

Sid nodded knowingly.

'Yeah, I read about it in the columns—when you did that first picture together.'

'That was bullshit.'

'Yeah, well, sure I know that,' Sid pursuing it with an odd delicacy and restraint, 'but you must of ... must of, uh, *made* it with her sometime.'

Boris looked at him, shook his head, and sighed. 'She's *lez*, Sid—*you* know that.'

'She's *lez*, she's *lez*,' Sid's exasperation exploded. 'She's got a *cunt*, ain't she?!? I mean, down there between her legs, there's a *hole*, right?!?'

Boris remained patient. 'Sidney ... *she does not dig men.*'

'So she doesn't dig men. I mean, if you're so *close* she ought to let you fuck her *anyway*. Who knows, maybe she'd like it.'

'Who wants to fuck a dyke?' asked Boris, and leaned back, closing his eyes.

Neither spoke for a moment or two, then Sid blurted it out: '*I* do! I'd *love* to fuck a dyke! A beautiful dyke! Can you imagine making a beautiful dyke *come*? It must be fantastic! But more than anything in the world I'd love to fuck *her! Arabella!* I mean, didn't you ever look at her *ass*? Those *tits*? Her incredible *legs*? That *face*? You can't tell me she doesn't need to be *fucked!* I swear to God, B., and this is no shit, I had fantasies, wet dreams, a million jerk-offs, you name it, about that broad for the last *twenty years!* Ever since *Bluebird of Happiness*, her first picture, seventeen years old!' He paused, shook his head, and continued sadly: 'Even after ... after I knew she was lez, I still wanted her, maybe more than ever. I kept thinking "If I could just *get it in her*, it would change everything"!' He threw up his hands in helpless despair. 'So now you know. Christ, I must really be sick in the head, huh?'

Boris laughed softly, reached over, and patted his arm. 'No, no, no, Sid, you're just a *good* ... *red-blooded* ... *American* ... *boy*. Wanting to fuck all the dykes and save them. Very commendable I'd say—a sort of one-man Salvation Army.'

Sid had to chuckle at the image, then they both looked up at the sound of the approaching jet.

'Well, speak of the dy—, I mean, *devil*,' said B., and Sid rapidly began to straighten his scarf.

'Listen, B.,' he pleaded, 'promise me you won't say anything to her about that ... I mean, jerking off and everything. Okay?'

77

'Okay,' said Boris, opening the door.

'I still have hopes, you know,' said Sid, only half jokingly.

'I know,' said Boris, and laughed. 'Lottsa luck.'

7

For Arabella, it was soon apparent, Liechtenstein was a place of tender memories—because it was here, many summers before, as a schoolgirl on holiday from her Paris *lycée*, she had frequently come to visit her cousin, Denise. And it was here, too, she had first known romance.

'There was the most wonderful place,' she was saying to Boris now, as she moved about the room, unfolding things from a suitcase which lay open on the bed, and hanging them in the closet—doing this in a smoothly efficient manner, swift but unhurried, with no wasted movement, and the grace of a cat, '. . . a beautiful place,' she continued, 'where we always went for . . . *picnic.*' She smiled at Boris, uncertain of the word. 'Picnic, yes?' Her accent was slight, and altogether delightful, her voice melodious—and though her English was nearly perfect, the care with which she selected each word gave her speech a charmingly tentative quality, deceptively coquettish.

Boris lay back on the couch, hands clasped behind his head, watching her. 'Yes,' he nodded, '*picnic.*'

'I will take you there,' said Arabella, hanging up a velvet jacket the color of blood. 'It is ten minutes by car from Vaduz.' She turned and leaned her back against the closet door, closing it. 'Now tell me about the picture—do I wear lots of beautiful beautiful clothes?'

'You *take off* lots of beautiful beautiful clothes.'

'Oh yes,' she laughed and crossed the room. 'Well, it

78

would not be serious picture unless I did that, would it? Now tell me, did my car arrive from Paris?'

'It's parked in front of the hotel,' said Boris, regarding her with amusement. 'Didn't you *notice* it when we got here?'

'No,' she said, raising her brows in an exaggeratedly imperious manner, and playfully mimicking his own flat weary tones, 'I did *not* "notice it when we got here." I *never* notice things like that.' She bent over and kissed his cheek. 'And, *chéri*, when I am with *you*, I do not notice anything else at all!' She glanced at her watch. 'Now listen to my good plan. It is almost time for lunch, yes? We go to the *charcuterie*, we get nice things—*pâté*, *artichaut*, cold duck, cheese, whatever you feel . . . we get a nice bottle of Pouilly Fuissée . . . then I take you to my picnic place—my secret picnic place,' adding this last softly, not looking at Boris now, but out the window, and speaking as though from a distance, '. . . it is suddenly important to me . . . I feel it strongly.' She turned to him again, with a special smile— one that reflected a genuine camaraderie, along with just a touch of the bittersweet remembrance of things past; in her own way, she was extremely romantic. 'It is good, yes? My plan? And you can tell me about the picture.'

Boris nodded. 'It is *very* good, your plan.' He stood up and stretched. 'How about if Wardrobe gets your measurements before we go? It'll only take a second.'

Arabella drew herself up to her full hauteur once more. '*My measurements?*'

'Does Helen Vrobel know them?'

The news seemed to interest her. 'Helen Vrobel is on this picture?' Then she dismissed it with a shrug of let-them-eat-cake indifference. 'Helen Vrobel knows my measurements,' she said matter-of-factly. 'Helen Vrobel has my *patterns*—for everything.'

'All right,' said Boris, putting his head to one side, studying her body. 'They can't have changed much. Looks okay to me. Let's go.'

Arabella laughed, ' "Looks okay," does it? Good.' She

took his arm, and they started out. 'My measurements,' she said distinctly, 'have not changed *one centimeter* since ...' She searched for it.

'Since *Bluebird of Happiness?*' suggested Boris.

She threw him a quick look of astonishment, but he only smiled. '*Exactement, chéri*,' she said evenly, 'not one centimeter since *Bluebird of Happiness*.' And she leaned over and, very gently, bit his ear.

8

The pearl-blue Maserati sucked at the surface and whined over the empty Alpine road like an artillery shell, drifting through the long sloping curves as if it were making turns inside a pneumatic tube. It was Arabella's claim, and probably true, that Fangio himself had taught her to drive. Be that as it may, her skill was extraordinary. To say that she drove like a man would be misleading; with the finesse of a Grand Prix driver, yes, but loose, no sign of the uptightness that may accompany intense concentration—driving, it seemed, with more ease and grace than a man, allowing her to maintain her animated, half-theatrical monologue without interruption, even to the point of favoring Boris with a brief but devastating smile while she shifted down going into a seventy-mile-an-hour curve.

He watched her face, aware of her mild exhilaration, and long since satisfied about her motives.

'I make the car *respond* to me,' she had once explained, '... like a *woman*, yes? With another woman, *I* am dominant, *n'est-ce pas?* With the car, it is the same—I am master —that is why I like it. You understand?'

The picnic place of Arabella's childhood proved to be as remote as it was lovely, lending it, as she had already recalled, a 'secret' quality, Shangri-la style.

After turning off the main road and following a secondary one until it stopped at an impenetrable wall of trees, they left the car and walked into the forest, along a soft pine-needle path, above which the boughs of the very tall trees intertwined, forming a canopy which blocked out the sun; so the passage was like a tunnel that appeared to lead nowhere, but from which they emerged into a picture-book setting—the grassy banks of a sparkling mountain lake, surrounded by pines, and, rising above on every side, the silver-blue Alps.

'This is the place,' said Arabella, moving toward the shade of a huge evergreen.

Boris surveyed the whole scene, then nodded. 'This is the place all right.'

While she took out the things they had brought, and arranged them on the grass, he opened the wine.

'We pour one glass,' said Arabella, 'then we put the bottle to chill in the lake, yes?'

'Good idea,' said Boris, pouring a glassful and putting the cork back in.

'Like Jake and Bill, yes?' said Arabella. 'Very romantic.'

'Jake and Bill?'

'Yes, in Hemingway—*comment s'appelle? Le Jour Se Lève?*'

'Ah yes,' said Boris, remembering, 'when they went fishing . . .' Then he laughed, 'Why do you say "romantic"—you think they were fags?'

'Oh no, no, no, I mean *romantic*—in the classical sense! *Fags!* Mon dieu!' She shrugged as she unwrapped the Camembert. 'I don't know, were they *supposed* to be fags? . . . but he couldn't do it, could he? Jake? His thing was gone—wasn't that the story?'

'Hmm.' Boris thoughtfully stared at the chicken leg in his hand, then began to eat it.

'Of course,' said Arabella, frowning down as she studiously applied *pâté* to a small, thick, torn chunk of bread, 'they *could* have done it—Bill could have made love to Jake, and Jake could have *kissed* Bill . . . how do you say *"sucked him"*? Yes?'

Boris smiled. 'Yes.'

'Or "sucked him *off*"? How do you say? Which do you say?'

'Either one.'

She nodded gravely, scholar of linguistics, serious actor ever in search of *le mot juste*, slowly chewing, then taking a sip of wine.

'Listen,' said Boris, 'who, in all the world, had you rather make love to?'

She looked up at him, stopped chewing for only a second, then answering without hesitation:

'Angela Sterling.'

'Sorry, she's already spoken for. Who, next to her?'

' "Spoken for"? What does that mean, "already spoken for"? And what are you talking about anyway?'

'Well, you know the part, in the movie, *your* part—I told you it was a lesbian sequence . . .'

'Yes?'

'Well, I thought it might be good to get someone to play it with you who you had always . . . had eyes for, so to speak . . . someone you'd always wanted to make it with, you know, make love to. *Compris?*'

Arabella was delighted. 'What a *marvelous* idea!'

'That way, you could sort of *have more feeling* for the scene, right?'

'*Mais exactement!*'

'Okay, who . . . besides Angela Sterling?'

Arabella brushed her hands and settled to the obviously savory task of thinking this through. '*Eh bien*, let me see now . . .' and after perhaps three seconds, 'ah, how about . . . Princess Anne?'

'*Who?*'

'*Princess Anne . . . of England!*'

'You mean Princess *Margaret?*'

'No, no, no, Princess *Anne! La petite!* Mon Dieu!' She turned away with a show of annoyance.

'Wait a minute,' said Boris, standing up, 'let me get some more wine.' He came back with the bottle. 'Now, I'm sorry —two things I should have made clear: one, she has to be an actress; and, two, she must be at least eighteen.'

'She *is* eighteen,' said Arabella from the depths of her pique.

'Yes, well the thing about someone like her is that she's not an *actress.*'

'All the better—*I* will teach her . . . *everything.*'

Boris sighed. 'She'd never do it. It's a nice thought, but she'd never do it.'

'Not be in a film of Boris Adrian? She would be *mad!*'

'The only people who will be in this film,' explained Boris, 'are people who need *money,* and *actors* . . . actors like you . . . *artists* who want to be involved—for one reason or another. She is neither.'

Arabella shrugged, morosely.

'And then there's the *Queen,*' Boris added as a clincher, 'think how *she'd* feel.'

'Ah, yes,' Arabella was impressed, 'the Queen. It's true, it could upset her.'

'Break her heart,' murmured Boris, smiling at the thought. 'No, you'll just have to come up with someone else.'

'A compromise . . .'

'I'm afraid so.'

'All right, I will think.'

They continued eating, in silence now—Boris pursuing a fantasy about a lesbian and a princess, while Arabella explored her own world of dark writhing images for a suitable cohort.

Neither spoke for a while, until Arabella, having finished the last of the cheese, lay back on the grass, and sighed.

'You know,' she said after a moment, 'it is here, in this place, I make love for the first time.'

'You mean with a *girl?*'

'Certainly, with a girl! What did you *think* I meant—a *donkey?*'

Boris lay back beside her, one hand behind his head, the other resting his glass of wine on his chest. 'Who was it—that cousin you visited every summer?'

'Yes . . . *Denise,*' she said the name as though tasting it.

'Hmm. Right here, huh?'

'Right here exactly.'

He waited for a long moment, looking up at the sky.

'What happened?' he finally asked.

'What happened?' she repeated, shaking her head as though no longer certain, or as though it might be too intricate to recreate—or, yet again, as if at that very moment she was actually reliving it. Then she sighed. 'I was fifteen,' she said, 'Denise a year younger. She was my cousin, and we were together every summer for as long as I remember. I can't tell you, I can't express how close we were. She was an enchanted thing—strange, delicate, pure . . . a child of nature, or like something out of a ballet. And so . . . *exquisitely* beautiful. I *adored* her, because she was completely . . . *unselfish,* completely unaware of the material world. I was the opposite, like my friends in Paris—ambitious, always driving ourselves to the brink, obsessed with the idea of perfection and success. But I was her *idol*—I was already working in the theater, and studying . . . to her I represented all the mystery and excitement of Paris.' She paused for a moment, smiling softly. 'You know, young girls—beginning about twelve years old—have an extraordinary interest in the development of their bodies. Every day they examine their breasts to see if they've grown anymore. And if they have a close friend, about the same age, they show each other and compare. Well, that's how we were, Denise and I, except that I was almost a year older, and mine came first. Also I was naturally more . . . precocious in that way. In

any case, by the time I was fourteen, my breasts were nice,'
she involuntarily cupped her hand over one of them and
looked down at it, 'very nice, in fact, while Denise's were
still just beginning. Then I came back the next year—now
she was fourteen—and her breasts had changed completely,
they were marvelous. That was the first thing she did was
show me, even though she was a little shy about it, because
they were *perfect*—exactly the way mine had been the year
before. So. That day we had our lunch here, just like this,
and then we went in swimming, as we always did, not wearing anything. And that's when it happened, when we came
out of the water, and we were looking at her breasts again—
and now fascinated, of course, at the way the nipples stuck
out because of the cold water. We both touched them, and
mine, laughing a lot, and I said I'd like to see how it felt to
kiss one, while it was all hard and sticking out like that. And
Denise laughed and said all right, and that she would too.
And we did, and it felt wonderful—I mean, her nipple in
my mouth felt wonderful . . . so hard and cold from the water, yet underneath it warm and alive, and so *sensitive*—I
could feel it getting harder and bigger as I kissed it. I think
that's how it began—the *response*, feeling her *respond* like
that. And then I had this overwhelming desire to kiss her on
the mouth—which we had actually done before, but never
seriously—with the tongue and everything—but just sort of
practicing, for how it was supposed to be with boys. But this
was different—I wanted to kiss her very deeply now, and I
wanted to feel those hard nipples pressed against my breasts.
So I began kissing her, while we were still standing, exactly
here, and caressing her—her sides and hips, and legs . . . and
finally, her thing. And then I said to her I didn't know why,
but I would like to kiss it. And she said all right, and I
dropped on my knees and began kissing it, her clitoris—and
then we lay down, here, and kissed each other's.' She reached
out and gripped Boris's hand. 'It was so wonderful . . . so
fantastic. We were delirious. Oh, we had both played with
ourselves before, and maybe had something like an orgasm,

85

a little one, but this was incredible—the way she would moan and twist, and then sob when she came. It gave me such a feeling of *power*, being able to affect her like that. Finally it was just me kissing her, making her come over, and over, and over . . .'

She fell silent, toying with a blade of grass.

Boris, resting on one elbow, studied her celebrated profile. She was considered to have the most beautiful mouth in France, where it had been immortalized in a famous tooth-paste advertisement when she was sixteen, and was still used—just the full, wet, red lips, and the strong, white perfect teeth. He felt himself getting an erection. 'Tell me some more,' he said softly, 'I mean did you do it all that summer?'

'Yes, in bed at night—but we had to be careful because she couldn't keep quiet. And then a terrible thing happened. My uncle—it was her stepfather, a gross horrible man—found out. I suppose he heard something, in our room at night, I don't know, but then he saw us—he followed us here one day and watched. Then, that evening, he got me alone and told me he had seen. He said he would tell my parents . . . unless I let him be alone with me. I told him that I had never been with a man, that I was still virgin—but I know he didn't believe me . . . he just kept saying he would-n't hurt me. I asked him how he could do it without hurting me if I was a virgin, and what if it made me pregnant—and then he said he wouldn't make love to me, he would just embrace me, hold me close. Well, I was so frightened and confused . . . I mean, I thought it would *destroy* my parents to find out. So the next day was Saturday, which was the day we, that is, the women—Denise, and I, and my aunt—always went to the village, to do the marketing. He told me to say I was sick and couldn't go—and to stay in bed.'

It seemed for a moment that she didn't want to continue, but Boris now had his own reasons for pursuing it.

'Yeah?'

'Well . . . I stayed, the way he said, telling them I felt sick, so they left for the market without me . . . and I lay there, listening, waiting—it was horrible—then I heard, in another room, his shoes drop against the floor—heavy shoes that farmers wear—and I knew he was coming, I closed my eyes, it was unbearable, and he came in, very quietly, like he might be on tiptoe.

' "Pretend you are asleep," he said in a whisper, as though he thought someone would hear us, but, of course, he knew there was no one for miles—and he got into the bed, with his clothes on, except for his shoes ... he unbuttoned the top of my pajamas—I just lay still while he did that, but then he began to pull off the other part, and I tried not to let him, but he kept saying, "I won't hurt you, I just want to hold you"—I still had no idea what he was going to do—then he was on top of me, pulling my legs apart and pressing himself in between them ... and his thing, his penis, was out, hard, pressing against me, already hurting, and I tried to pull away and said, "You promised you wouldn't," and he said, "I just want it to touch you," and he was trying to force it inside, but it wouldn't because I was dry and everything, and he put saliva on the end of it and forced it in, very hard —oh, it was unbearable, it was such pain—and I was crying and he kept saying, "Is this how your lover does it?" and "Is mine as big as your lover's?" and terrible things, I would gladly have died to stop it. I didn't even have the presence of mind to ask him not to come inside me—not that he would have listened ... so anyway he finished, and he looked at the bed, for blood, but of course there was no blood—a ballet student loses her hymen on the first *plié*, and I had been dancing for six years. Well, he was relieved that there was no blood, but I was still crying, almost hysterical, and now that it was over, he began to be afraid I would tell—so when I said I wanted to go home, he took me straight to the station. Later he told my aunt and Denise that I was sick and had insisted on going home. Afterward I saw Denise a few times, in Paris, and we made love, but I never went back to stay with her again.'

She looked over at Boris and smiled faintly. 'So, Mister

B., there you have my story—"The Loves of Arabella"—or at least the first chapter.'

Boris was somewhat astonished to find himself thinking along the very lines for which he had earlier chided Sid.

'Well,' he asked, 'did you ever, uh, you know, try it again? With a *man*?'

'Yes. When I was still very young, before I had accepted myself. I tried it twice, as a matter of fact—and each time should have been ideal . . . each time it was with someone I was very very fond of . . . someone gentle and loving . . . someone I wanted to please. And each time it was terrible —I could feel *nothing* . . . except fear and resentment. I couldn't even *begin* to *relax*, much less . . . to *give* anything.' She turned to Boris with her famous smile. 'Well, Doctor?'

Boris shook his head. 'Incredible,' he said softly.

'Incredible? You mean you don't believe it?'

'No, no, I mean it's . . . *astonishing* . . . it's *great*. We've got to *use* it—for your sequence in the film.'

'You can't be serious—what about the story you already had prepared?'

'Mickey Mouse compared to yours. No, we didn't really *have* a story—just some ideas, images mostly, about two girls making love. This way we can use the *uncle* as well. It'll be terrific—something for every taste.'

'But I couldn't—not with the uncle, I mean, I simply couldn't do it.'

Boris had a sudden wild notion of suggesting *Sid* as the uncle, but then thought better of it.

'But don't you see, the *abhorrence* you would feel would be *perfect*—it would be exactly what we'd be trying for.'

She shook her head, not looking at him. 'No, it is not possible. I would do anything for you, Boris—I'll do it on camera with the girl, kiss her, make love to her, do anything you want . . . because I *believe* in it . . . I *feel* it . . . and because I know it is for *art!* But I just *cannot* do the other— please don't ask me.'

'Hmm,' Boris considered it, then sighed. 'Okay, we'll use

doubles on the inserts—when we cut to the close-ups—erection, penetration, and so on, we'll use somebody else's. I'm sure you'll be able to do the face stuff great.'

'Oh, I *will*,' she said, reaching out and touching him in gratitude. 'I *promise* you I will, Boris.' She raised her great gray-green eyes to him, and smiled sadly. 'I'm so sorry, Boris—you know how I always try to do anything you want. I love you, you know,' she added softly, lowering her eyes.

Watching Arabella closely as she went through these various changes, and still aware of his quite serious erection, Boris suddenly found himself seeing her through Sid's eyes, recalling the intense imagery he had used—'fantastic to make a beautiful dyke come,' and so on, and he fleetingly considered the notion of trying to actually *experience* it vicariously from Sid's attitude—but, more than that, being so genuinely fond of her, and feeling such an urgent demand between his legs, he found it almost impossible to believe that she wouldn't enjoy it. He wondered what would happen if he asked her . . . *begged* her . . . *pleaded* . . . appealed to her friendship, loyalty . . . swore it was a matter of life and death . . . or perhaps if he said *she could be on top*—then she wouldn't feel dominated. His erect member had arrived at the state sometimes described (by hacks) as 'pulsating tumescence,' and he realized, too, with a certain disquiet, that due to the press of events of the last two weeks—the script preparation and the pre-production work generally—he had neglected to get laid during that entire period.

'Do you know why I'm so fond of you?' asked Arabella, looking at him again, 'or anyway one of the reasons I'm so fond of you? It is because you have always *accepted* me for what I am. Yes?'

'Hmm,' Boris murmured, no longer too certain of this, and shifted uneasily.

'And *I* know you like women,' she went on, 'and that sometimes you may think of *me* that way—as a woman. Well, I do have certain feminine qualities, or let us more properly say, certain *Yin* qualities.' And whether through a wondrous intuitive awareness, or whether she actually perceived it, she reached out and gently rested her hand on his trousers and thé taut wood-hard muscle beneath, raised her beautiful face to him with a smile that was radiant and benign. 'Is that for Arabella?'

Boris, who was ordinarily rather blasé in these matters, felt an unaccountable tinge of chagrin when his member throbbed and reared at her touch as though from the slightest electric shock.

'I'm beginning to think that it is,' he admitted.

'Oh Boris, you're wonderful,' she said with a marvelous laugh, and slowly pulled down the zipper, and took it out—holding it carefully, studying it. 'Just look at it—all throbbing and eager, and no place to go.'

'No place to *come*, you mean,' said Boris, trying to maintain a cavalier mien—he was beginning to suspect her of being one of the world's great prick-teasers.

'Why do they have to be so big?' she said, her head to one side regarding it with a little-girl pouting expression. 'Maybe if they weren't so big I could do it.'

'Sorry,' said Boris.

'No, no, *chéri*,' she laughed, 'it's *perfect*. I wish *I* had one exactly like it. And look, it's so hungry,' she touched a small glistening drop on the head, 'it's drooling.' She sighed, and looked at him, now holding it very firmly in her right hand. 'Yes, I promise you one day we will—not now, it would upset me too much, would be bad for the picture, but one day . . .' she giggled, and added, 'maybe if I am on *top* . . .' Then she returned her attention to the member straining in her grasp. 'But now we've go to stop it from throbbing and aching and everything, yes?'

'Yes,' Boris agreed hopefully.

'It *is* a beautiful thing,' she admitted, and closing her great lovely eyes, and moistening her heavy red lips, she opened her mouth and slowly, tenderly took it inside.

Boris sighed with relief that it was actually going to happen; he was ready to come immediately, but felt this would be unfair, in some absurd way, to *Sid*, and to himself, and, even more absurd, to the countless unseen Sids all over the world—so he settled back to watch this super-beautiful internationally famous face suck his cock, so to speak, trying to get some erotic mileage out of that notion, or reality.

It also occurred to him that the erotic content of the experience might be further enhanced by accentuating to the ultimate its *female* qualities (so that his id, ego, or whatever other hidden agency evaluates these things, could not possibly mistake it for some kind of madcap fag-suck) and to this end he carefully undid the two top buttons of Arabella's cardigan, gently slipped his hand inside, and firmly cupped her no-bra perfect left breast—just holding it for a second before tenderly taking the nipple between his thumb and forefinger. At the pressure, slight as it was, she almost imperceptibly recoiled—but then relaxed, yielding, even coming forward a little, as the nipple began to swell and distend while he softly squeezed and rolled it between his fingers. This 'submission'—allowing a man to fondle her breasts—as insignificant as it might seem, had an effect on Arabella that went quite beyond whatever immediate sensation it may have produced, and caused her to apply herself with obviously real and mounting excitement. While she continued, closed-eyed and breathing hard, her hands groped, opening the top of his trousers, taking them down enough to put her hands inside and grip his bare waist, and then his buttocks, urgently pulling him toward her, sucking voraciously, with gasps and moans, like a woman being made love to, almost painful—though occasionally taking so much that she gagged (but, as Boris noted, even when she gagged, she did it—consummate artist that she was—with a certain classic *élan*).

And Boris now, with her breast in play and this convincing show of passion, could only think of her as *purely woman*, and wondered if this moment might not be extremely opportune for the emancipating experience (he now felt) she needed, which he wouldn't mind performing, and his inclination toward this was heightened as he looked down on the lithe curve of her body, curled spoon-like, the black chinos taut over her perfect rounded bottom, beneath which he could faintly discern the panty-line, and wondered fleetingly if they were black too—he also wondered if she were *wet*, and his hand almost went out involuntarily to touch her there (thinking if her nipple responds, why not her clit?) but then, on a stab of intuition, he withdrew—touching her there, he was suddenly sure, might blow the whole thing ... she probably wasn't ready for that yet ... and then there would be the awkward hassle of getting the slacks off (*and* the sandals), precisely the kind of untimely deal-breaking catalyst to avoid. He made a mental note to use such a situation in a film sometime, and a second note to be sure and *fuck* Arabella as soon as possible—then he returned his attention to her fabulous head, and as he did, she stopped for a second and looked up with a soft smile, all breathless, dewy-eyed, and shimmering wet lips. 'Are you going to come in Arabella's beautiful mouth?'

'Uh, something like that,' said Boris, thinking, My God is she going to stop now?

She nodded, closed her eyes, opened her mouth, then looked up at him, assuming her little-girl pout. 'I guess she has to *swallow* it, doesn't she?'

'Yep.'

She smiled her secret smile. 'Good—she *wants* to swallow it.'

She resumed in earnest, Boris fondling both nipples, squeezing them hard, and she reacting more ravenously the harder he squeezed. When he started to come, he let go of her nipples and took her head in his hands, holding it and pulling it to him, wanting to come as deep inside her famous, beautiful mouth as possible, to explode against the very back of her virgin throat. And she devoured it, gulping and sucking as in some insatiable desperation, until every drop was drained—and Boris, in a state of collapse, weakly pushed her head away.

'*Wow*,' he murmured.

Arabella looked up at him, her huge eyes shimmering, happy knowing she had pleased. 'Hmm,' her pink tongue moved around her glistening lips, 'it's strange, I always thought there would be more of it.'

'Well . . . it's very *rich*.'

'Oh, it's fantastic, it tastes so . . . I don't know, so *alive*.'

Boris, eyes closed, reached out and found her hand.

'Yeah, I guess it would at that.'

Arabella laughed softly, closing her eyes too, and snuggling up to him, and together like that, they fell into a deeply peaceful sleep—there on the cool grassy bank of the silver mountain lake.

9

Lazlo Benvenuti, Boris's great cameraman—or more correctly, his director of photography—arrived from Los Angeles that afternoon, and with him two camera operators, a three-man lighting crew, one soundman, and a couple of tons of equipment, including a gigantic BMI studio camera.

'Why the hell didn't you get that from Paris or Rome?' demanded Boris.

But Sid deprecated the idea with a Mussolini-type gesture and a hasty glance at Morty for support. 'Quicker,' he said, '*and* safer to get it from the Coast, believe me, I know, I done business with the frogs and eyeties before. Besides, Hymie Weiss gave us a good deal on this Mitchell. Right, Morty?'

'Right, Sid.'

'You mean a good kickback,' said Boris, examining the camera. 'Did Lazlo check it?'

Sid made a circle with his thumb and forefinger, and winked. 'A-Okay, B.'

'What about the Arries?' asked Boris.

'We got two Arriflexes due in from Paris this afternoon. For Arries, I trust the frogs—not for my big Mitchell. Right, Morty?'

'You can say *that* again, Sid!'

Boris looked from one to the other with a weary smile. 'You guys are too much—you ought to have an act.'

Sid guffawed, nudging Morty, and rolling his eyes. 'Maybe we *have*—right, Morty?'

Morty grinned insanely, 'Right, Sid!'

10

Because of the delay in completing the Casbah set, and the immediate availability of Arabella, the shooting schedule was revised so the lesbian sequence would be the first episode to be filmed. And that evening at dinner, after she had gone up to bed, Boris retold the story of Arabella, Denise, and the uncle to Tony, while Sid and Morty also listened.

Tony was delighted. '*Fan-fucking-tastic!*' And he immediately plopped his yellow-page pad on the table and began scribbling dialogue.

'Can she go that young?' Sid wanted to know.

'She can go that young,' said Boris, '—with Du Couvier she can go back to the cradle. It'll be beautiful.'

Du Couvier was the French makeup wizard—his specialty, of course, being the conversion of elderly actresses into the Maid of Orleans.

Sid snapped his fingers at Morty. 'Oblige the man.'

'It's okay,' said Boris, 'she already called him—he'll be here in the morning.'

'Relax, Morty,' said Sid.

'Who's going to play the other chick?' asked Tony, looking up from his yellow pad.

Boris smiled. 'Would you believe . . . Pamela Dickensen?'

This set them all agape.

'*Pamela Dickensen!?!*'

'You gotta be kidding!'

'Why that's too *fan-fucking-tastic!*'

Pamela Dickensen was a lovely young British actress, Suzannah York style, of about twenty-two, whose role was consistently that of the nineteenth-century ingenue, all petticoats and lace—virginal, prim, even prudish.

Tony couldn't get over it. 'Wow, whose idea was that?'

'Arabella's—that's who she decided she'd rather make it with . . . after Angela Sterling and Princess Anne.'

Sid was flabbergasted. 'Princess *Anne?!?* You mean Princess *Margaret*, don't you? Huh?'

Boris, slowly turning a glass of cognac around and around in his hand, studied Sid's face carefully.

'Huh?' Sid repeated.

'Yeah, sure,' said Boris, '. . . listen, Sid, how'd you like to play the *uncle?*'

'You gotta be kidding,' said Sid, then looking at Tony, 'he's kidding, right, Tone?'

'You better fucking believe it, he's kidding,' said Tony, looking somewhat disturbed as he mashed out the cigarette he'd just lit.

Boris shrugged: 'She said Sid reminded her of her uncle.'

Tony dropped his pencil and went into his Lyndon Johnson accent: 'Ah ain't writin' *no* dialogue fer no Sid *Krass*-man! He cudn't talk it nohow! Hot dang, Viet Nang!'

'We'll *loop* it,' said Boris, 'we'll stay on *her* face, and we'll loop it. The thing is, she thinks he *looks* right. Man, it could bring a fantastic performance out of her—a real *psychodrama!* What do you think, Sid?'

Sid was ambivalent—flattered at the attention, but somewhat hurt that she should think of him as so much older. 'She said that, huh—that I reminded her of her uncle'?

'Not *now*, schmuck,' Boris reassured him, 'when she was *fifteen* years old.'

'Now it's her *granny*,' said Tony.

'No, no,' said Boris, 'now she's very attracted to you, probably . . . I mean, you know how those things are, the narrow line between hatred and love . . . between repulsion and lust . . . what's the matter with you? I thought you had such big eyes for her.'

'Yeah, but you said you're going to use doubles for that—I mean, for the actual thing.'

'Well, let me put it this way, Sid—*before* we cut away, for the penetration shots, we're going to shoot a *lot of film*, right? A lot of film of him—that is, of *you*—on top of her, moving in a manner that suggests, even *convinces*, the audience that he *is*, in fact, making it with her. Now that's the situation—your both naked, you're on top, between her legs . . . nothing between her wonderful, perfect cooze and your coarse animal member, right? Well, if you can stick it in, *stick it in*—and we'll see what happens. Just don't make her come too much, okay?'

Sid guffawed so nervously that he went into one of his coughing fits. 'Holy Christ,' he kept saying, 'holy Christ!'

Sid's got a thing about dykes,' Boris explained to Tony, 'can't resist making them come.'

'Holy Christ, holy Christ . . .'

'Well, Sidney, even if she doesn't *come*,' said Tony, 'it should at least put you on a *first-name* basis—I mean, pressing against her like that, your coarse animal member and her wonderful cooze . . .'

'And *knocker*,' Boris reminded him, 'all the bare knocker you want . . . sucking those perfect pink nipples . . .'

'Sounds like the chance of a lifetime,' Tony agreed.

Sid laid his face down in the crook of his arm, moaning.

'Oh, you guys . . . you guys are crazy . . . Morty, what are they doing to me?'

Morty gleefully threw up both hands. 'That's some *break*, Sidney—great actress, great director—you gonna do it for *scale* awready?'

'Aw come on,' said Tony, 'he may even get a piece of the action—get it, Mort? "Piece"? "Action"? Haw-haw.'

'Oh you guys,' Sid half sobbed. 'don't you guys care about anything? I don't know what to believe.'

11

The stillness of the summer morning was broken as the clapboard marked '*The Faces of Love*, Scene 1-1, Take 1' banged shut.

'Running,' said the operator.

'Speed,' said the soundman.

'Action,' said Boris—and on the blue-grass bank of the silver lake, the famous Arabella and the beautiful Pamela Dickensen begin leisurely unbuttoning their blouses, and stepping out of their skirts—while the director, two camera operators, the first and second assistant directors, the director of photography, the writer, the sound man, the prop man, the makeup man, the script supervisor, the hairdresser, the producer, the producer's assistant, the wardrobe lady, three electricians, and a man holding a microphone on a boom, carefully assume deadpan expressions of professional interest.

The shot called for the girls to undress, and to dance joyfully hand in hand toward the water—one camera shooting from behind, the other from the side—and this movement would then be shot from two other angles before they actually went into the water, thus conserving their makeup for as long as possible.

Neither girl was wearing a bra, so the garments were discarded in the order of blouse, skirt, sandals, and panties. And as each stepped out of her pants, with just the right show of maidenly coyness, clasped hands, and started toward the water, Tony leaned forward and whispered something to Boris, who nodded and stood up.

'Cut,' he said to the cameraman, and to the actors. 'Hold it a minute, girls.'

Helen Vrobel, the wardrobe lady, immediately went out to the girls, carrying two terrycloth robes, which they put on, Arabella quite casually, Miss Dickensen rather hurriedly.

'That was beautiful,' said Boris as he approached them, 'but I think Tony's right—it'll be more effective if you leave your pants on, so that when the seduction occurs, it'll be that much more erotic, Pam, with Arabella very slowly, sensually, pulling your pants down. Do you follow?'

'Hmm,' Pam agreed, somewhat vaguely, as though she might simply be glad for the moment to get her pants back on. Hers was a curious beauty—or more of a *cuteness* perhaps, but of the turned-up-English-nose variety so highly prized in certain circles, the eyes twinkling with self-satisfaction and a trace of mischievousness, the lips full but curved with conceit, almost with disdain.

'I would like to *change* that look,' Arabella had said, '. . . that *haughty* look, first into *ecstasy*, then into *abject adoration*.'

And Miss Dickensen's body, needless to say, was super—a thought which occurred to Boris now as she half turned away from him to put on the panties which Helen Vrobel had retrieved and handed to her.

'Let's see how it looks, Pam.'

She obediently turned around and opened the robe, with only the suggestion of a sigh which seemed to say: 'I suppose you're enjoying this.' At this range Boris saw the pants clearly for the first time—black with delicate interlacings of red—and he wheeled around frowning at Helen Vrobel. 'Who the hell put her in those *hooker* pants?' he demanded. 'Helen, the girl is a *virgin*, living in the provinces—and you've got chorus-girl underwear on her!'

Helen Vrobel grimaced to warn him, but not in time.

'They *happen* to be my own,' Pamela said icily, closing her robe.

'Oh . . .' Boris turned away for a moment, thinking that's great, not even one shot and already alienating the actors. 'Sorry, Pam,' he said, 'I didn't mean that the way it sounded . . . they're really very, uh, attractive . . . it's just that I think we better have something not quite so, uh, *sophisticated*.' He turned to Helen Vrobel, and spoke with exaggerated patience: 'Get her some white ones, okay? Just nice, plain, white pants, like a nice, plain, uh, or rather in this case very very *beautiful*, fifteen-year-old girl would wear . . .'

'I *do* have some white ones, of course,' said Pamela, 'and I *would* prefer to wear my own.'

Arabella, having joined them in time to overhear this last remark, was quick to agree. 'Oh yes, please,' she said, 'I too would prefer that they be her own . . . *things*—that way it is more real . . . for me as well, yes?' She flashed a radiant smile at each of them, and squeezed Pamela's arm, before turning away. 'Excuse me, I get us some coffee.'

They watched her for a moment, then Boris returned his attention to the problem at hand. 'Well, we'll have to send someone to the hotel to get them,' and he immediately thought of gross Sid rooting about among Pamela Dickensen's precious underthings, maybe even doing something weird or obscene with them.

'I hope that won't be necessary,' she said coolly. 'Unless I'm quite mistaken, I have some in my bag, in the dressing room.'

'Great,' said Boris, and they started walking slowly across to the caravan of trucks and trailers, two of which served as

99

dressing rooms for the actors. As the crowd of technicians parted to let them pass, some of them nodded and smiled at the director and the movie star. After acknowledging one or two of their greetings, Pamela looked at Boris for a moment, then spoke in her crispest tones: 'Mr. Adrian, I was wondering if it is absolutely essential that *all* of these people be on the set.'

'Oh no, they won't be on the set.'

'But they *are* on the set.'

Boris looked perplexed. 'You mean *now*? Because of the nudity?'

'Yes.'

'I see. Well . . . I had planned to clear the set when we started doing the love scenes . . . but if it bothers you—just being nude, I mean . . .'

'But isn't it customary, when nudity is required of an actor, the set be cleared of all nonessential personnel? In fact, unless I am very much mistaken, it is a guild regulation.'

They reached the door of the trailer and stood there.

'Hmm,' Boris murmured. 'Well, I was just thinking it might . . . loosen things up a bit.' This was almost true; the psychological strategy, which he had contrived with Arabella, had been simple: the more they could get Pamela Dickensen to do in front of a crowd, the more they could then get her to do when alone. But there was another reason as well.

'You see,' she continued, 'this is all quite new to me . . . I mean, I consider it a very great privilege, an *honor* really, to work with you—*and* with Arabella, whom I've always admired tremendously—and I understand what is required of me in the love scenes, and I'm prepared to do that—I admit I'm not entirely certain about what you . . . well, what you hope to achieve by being so *explicit*, but I have confidence in you . . . in your integrity, and in your artistic ability, *and* in Arabella's. What I do *not* understand is why you allow all of those idle people to stand there, ogling the undressed actors. I simply can't believe that *Arabella* hasn't complained.'

'Not a peep.'

Pamela shook her head, and sighed. '*Astonishing.*'

Boris smiled. 'Maybe we should *all* undress—how would that be?'

She managed to return the smile, rather weakly. 'Somehow I don't feel that's the solution.'

'Okay, we'll clear the set. Just me, Tony, the cameramen, and the soundman. How's that?'

She seemed greatly relieved. 'Thank you,' her smile warmed considerably. 'I'm sorry to be such a prude—but I was afraid it would affect my performance.'

'Yes, well of course that's the most important thing of all. And I know you'll be great.'

She touched his arm. 'Thank you again—excuse me, I'll just see about the underpants.'

Boris watched her step up into the trailer, satisfied that when he cleared the set now, she would feel considerable obligation—which was the real reason, of course, for not clearing it in the first place.

12

After reshooting the girls' approach to the water, from the rear and the side—this time in their panties (Pamela's white, Arabella's light blue)—both cameras were moved out onto the water.

In the first shot, the girls had gone into the water only up to their thighs.

Helen Vrobel dried their legs, and it was shot again, this time from the front angle. In order to get the proper perspective on this shot, it was necessary to have one of the cameras well in front of the actors, almost, in fact, in the middle of the lake. This was anticipated, and a twenty-one-foot motor launch had been brought to the site that morning. The setup, however, proved unsatisfactory—the motion of the boat, though extremely slight, caused the image to waver—and for a while it appeared there was nothing for it but to construct a stationary camera platform atop sunken pilings . . . a job which, under the circumstances, could have taken half a day. Sid was flipping. 'For Chrissake, B., if we have to keep those two broads an extra day, it's going to cost us *thirty fucking grand!*'

'I need that shot, Sid.'

'Oh Christ, Christ, Christ . . .'

But then Boris solved the problem—by placing the camera on the opposite shore of the lake, and shooting with a six-hundred-millimeter lens. This time the girls went into the water over their breasts, and then, without getting their hair or faces wet, made the first motions of swimming, before the scene was cut. This completed their approaching and entering the lake; the next three shots called for: (1) playing and swimming in the water, (2) coming out of the water, and (3) making love. In order to better control their appearance of hair and make up—Boris decided to shoot the love scene *before* shooting the swimming sequence.

'I guess we'd better talk about this,' he said, and he told the first assistant, Fred Johnson—best known as Freddie the First—to call a tea break, while he and Tony sat down on the grass with the two girls—who now looked so very young it was unnerving. Du Couvier, the facial magician, had transfigured them into the quintessence of fifteen-year-old schoolgirls—giving Arabella the classic Parisian *gamin* look of straight black hair, short with bangs that came just to brows above dark eyes sparkling with intelligence and mischief . . . and to Pamela, auburn tresses which fell past her shoulders in two marvelous braids, a pink ribbon in each. Miraculously, neither face appeared to have on it a trace of makeup, but looked freshly washed, radiant with milk-fed health, and very very young.

102

'Did Arabella tell you,' Boris asked Pamela, 'that this is a true story—that it actually happened to *her*, right here?'

'Yes, she did,' said Pamela, flushed and nervously vivacious, 'I think it's absolutely *charming* . . . and in such an *enchanted* place!'

Arabella reached over and squeezed her hand. 'Pamela,' she said, 'you remind me so much of *her* . . .'

Pamela averted her eyes. 'I'm glad,' she said softly, quite embarrassed.

'. . . but you are even more *special*,' Arabella continued, 'more *beautiful*.'

Now Pamela was blushing, exactly like the schoolgirl she appeared to be. 'Thank you,' she murmured.

'Well,' said Tony, 'this looks like it's going to work out all right.'

Pamela giggled awkwardly. 'It's all so strange,' she said.

The second assistant arrived with tea in four styrofoam cups.

'Good tea,' said Boris, after trying it.

Tony took a sip. '*Fan-fucking-tastic*,' he said dryly, poured it out, and half filled his cup from a pint bottle of Scotch he had in his pocket.

'Tell me,' Boris continued gently to Pamela, 'have you ever had any . . . *experiences* like this—I mean, you know, with a woman?'

She shook her head, the two ribboned braids wagging childishly. 'No . . . no, not really. Certainly not like in the script, I mean, being kissed that way and everything.'

'Are you going to pretend,' asked Boris, 'that it's a *man* doing it?'

Arabella was sharply annoyed. 'That *won't* be necessary,' she snapped, 'just let her *respond* quite naturally. It will be all right, I promise you.'

'I really don't know,' said Pamela, 'I'd like to do it in a sort of, you know, *method* way, if I can. In any case, I'm sure I can handle it somehow—now that all those people are gone. Thank you so much for that, Boris.'

Arabella reached out for her hand again. 'It will be fine, you will see.'

Pamela managed to return her smile—weak but brave, lamb-going-to-slaughter style.

'Okay,' said Boris, standing up, 'let's give it a whirl.'

The script called for the girls to come out of the lake, holding hands and laughing, both admiring Pamela's breasts and commenting on how much they had grown since last year.

'Go back in the water for a minute,' said Boris, before they started the shot, 'just up to your waist—we'll take care of the rest.'

When they came out, he pointed to a spot on the ground, '. . . now here's where we'll play the scene,' he put a leaf on the grass, 'this will be your mark, Pam—you'll be standing like this, a three-quarter profile into the camera, when she starts, you know, *caressing* you, okay? And Arabella, you'll be like this, three quarters away, and cheat a little to the left with your body, so we can see what's happening, you know, between your hands and her breasts and all that, okay?' Without waiting for a reply, he turned to Du Couvier's assistant, a curious-looking man who was standing nearby with a large makeup case. 'Okay, get the top part of them wet, and fix the nipples. Be careful with Arabella's face.'

The young man came forward with his case, took out an atomizer, and sprayed each upturned face with a glycerin solution, which stood on their skin like drops and droplets of water, but with a more positive light refraction, and with no effect on their makeup. He then repeated it on the rest of their top parts, front and back.

'How are the legs?' asked Boris.

The assistant shrugged. 'My mix always better,' he said in a heavy French accent, and added sardonically, 'if you want the serious *realism*.'

'Okay,' said Boris, 'go.'

The assistant took a towel, and began vigorously wiping

104

the water off their legs, to prepare them for the glycerin spray.

Tony, nearby, laughed at the irony of it, quaffed a big swig from his styrofoam cup, and muttered, '*in-fucking-sane!*'

Next came the nipples. The assistant supplemented the traditional Folies Bergère (and Krassman) technique (ice cube with hole in center, twirled about nip) with an immediate follow-up of Supercainal, an aerosol pain-killer containing a super-powerful 'freezing-agent.'

Pamela Dickensen, who was familiar with these methods only by remotest hearsay, drew back indignantly when the assistant seized her superb left breast in one hand and started to apply the cube with the other.

'I *think* I can manage that myself,' she said, with a toss of her head more suited to a powdered coif than her own present pigtails.

The assistant gave a mighty shrug of disdain and handed her the ice. '*Avec plaisir, mon chou.*'

While Pamela daintily applied the ice to herself, Arabella allowed, or rather supervised, the assistant—thrusting her own proud breasts forward, speaking rapidly and imperiously in French: '*Encore pour l'autre! . . . Pas si vite! . . . Doucement! . . . Maintenant plus vite! . . . Les voilà! Bon . . .*'

When it came to the Supercainal, however, it was she who protested—not Pamela.

'No, no, no,' she said to Boris aside, 'she will not be able to *feel* anything in her breasts if you use that! I *need* her feeling for the *response!*'

'Well, we've got to keep those nipples out there, you realize that, don't you? Otherwise, we'll lose the shot.'

'They will be out there, Boris, I promise you that—the *ice* will *put* them out there, and *I* will *keep* them out there!'

'Hmm,' he supposed she was right. He glanced down at her own breasts, and nipples, which seemed to be literally *pouting* forward in annoyance.

'How about *you?* Are they going to stay like that?'

She looked down as though she had forgotten about them. 'Ha, you see! Mine will keep out there too! *Certainement!* I am very excited, *chéri!*' And she impulsively leaned forward and kissed his cheek. 'It was good, *chéri*,' she whispered, 'the coming in my mouth. I can still taste it. Now I let you try anything, sometime. Soon. But do *not* permit them to freeze her nipples, yes? *Je t'adore!*'

The first take went pretty much as planned. The girls tripped in, toward camera, from water's edge, hand in hand, dripping, laughing, shaking their hair, wet panties clinging, nipples standing out like four rosebuds.

Because of the nature of the sequence—its content, the character of the girls, and the obvious Alpine background—Boris had decided it would have to be a French setting. The dialogue therefore would be in that language. Pamela, of course, did not speak French well enough to make a master track, so it was decided since this was a medium shot, wherein lip movements are not critical to sound-sync, that Arabella would speak French, and Pamela—who, beyond a certain amount of very girlish sighs, moans, and sobs, didn't have much dialogue anyway—would respond in English, which would later be dubbed into French. In this way, Boris felt, neither would be distracted, or inhibited, by having to think about saying something very personal in a foreign language.

The scene opened with the goddesslike Arabella affectionately teasing, cajoling, flattering, and high-jiving the enchanted Pamela—while they both joyfully admired her newly developed breasts, with Arabella playfully touching the nipples, fondling them, and finally, kissing them, circling each slowly with the tip of her tongue. She stopped and raised her lips to Pamela's mouth . . . gentle and tentative kisses which soon became deep, tongue-probing, lip-biting, almost carnivorous—while her hands moved over Pamela's body, as gingerly and electric as a Geiger counter . . . but then began to grasp and squeeze, causing the girl to wince with pain, either real or assumed, remaining ecstatically

106

closed-eyed as Arabella began her sensual descent ... from the lips, to the throat, to the shoulders, to the breasts ... and down, slowly, to the navel, tonguing there, and along the top of the precious panties—whereupon began a new line of action ... hands gently peeling the panties down, and the famous mouth-tongue covering every inch of perfect Pamela-tummy as it was gradually unsheathed.

'You better cut it,' said Lazlo, 'I'm not getting anything but the back of her head.'

'It's okay,' said Boris, 'I just want to let them warm up—put it on Pamela's face.'

Watching Pamela's face, it was impossible to tell where the acting left off, and the reality began. The action called for her to remain standing for a moment after Arabella had dropped to her knees and started kissing her. She was to respond in a tenderly affectionate way, gazing down at Arabella, gently stroking her hair with one hand, the other instinctively raised across her own breasts—though not concealing either of them. Then, as her feelings of affection gave way to those of excitement, she was to go closed-eyed, head back, both hands down now, one on Arabella's head, the other on her shoulder. And as she gave herself over completely to the feeling, she would allow Arabella to gradually pull her down to lie on the grass. The transition was carried out quite gracefully, so that Pamela now lay on her back, and Arabella knelt beside her, fondling her breasts and kissing her clitoris.

'Get in tight on Arabella's face now,' Boris whispered to Lazlo, 'try to get her mouth ... her tongue.'

The assistant cameraman slowly turned the focusing ring, but Lazlo shook his head. 'It's not registering—we'll have to light it from the side ... somehow.'

And it was about then that Pamela reached her saturation point, at least for the moment.

'Please ... ,' she said, 'can we stop for a moment ... '

'Okay, cut,' said Boris, and went over to where they were, helping Pamela with one of the robes Helen Vrobel brought

107

out to them. 'That was beautiful,' he said, 'really beautiful.'

'I'm sorry I had to stop,' said Pamela, 'I just felt it was getting out of control – I wasn't able to concentrate on what I was doing.'

'How did it feel, *chérie?*' Arabella wanted to know.

'Well, it's really quite extraordinary . . . I mean, that's the difficulty, it's so terribly *distracting.*'

'Maybe you should just sort of go along with it,' suggested Boris.

'Well, I *did* . . . up to a point, then it seemed . . . well, it just got to be a bit *much.*'

'But you didn't *come, chérie.*'

This thought seemed to agitate Pamela considerably. 'Well, I didn't *come*—no, of course not . . . I mean, I don't very well see how I can do *that*, and still know what I'm doing. Good heavens, I practically forgot where the *camera* was just now!'

'Don't worry about the camera,' said Boris. 'Just try to relax and enjoy it.'

Arabella agreed heartily. 'Oh yes, if you just relax and enjoy it, it will be such a wonderful scene . . . so beautiful.'

Fred the First came over then and said that Du Couvier was waiting in Arabella's trailer, to check her makeup.

She kissed Pamela on the cheek before getting up. 'You are ravishing,' she whispered, and hurried off.

Pamela sighed. 'Oh dear, I just wish she weren't quite so . . . *zealous* at it—I'm not at all sure I can cope.'

'How do you mean, "zealous"?' asked Boris.

'Well,' said Pamela, somewhat at a loss, 'I really don't know—I mean, I guess I just didn't know they did it like that—l thought it would be more of a . . . *kissing*, instead of . . . that.'

Boris was intrigued. 'Instead of *what?*'

'Well, I'm not entirely sure, you see—it feels more as if she were sort of . . . well, *sucking* it, and then sort of, I don't know . . . *biting* it. I must say, it's the most unnerving sensation I've ever experienced.'

108

Boris regarded her quizzically. 'Didn't any ... *man* ever do that to you?'

'No,' said Pamela primly, 'decidedly not. *Kissing* it, yes—but not *that* ... not doing *that*.'

'Hmm ...'

'I'm not suggesting, you understand, that I've led a particularly *sheltered* life—I've had the usual number of affairs, etcetera—it is simply that I have not, or *had* not, encountered an experience—or sensation, if you like—such as this. Now you've both suggested that I just "relax and enjoy it" ... even to the point of having an orgasm—well, you don't need an *actress* for that, Mr. Adrian, you merely need a ... well, that sort of *girl*.'

Out of the corner of his eye, Boris saw the white terry-cloth robe as Arabella stepped from her trailer, in animated converse with Du Couvier. He felt he didn't have much time. 'Surely you can't believe,' he said to Pamela, after fixing her with his most darkly serious look, 'that there isn't more to the *role* ... the *character* ... than that? I *know* that you must recognize the *symbology*, and the *parable*, underlying the sequence—perhaps the *most important* sequence in the entire film.'

'Well, I *do* like to think that there's more to it than just ... well, of course I'm sure that there *is* more to it than that—otherwise, none of us would be here—'

'Right,' Boris said hurriedly. 'Listen, I'll tell you what—I'll ask Arabella to, you know, sort of *take it easy*, so to speak ... and *you*, in turn, try to ... well, kind of go along with it ... like *method*, okay?'

He gave her a solid wink of conspiracy, just as Arabella arrived, glowing.

'*Bon*,' she said, 'now we *work*, yes?'

Boris got up, and helped Pamela to her feet. 'Yes, let's,' he said in his best Laurence Olivier manner, 'we'll take it from the top, shall we?'

Pamela looked at him beseechingly, before moving a few steps away so he could speak to Arabella alone—but it was

Arabella herself who seized the opportunity. 'Well,' she whispered urgently, 'how did she like it?'

Boris nodded, gave the Sid sign of circled thumb and forefinger and a big wink. 'She *loves* it,' he said, 'absolutely *loves* it.'

Arabella was delighted. 'Oh wonderful, wonderful!'

'Yeah, it's beautiful,' said Boris, 'you just hang in there, you hear?'

She squeezed his arm. 'Oh, *chéri*, you can count on that!'

13

At one o'clock in the afternoon, Lips Malone returned from a two-day trip to Paris, and a mission of considerable import. It had been his task to comb the streets, clubs, and whorehouses of Montmartre and the Champs Elysées, in search of a girl whose legs and bottom resembled Arabella's —at least adequately enough that, in the close-ups of Uncle-penetration, it would not be discernible that it was, in fact, a different girl. He had succeeded remarkably well, considering the short time in which he did it. She was twenty—or so she said, and didn't look much over it—dark eyes, and the right skin coloring. After some painstaking work by Du Couvier, including an Arabella hairpiece, the resemblance was quite astonishing. Most importantly, however, she had Arabella's slender willowy waist, her long rounded dancer's legs, and her perfect derrière—the principal parts slated for the silver screen.

Her name was Yvette, and her price was one hundred francs (N.F.), about thirty-five dollars, for what she termed an '*acte normal*'—all deviations therefrom being negotiable. After learning the nature of the job, and that it might engage her for as much as two days, she made certain calculations and announced that her price would be 4,800 francs.

Lips, who was accustomed to getting things wholesale, or at least at a discount when buying in bulk, couldn't understand. 'Forty-eight hundred francs? That's fifteen hundred bucks, for Chrissake! How'd you figure that?'

'I think one hour per customer,' she said, 'that's one hundred francs per hour, times forty-eight hours, is forty-eight hundred francs.'

'But what about *sleeping?*' asked Lips, 'don't you ever *sleep?*'

She shrugged. 'Sometimes I go forty-eight hours without sleeping.' Then she added, 'Besides that, Arabella is rich, and so are movie companies.'

'Okay,' said Lips, 'what the hell.' Actually he had been prepared to go much higher than that for the right girl— and Yvette was right . . . as Boris and Sid agreed when they met her now back at the studio.

Sometime before lunch, it had started to rain, putting an end to shooting at the lake for the day; so the company had returned to the studio—which was perhaps just as well, since Pamela had twice reached the breaking point, and very nearly the point of *collapse*.

On the first retake, she had been more relaxed, in the beginning—lying there closed-eyed, her hands back alongside her head as though pinioned at the wrists, her body writhing slowly in, presumably, feigned response . . . while Arabella, kneeling between her legs, massaged her breasts and ran her tongue up and down the lips of her vage, pausing at the top every second or third time to dart it playfully against her clitoris.

Then, as the camera came in very close, she dropped her hands from the breasts to the lips of the vage, and slowly drew them apart.

'Are you getting it?' Boris asked Lazlo in a whisper, referring to the glistening pink-pearl clit which the opened lips revealed, while Arabella paused momentarily, just gazing at

111

it, as in anticipation, before reaching out to it with her equally pink tongue.

'Got it,' Lazlo whispered back, 'the highlight was beautiful.'

The shot had been lit for exactly that—to catch a point of shimmering light on the top of the clitoris—and Arabella had been instructed to pause momentarily before flicking her tongue out lizardlike, and then slowly obscuring it with her whole beautiful mouth.

Afterward she placed her hands under Pamela's buttocks (which she had earlier described as 'like two foam-rubber cantaloupes') and applied herself, lips and tongue, with renewed zeal, while the distressed Pamela sighed and moaned, eyes closed, her head thrown back, moving from side to side.

'Now, Pam,' said Boris, 'as you get more excited, bring it up to meet her—bring your thing up to meet her mouth. And raise your legs a little more.'

It was a sound-take, of course, but they would lose his voice in the cutting—and Pamela obeyed, straining upward from the waist down.

'That's it,' said Boris, 'now put one hand—your *left* hand—on her head, and pull it toward you, and move your right to your breast and hold it. Beautiful. Now just try to go with it, Pam. Please.'

'I am, I am,' she murmured, almost painfully, 'Oh, God . . .' and her breath began coming in gasps, and then she was moaning, biting her lower lip and tossing her head from side to side, before her body was seized with a violent shudder and her head back, her mouth opened in a soft wail, '. . . *oh God, please, please, oohhhh* . . .' and she gave a great gasp and began to sob, pulling away from Arabella, and putting one hand protectively over her vage.

'Okay, cut,' said Boris, quietly, and went out to comfort the girl, who was crying profusely.

'It was *beautiful*, Pam,' he said softly, 'absolutely *beautiful*. You're a really *great* actress.'

112

'What does *acting* have to do with it?' she asked tearfully, but it was apparent that the compliment had at least a modicum of appeasing effect on her, and she began dabbing at her eyes.

Helen Vrobel noticed as she arrived with the robes, and called out over her shoulder: 'Makeup—tissues please!'

'I mean it, Pam,' Boris continued, 'it was terrific—you too, Arabella,' he added, putting an arm around his superstar, she who seemed vaguely annoyed.

'But why did we *stop?*' she wanted to know.

Boris looked at Pam. 'Yeah, it was so great . . . I mean, I thought you were going to *come.*'

'But I *did* come,' exclaimed Pam, looking from one to the other in astonishment. 'Good heavens, couldn't you tell?'

Arabella's hurt and sullen expression stayed the same. 'But that's no reason to *stop,*' she said, 'and to push me from you—that way it looks like you did not enjoy it.' She turned to Boris. 'Is it not true, Boris?'

'Well—'

Pamela couldn't believe it. 'But I thought I was going to *faint* or something. I mean, *surely* you don't believe I could have kept that up?'

'Well, the thing is,' said Boris, 'we need to go out on your *submission* to her—I mean, we can't go out on your *rejecting* her, can we?' He thought about it for a second. 'You know, the *fainting* thing might not be a bad idea.'

'Well,' said Pamela ruefully, 'I can't very well *faint* if she doesn't *stop,* can I?'

'Yeah, well maybe not *faint* exactly, but just sort of look . . . you know, *satisfied.*'

'But that's what I'm *saying*—I can't do *anything* if she keeps on doing it . . .'

'You mean after you come?'

She sighed, and demurely looked away. 'Yes.'

'Well . . . what if you come twice?'

This suggestion caused her to burst into tears anew. 'Oh, I just *couldn't,* I *couldn't,* I *couldn't* . . .'

'Okay,' said Boris, 'we'll work it out.' And he smiled to himself. Great, at least now she had accepted actually having an orgasm as part of the scene.

The third take went according to plan—except, of course, that Arabella didn't stop as promised, and Pamela came twice—the second time, almost hysterically, when Arabella inserted two fingers while still sucking and biting her clit—and then she fell limp like a broken doll.

14

The cover-shot—that is, the shot which was scheduled as an alternative to the lake sequence in case of rain—was the love scene between Arabella and her uncle . . . uncle to be played by a certain gross Sid Krassman.

'If Sid actually tries to stick it in her,' Boris was saying to Tony, 'she may get pretty uptight—I mean, like actually violent . . . you know, *scratch* his face, try to *disfigure* him, or something.'

Tony went into his deadpan minstrel routine: 'Now, er, uh, Mistah B., does yoah mean dis-*figure*, or does yoah mean dis-*membah*? Hee-hee-hee!' and he did a quick soft-shoe two-step.

'Well, the thing is,' Boris explained, 'we ought to get one shot of his face while he's *coming*, right? Now, the only way to be sure of getting that is with the *other* girl . . . Yvette—I mean, we can't count on *Arabella* to stand still for that sort of thing, can we? And most of all we can't risk her blowing her stack, and walking off the picture. No, we better shoot all the stuff with Sid and the hooker first—you know, all the penetration stuff.'

Sid, understandably, was somewhat nervous, making his screen debut in such an auspiciously questionable manner.

'You look great, Sid,' Boris told him, when he came out of wardrobe.

Sid studied himself—dirty, faded coveralls, gray workshirt, and big brogans—in the long mirror. 'Christ, I must be outta my mind, letting you guys talk me into a thing like this!'

Tony feigned astonished admiration. 'Now I can *see* it, Sid—your true and fundamental nature! A man of the soil! From the great heartland of America! "... plowing your swift, broad acres ... as the wind carries the smell of pine and dung across the fields, and the rhythm of an old, old work enters your soul." Underneath that veneer of cynical corruption, Sid Krassman, you're a *simple honest farmer!* The backbone of this grand land of ours! How's about a *quick cornhole?!?*' And he rushed against Sid's great bottom with outthrust pelvis.

Boris broke up, but Sid was not amused. 'Will you guys be *serious*, for Chrissake! Here I am, about to make a *real schmuck* outta myself, and you guys kid around ...'

'Now come on, Sid,' Boris assured him, 'you know I wouldn't ask you to do anything like that. Don't forget, you're going to get a shot at Arabella's fabulous cooze—her whole *store*, man, right there, *open* for you! And besides that, you're doing it for the sake of *art*.'

'Art *Linkletter*, that is,' said Tony.

'Art, my ass,' said Sid, 'this is a *dirty movie*, that's what this is! Aw, what the hell—come on, let's get it over with.'

Nicky had designed and built the set exactly as Arabella had remembered and described it: a dark-walled Provençal room—small, with a high ceiling and one wide, white-curtained window, a big four-poster bed and quilted eider-down, small stone fireplace, dark wide-board floor, marble-top washstand, earthenware pitcher, and a kerosene lamp with a cracked chimney.

When Boris, Sid, and Tony arrived, the eiderdown was crumpled on the floor at the foot of the bed, along with the bottom part of Yvette's pajamas—while their cutie-pie owner, lying on the bed, wearing only the unbuttoned top, was being lit by Lazlo and focused by the operator.

Tony gave Sid a nudge. 'Wow,' he whispered, 'dig that! Ready to dip in, Sid?'

This shot was to begin where another, which had not yet been done, left off—that is, just at the moment of penetra-tion; in other words, everything *prior* to penetration (un-buttoning the top, fondling the breasts, pulling off the bottoms, etc.) would be done later, with Arabella.

'Okay,' said Boris, motioning Sid to accompany him toward the bed, 'you want to take them off now?' He was referring to the coveralls—since, for the sake of good cine-matic imagery, Boris and Tony had decided, poetic-license style, to alter Arabella's version somewhat, and have the uncle naked during the scene.

'Christ,' Sid exclaimed, 'I don't think I can get a *hard-on*, for Chrissake!'

'Oh, *she'll* know how to do that, all right,' Boris assured him, 'what do you think she's getting fifteen hundred bucks for? Now come on, Sid, you're holding up the shot.'

'And if you're holding up the *shot*,' quipped Tone, 'you're holding up the *picture*. Right, Sid?'

'Well, wait a minute,' said Sid anxiously, 'at least lemme work up a little *heft* to it!' and he stopped and reached down and began squeezing his penis beneath the coveralls.

'Okay, Sid,' shouted Tony from the edge of the set, 'get that coarse animal member out front! Let's see some action!'

'Well, just look at her, Sid,' said Boris when they reached the bed. 'She looks like *Arabella*, for Chrissake! You can pretend you're fucking *Arabella*.' And to the girl: 'Baby, you look marvelous—see if you can give our friend here a nice big fifteen hundred dollar hard-on, okay?'

'*Heart-on?*' asked Yvette, 'what is this "*heart-on*"?'

'*Hard*-on,' said Boris carefully, as though for a lip-reader, and pointed to where Sid's hand was still squeezing.

'Ah yes, *hard*-on,' she said, face alight with understanding, 'yes, I *know hard*-on! Come, *chéri* . . .' and she reached out her hand for Sid, 'come into the bed, Yvette give you nice big *hard*-on.'

'Yeah, go, Sid,' said Boris.

Sid resignedly began taking off his coveralls. 'You know,' he muttered, 'I never liked getting into bed with a broad without a little *heft*—I don't like to a have a full-on *erection* when I get into bed with a broad, but I *do* like it to have a little *heft*.'

While Sid got into bed, Boris arranged the coveralls on the floor, so that the crude, dirty garment was slightly en-twined with the delicately flowered, girlishly innocent pajama-bottom. He called Lazlo out, and pointed to it. 'We'll hit that on the way up, okay? We'll go for a beauty-and-beast feeling on the whole thing.'

'Terrific.'

Boris stared down at the two pieces of clothing. 'Maybe

117

hers ought to be *torn* a little,' he said half aloud, then called Tony out, and asked what he thought.

Tony shrugged. 'I don't think he *forced* her, I think he *tricked* her.'

'Yeah, you're right.'

They started back to the camera.

'But wait a minute,' said Boris, stopping. 'Suppose he tears them *before* he tricks her—I mean, he can start pulling at them, and she instinctively resists, and he pulls harder, and that's when they tear—*then* he tricks her, you know, telling her he just wants to hold it against her, and all that bullshit. Right? I mean, it's such a great image—a girl's torn pajama-bottoms.'

'Sure, that works.'

They went back to the bed where Yvette was simultaneously massaging and sucking Sid's organ. Her Arabella make-up caused Boris's mind to do an instant replay of the previous day's big event. 'Wow,' he said, 'she sure looks a lot like Arabella, doesn't she?'

Tony considered it. 'Hmm. Well, if she were doing anything other than *sucking a cock*, she would—I mean, I can't quite see Arabella *sucking a cock*.'

'You can't huh? And you're supposed to have all that imagination.' He leaned over and picked up the pajama-bottom. 'Now where the hell should it be torn?'

'Right at the top.'

He held it in both hands at the top, where the drawstring was, and pulled.

'Christ, they won't tear—whatta drag.'

Tony reached out for them. 'Let me try . . . hmm, you're right.'

'Wait a minute, they'll tear at the bottom of the opening.' Boris took them back and tore them slightly at the fly. 'That'll make a nice *shot*, too, when it happens—a close-up of it tearing, gradually revealing her young cooze.'

'*Young* cooze? How you going to make it look *young?*'

118

'Hmm. We'll have to *trim* it.' He waved at Du Couvier's assistant: 'Hey, Makeup! Bring your *scissors!*'

'Terrif.'

Boris replaced the garment, and arranged it to his satisfaction—while Tony leaned forward to peer at Sid and Yvette, or rather at Yvette's head and Sid's member. She raised her eyes to him without stopping, which produced the rather odd effect of a five-year-old looking up wide-eyed and inquisitive from the popsicle in her mouth, while now, hovering over her in the manner of a horror-film surgeon, the assistant makeup man adroitly and selectively thinned the beaver.

Tony reached out and touched her hair, smiling. 'Listen, come around to my place when we break—I want to talk to you about your part.'

Sid broke up their little tête-à-tête with a gruff shout: 'Will you get the fuck outta here, fer Chrissake! I'm just about to get a good hard-on!'

Tony winked at her as he turned away, crooning under his breath: ' "*You ought to be in pictures . . .*" '

Boris, kneeling and absorbed in the minutiae of arranging the torn pajama-bottom to best advantage, stood up, still looking down at it, hands on hips. 'We'll have to come in *very close,*' he said half aloud, '*very close . . .* or it won't make any sense . . . we've got to see the *fibers,* the *thread fibers,* right where it's torn . . .' and he turned to walk toward the camera, Tony following—but they were stopped short by a shout from behind: 'Hey, you guys, get a load of this! Some whopper, huh?' and they turned to see Sid flashing—in fact, flaunting—a quite serious erection, proffering it forward to best advantage. 'How about *this,* huh? Like to see *you* guys match *this* blockbuster!'

Boris, thinking of other things, cast a look merely in response to the noise. 'That's great, Sid,' he said, without much enthusiasm—then, more seriously, stopping and looking back at the sucking Yvette, he intoned in a slow shout: '*Don't let him come! Not yet!*' and, by way of insurance, repeated it in French: '*Attention, faut pas le faire jouir! Pas encore!*' Then he and Tony continued walking back toward the camera. 'I think it can be a fantastic scene, Tone,' he said, so serious it was almost morose. Behind them Sid was still yelling: 'Hey, you guys, Yvette says it's *perfect!* "*Parfait*," she says! You hear that, Tone? *Par-fucking-fait!* Haw!'

The shot to precede the present one would be of the pajama-bottoms coming off and falling to the floor, crumpled and torn. The camera, after holding on that poignant image, would pan up and in close to where the uncle was trying to force penetration.

'Okay, Sid,' said Boris, 'put it just on the edge of the cooze, like you're trying to push it in but it won't go ... that's right. How is it, Laz?'

'It's all *wet*—I'm picking up a lot of glisten ... it's still wet from her mouth.'

'Oh, Christ,' then yelling to Sid: 'Okay, Sid, wipe it off.'

'Huh?'

'Your *cock*—it shouldn't be *wet* yet, for Chrissake.' He turned to Du Couvier's assistant, 'Makeup—tissues, please.' And the young weirdo rushed out with a handful of Kleenex.

'I'll take care of *that*, Buster,' Sid growled, snatching them out of his hand, when he proffered personal assistance.

'Now, that's it,' said Boris after the action was underway again, 'keep pressing, Sid, trying to get it in. How is it, Laz?'

'Great.'

'Okay, turn it. Keep going, Sid, we're shooting. Yvette, keep your legs *down, down. down* ... try to keep them *together* ... remember you're a nice girl, you're a virgin, you don't know what's happening ... you don't like the idea of him being between your legs ... okay, Sid, now slowly, see if it will go in ... actually try to put it in ...'

In order to prevent full pen from occurring too quickly, not only had Yvette's vage been thoroughly dried with terrycloth, but it had received a liberal douching of a strong

120

alum solution—known to have a severe drawing or puckering effect, and which now proved itself quite handsomely, as Sid strove with genuine ardor to get it in.

'Christ,' he called over his shoulder, 'I've heard of *tight pussy*, but this is ridiculous!'

'Don't give up, Sid,' Boris directed, 'remember, it's *Arabella* . . . you've *got to get it into her* . . . that's it, now it's going . . . keep on . . . forcing, forcing . . .' and aside to Lazlo, 'Are you on it?'

'Yeah, yeah, great.'

'Okay, now out a little, Sid, then back in . . . all the way . . . *to the hilt, Sid, to the hilt!* That's it, that's it! Terrific!' Then his face fell. 'Oh Christ, cut, cut, cut!' He turned to Tony. 'Did you see *that?* She *threw it up to him!* She threw it up to him like a *hooker*, for Chrissake! A frightened virgin, and she throws it up there like some kind of *nympho hooker!*'

Tony shrugged. 'Breeding will tell.'

Boris walked out to the bed, 'Yvette baby . . . you must not *push up* like that . . . remember, you're a *virgin* . . . it's *hurting* you . . . if anything, try to move *away* from him, okay?' Then he called Tony out.

'What about some *blood?*' he asked. 'You know, for the virginity bit? Don't forget, it's in living color.'

Tony made a face. 'Turns me off.'

'Yeah, to hell with it,' said Boris, then leaning over to peer at the org-vage-pen itself. 'Hold it, Sid—take it about halfway out . . . that's it. We gotta get some glycerin spray on there—looks all dry,' and he signaled Du Couvier's assistant, who rushed out and made the application.

'Now hold it just like that, Sid, don't put it in all the way till we get this shot.' He hurried back to the camera and looked through the lens, which was tight on pen—the member sparkling with what appeared to be genuine juice of cooze. 'Beautiful,' he said, 'turn it, Laz.'

'Turning,' said Laz.

'Okay, Sid, do your thing . . . and Yvette, you lie still,

keep your knees down . . . it's hurting, it's hurting . . . that's it, Sid, get in there *deep*, it's *Arabella* . . . *you're fucking Arabella* . . . put your hands under her ass . . . don't let her get away, pull her close . . . okay, now try to get her legs up . . . *deep*, Sid, get in there *deep* . . . hold it, hold it . . . cut, cut. Listen, you started moving too fast, Sid, it made it look like you came . . . now, let's take it from the top, and just move in a kind of *slow, rhythmic* . . .' Face fell again: 'What, you *did* come?!? Oh, for Chrissake, Sid!'

Tony guffawed. '*Very unprofessional*, in my view.'

'Okay, makeup,' Boris continued morosely, over his shoulder, 'tissues, please,' then added, '. . . yeah and bring the *splint*.'

THREE

*On the Possibility of
Certain Side Effects
From Smoking Catnip*

1

The residents of Monte Carlo, that is to say the citizens of Monaco, are not allowed to enter the casino—source of seventy-eight percent of that country's revenue—thus sparing the conscience of the government any guilt for whatever individual tragedies may be wrought through excessive loss at the tables. So the Prince sleeps easy, secure in the knowledge that these tragedies have befallen not his own subjects, but foreigners of questionable motivation.

In regard to the film, *The Faces of Love*, and its ultimate presentation, a similar covenant had been formed between the Prince of Liechtenstein and the Church—the latter having been fairly opposed to the project from the outset, but naturally unable to withstand the pressure of commerce, brought in the name of the government and on behalf of its citizenry. 'For the common good,' said the Prince, 'of this proud land, this Liechtenstein.'

The gist of the agreement was that the citizens of Liechtenstein would not be permitted to see (or '*be exposed to*,' as the document read) the film, except by special dispensation from the Church, to be granted under only the most extraordinary circumstances. In this way were they to be protected against any influence the film might have on them, corruptive or otherwise—though at no loss, certainly, to the massive influx of tourist dollars, pounds, marks, and francs they hoped to attract. On the contrary, it was deemed, by the hot-shot West German publicity team which had been engaged, that this curious (perhaps unique) national 'restriction' would garner 'a million dollars' worth of wire-service releases,' and would 'psychologically enhance the taboo-potential of the film tenfold—a definite *plus*, motivation-wise.'

The relationship between the film company and the heads of the Church—or specifically, the aging Cardinal von Kopf—had been tenuous and delicate from the beginning. A thin and hawklike man, one of those scions of Austrian aristocracy, he had showed extreme annoyance when he learned about the hookers-in-the-hearse episode. Not that he was a particularly superstitious man, but rather that his notion of impropriety was fairly rigid. Also, by unfortunate mischance, three days later, he himself had occasion to engage the vehicle—like the ambulance, the only one in Vaduz—for use in the burial of his mother.

'Still warm from the heat of their vile writhing bodies!' he had bitterly complained, and swore moreover that the 'fetid stench of musk and tallow yet hangs heavy in the air, like the *shroud* itself!' A proud and eccentric man, he had secretly sworn vengeance against the film company, and above all 'against the gross Leviathan,' by which he presumably meant a certain grand guy, Sid K. Krassman.

To date, however, his only effective interference had been in denying them the use of two sixteenth-century chateaux which Morty and Lips had located, and which happened to belong to the Church.

'He's anti-Semitic,' said Morty, 'the lousy wop cocksucker!'

'*He* ain't no wop,' said Lips.

'He's a *Catholic*, ain't he? And he sure ain't no *mick!*'

'Yeah, but he ain't no *wop* either—he's some kind of *kraut.*'

'Oh yeah?' said Mort wisely, 'well, if he's *Catholic* and he ain't no *mick*, then in *my* book he's a fucking *wop!*'

'Wait a minute—maybe he's a *Nazi*, for Chrissake!'

This notion excited Mort. 'That's *it!* He's a lousy Catholic kraut *Nazi!* You may of put your finger right on it, Lips!' He grabbed the phone. 'We'll get Sid to check it out!'

Another thing which had enticed the ire of the Cardinal was a piece of information, or misinformation as it proved to be, that he had received on the very first day of filming. As it happened, two of his parishioners, a middle-aged couple who owned a restaurant in town, had the catering concession for the film company, preparing breakfast and lunch for them from a makeshift lunch-wagon, and maintaining the urns of hot tea and coffee which were available throughout the day. While they were not allowed on the set itself, they did, of course, have occasion to see the principals namely, Arabella and Pamela Dickensen—when they passed near the lunch-wagon. They did not see them for the first time, however, until *after* their magical make-up job—and so the good couple, understandably, failed to recognize the famous movie stars, and saw them instead (as they later reported to the Cardinal) as 'two girls of the region . . . girls who could not possibly be more than fifteen or sixteen years old.'

Naturally, this had not gone down too well with the Card —who went straight to the Prince and lodged the strongest sort of complaint, which ultimately put him in the embarrassing position of having treated hearsay as fact. And for this, too, he blamed Sid and the others.

2

As the mystery of night is followed, generally speaking, by glorious morning, so the dark-eyed Arabella departed Vaduz only an hour before the arrival of the golden Angela Sterling, and seventeen pieces of luggage.

Boris met her with the big chauffeured Merk, while Lips Malone, driving a Citroën station wagon, took care of the luggage.

'Gosh, I just can't *wait* to see the script!' Angela said excitedly. 'From what you and Mr. Krassman told me in Hollywood, it seems so . . . *daring!*'

'Well, uh, yes, we like to think so. At least, it's . . . *different.*'

'Oh, of course! My goodness, what Boris Adrian picture isn't!?!'

'Tony Sanders is working on it, too—you know him, don't you?'

'Oh yes, he's simply wonderful—he wrote one of *my* pictures. It got all sorts of awards . . .' Then she sighed and gave Boris her brave little-match-girl smile, renowned throughout the world, '. . . none of them, of course, for "Best Actress".'

In a blue miniskirt that matched her eyes and lay halfway up milk-white thighs almost the color of her teeth, she was quite adorable. Boris returned her smile, reached out and squeezed her hand. 'Don't worry, Angie,' he said seriously, 'I think you may have better luck this time. It's a very serious film.'

'Oh I know, I know,' she exclaimed happily, 'and I simply can't tell you how much I appreciate the opportunity.' She pressed his hand between both of hers, resting in her lap—which, in the twelve-inch-above-knee skirt, was comprised of her two bare thighs, backed up briefly by Pucci panties. Like alabaster, thought Boris, visualizing them against the pink satin sheets and entwining around thrusting black buttocks—at the same time was quite surprised to feel along the side of his hand she held in her lap how very warm and soft they were . . . not like alabaster at all.

In New York, on the morning Angela received the cable from Boris saying they were ready to shoot her sequence, the first thing she had done was rush to Actors Workshop to tell her guru, Hans Heming, the wonderful news.

A passionate, bearlike man of Hungarian extraction, he

and his extraordinary teaching techniques were at once the scandal and the salvation of the industry, the center of a perennial storm of controversy among students and professionals of both stage and screen. For every person who considered him an opportunistic charlatan—and there were many—could be found another who thought he was a genius, in fact, a messiah. In any case, two things were incontestable: his Workshop was credited with having produced at least a dozen of the most celebrated actors in the profession; and secondly, his influence on them, and others, was profound. Angela Sterling was in this latter category; although the world's highest-paid star and top box-office attraction, she remained completely unproven as an actress. In fact, there were those who not only insisted that she was without a trace of talent, but went so far as to use her in their denunciation of Hans Heming—citing his professed interest in her as the final proof of his cynical deceptions and his artistic spuriousness. For his own part, he maintained that in Angela Sterling he could see purity and essence—something untrammeled, untouched. 'A blank page, perhaps,' as he was fond of saying, 'but a page of *vellum*.'

And she, in turn, idolized him to an almost fanatical degree.

'Isn't it just too *wonderful!*' she exclaimed through joyous tears, when she showed him the cable.

'I am so glad for you, kitten,' he said, hugging her to him. 'Boris Adrian is a great artist—it is the break we've been waiting for.'

'Oh I know, I know, I know,' she sobbed ecstatically.

Then he held her at arm's length, and fixed her with a somber gaze. 'A word of caution. What about the studio—you're under contract, aren't you? And your agent? What if they are against it?'

She seemed astonished. 'But why on earth should they be against it? They know this is what I've been working for . . . what we've all been working for—the chance to do something . . . *creative*—the chance to work in a . . . *serious film*

—the chance to work with a *great director* . . . isn't it?'

His face darkened slightly. 'Ah yes, but this picture . . . there are rumors . . . they say it is a . . . *strange* picture.'

'But *all* of his pictures are strange, aren't they?'

He shrugged. 'This one, perhaps more than the others. You understand, I only say this to caution you that the others—the studio, your agent—may try to dissuade you from it. You must be prepared for that, you must be prepared to resist their dissuasion.'

She looked at him in amazement. 'Are you *kidding?* You think I'd do that? You think I'd stand still for that?' In her eyes now was a glint of hardness and resolve. 'This is the break I've been waiting for, right?'

He smiled sadly. 'Yes, my dear kitten, it is indeed—but you must remember that the most cruel and ironic tragedy of life is our inability to do *what* must be done *when* it must be done . . . instead, we are like the reed, tossed about on the waves of chance.'

Angela shook her head gravely. 'Uh-uh, not *this* chickie— I'm not leaving *anything* to chance. Not anymore.'

He nodded benignly, releasing her and lowering his hands; then he placed one on her shoulder. With his large face and sad solemnity, he resembled a kindly Benedictine monk about to bless her. 'Good,' he intoned, 'I think my kitten is growing up.'

'You bet your sweet ass I am,' she agreed. 'My bags have been packed for a month.'

3

The contract between the government of Liechtenstein and Gray Eminence Films (the corporate name which Metropolitan was using for the picture) stipulated that 'all principal photography' was to be done inside the country. This had been interpreted, much to the dismay of Boris and Sid, as including 'second-unit' work as well. In short, instead of being able to send a small crew and camera to Tangiers to shoot exterior footage of the Casbah—mostly long or aerial shots—they were obliged, or so it had first appeared, to design and construct an entire village. It had soon become obvious however, that this sort of Cecil B. DeMille operation was not going to be feasible within their time and budget limitations—due mainly to the quality of the materials available and the inexperience of the local artisans. An exterior set used in anything more revealing than a medium shot almost invariably betrays itself as back-lot construction. It was a challenge even the ingenious Nicky could not rise to—beyond a few convincing façades, stone steps, and brief stretches of cobbled street—so that it seemed the all-important Casbah-sequence was in danger of being dropped from the script.

It was producer S. K. Krassman, however, who again saved the day—by dispatching Morty, Lips, and Nicky to London, Paris, and Rome, respectively—from whence they returned with six minutes of beautiful color footage, gleaned from a recent travel documentary.

'But will it *match*?' Lazlo demanded of Sid.

'Match *what*, for Chrissake—we haven't started shooting yet! Just make sure *you* match *it*, schmuck!'

So now they had the establishing shot—a beautiful aerial view of the Casbah, and a slow zoom in on one particular street, then on one particular building, and finally, one particular window. It was a simple matter for Nicky to re-create the street, the façade, and the window; so it would not be discernible where the travelogue stopped and the hot stuff began—to the untrained eye, natch.

4

'Hans sends his love,' Angela was saying, across the candle-lit dining table at La Marmite, Vaduz's *in* Frenchie restaurant—it being, again like the hearse, the only one in town.

Boris smiled. 'He's a great man,' he said, matter-of-factly, 'a great man.'

Angela sighed. 'That's what he says about *you*.' She put her head to one side and gazed at the candle flame with her wistful little-girl look. 'I hope somebody will say that about *me* sometime.'

Boris laughed. 'That you're a great *man*? Not likely.'

She raised her eyes, and her brave smile. 'That I'm a great actress,' she beseeched him, '. . . or not even great, but just *good*—instead of, you know,' she looked away from him, and her voice trailed off, 'what they say instead . . .'

'What, that you're a great piece of ass?'

Boris had a manner of speaking, whereby he could say something quite disarmingly personal to an almost total stranger without causing offense; it was the use of a tone which reflected a simultaneous detachment and concern, with no hint of lasciviousness, morbidity, or put-on. It had the ultimate effect of establishing an illusion of intimacy, in record-breaking time, to be followed, of course, by a profound trust—and it was this which enabled him not only to deploy actors like the proverbial pawns in a game, but to get from them even more than was in them to give.

'Is that what they say?' she asked after looking at him for a moment, but asking it softly and dropping her eyes again, knowing, of course, it was true.

'What do *you* think they say?'

She shrugged. 'Something like that, I guess.'

Boris smiled at her, and spoke with gentle deliberation: 'Angie . . . *they all want to fuck you.* You understand that, don't you? All the men and boys in the world want to fuck Angela Sterling.'

She looked at him, a cold, slow hatred coming into her eyes before she spoke. 'That's the image I want to *change.*'

'Yes, I realize that, and we *will* change it. But I need to know how it feels to be *you.* Don't you see, it's a fantastic thing, the pure phenomenon of it—boys in bathrooms, soldiers in all the armies of the world, prisoners of every country, all in their bunks at night, masturbating, thinking of *you,* having wet dreams about *you* . . . men making love to their wives, their girl friends, to whores, pretending it's *you.* You know how they have those statistics—like there's a murder in the world every eight seconds, that sort of thing— well, there's probably not *one second* passes, day or night, that there isn't a *gallon of sperm* discharged in your honor. Spurted out with your insides as the target! Isn't that incredible? Don't you *feel* all that collective desire? All the guys in the world wanting to fuck you? I mean, wow, the vibrations must be *fantastic.*'

Angela had followed his words—dumbly at first, in half disbelief at what she was hearing; but then, convinced of his genuine concern, she, too, could consider the image dispassionately, as though he were talking about someone else. She slowly ground out her cigarette, looking down at the tray. 'But that's just it,' she said, almost petulantly, 'it isn't *me* they want to fuck, it's *Angela Sterling.*'

'But don't you *identify* with her?'

'No,' she said firmly, 'not with *that* Angela Sterling. Definitely not.'

The slight piety in her reply caused Boris to smile, thinking back to a curious incident of several years previous—six, to be exact, at a moment when Angela was enjoying the first bloom of stardom, as well as the first anguish of the heart. The occasion had been a Sunday afternoon cocktail party at

133

Les Harrison's big beach brownstone, with both Boris and Angela present. Angela, in fact, had been living with Les for about six months, and was nominally the *hostess*—but she had just been tactfully informed that her Mister Wonderful had decided not to divorce his wife after all, but on the contrary, to return to her ('gotta try again to make a go of it with Ethel—we owe it to the kids') which was by no means true, but seemed to Les more considerate than just telling her to get lost. In any case, the news had caused Angela to sink into a veritable morass of self-pity and overindulgence lush-wise, so that she finally passed out on a bed in one of the guest rooms, after trying to phone her mother in Amarillo, Texas.

Also trying to telephone his mother that Sunday afternoon was a young man whom Boris had brought to the party—Grover Morse, from Macon, Georgia. Grover was a personable and star-struck boy of seventeen, who had been employed as a second assistant during the picture Boris had just completed—some of which had been shot on location in the Deep South.

The duties of a second assistant are those of an errand boy—bringing coffee to the director, chairs for the visitors, knocking on the actor's dressing-room door when the camera is ready, and, of course, the proverbial myriad other things. The qualities of a great 'second,' as they are called, are *one*, the ability to anticipate the requirements or needs of the members of the company; and, *two*, to attend to them without being asked, and to be quick and cheerful about it— though not so cheerful as to be obtrusive. Needless to say, a great second is far more rare than a good director or actor. Thus, when Grover Morse proved an exceptional talent at this most demanding and unrewarding of jobs, Boris suggested that he return to the Coast with the company and assured him he would have a lucrative future in the film game. Grover required no persuasion, but his doting mother did. Because he was an only child, just turned seventeen, who had never been further from home than the county line,

134

she was understandably apprehensive about his setting out for Hollywood, notorious sin-fest capital of the world. Boris, of course, had been able to give her countless reassurances—one of which was that her son would telephone her as soon as they arrived. As it happened, they arrived on Sunday afternoon—and because Boris had an appointment with Les Harrison, they went straight from the airport to his Malibu manse, where, as it happened, a party was in progress. Boris had immediately reminded Grover about phoning his mother.

'Use the phone in there,' Les said, indicating somewhat arbitrarily one of the closed bedroom doors nearby.

The young lad obediently went in, shut the door behind him, sat down on one of the twin beds, and started dialing. It was a large room, half in darkness because of the drawn shades, and it was not until the operator had said there would be a five-to-ten-minute delay, and that she would call him back, that he suddenly realized he was not alone. On the other bed was a prone figure, on her back, indistinct except for a shadowed glimmer of blond hair and one raised arm, back of the hand resting on her brow.

He hung up very quietly—but at the sound, Angela stirred and cast a narrow look at him from beneath the back of her hand.

'I don't know you,' she said in a drunken slur.

'No, ma'am—'

'Then what the hell are you doing in here?'

'I'm sorry, ma'am, I didn't see you when I came in—I was just using the phone.'

'You were, huh?'

'Yes, ma'am . . .'

When she continued to stare at him, or so it appeared, though actually just trying to focus, he felt obliged to add: '. . . I was calling my ma, back home. Operator said I'd have to wait.'

She gave a short, angry laugh. 'What's the matter—you in trouble, too?'

135

'Oh no, ma'am, I just have to let her know I got here okay.'
He stood up. 'I'll see if I can get hold of another telephone.
Sorry I disturbed you like that.'

She raised herself to one elbow and cleared her throat.
'Listen, sonny,' she said, more distinctly now, 'how'd you
like to fuck Angela Sterling?'

'Ma'am?'

'I said how would you like to fuck Angela Sterling?'

'You mean . . . the movie-star?'

'That's right.'

Grover, considerably flustered, shifted about uneasily,
darting furtive looks at her, coughed, scratched his head.

'Well, ma'am, I just don't rightly know what I should
say—'

'Say yes or no,' she said with a snarl, 'but just make goddamn sure it isn't *no* because I've had about all *that* shit I
can take today. Now lock the door and come on over here.'

'Yes, ma'am.'

And so, five or ten minutes later, when he was tucking in
his shirt and zipping up his fly, and Angela was in the bathroom straightening herself out, Grover's call came through,
and he was on the phone speaking to his mother:

'Yes, ma'am, everything's fine. Just like Mr. Adrian said
it would be. See there, Ma, you had no call to worry, after
all. . . . Oh sure, mighty nice, as nice a bunch of folks as
you'd wantta meet. . . . You mean right now? Well, I'm
with Mr. Adrian, we're over at a friend's of his house. . . .
Party? Well, I guess it's a kind of a party—*afternoon* party
. . . don't forget, we're three hours earlier out here than you
all are back home. Huh? Aw no, Ma, it ain't no *Hollywood*
kind of party, like you read about with them starlets and
everything. Shoot, that's all baloney anyway—like Mr.
Adrian said—they just print that stuff to sell newspapers.
Ain't nobody'd believe it but a dang fool. Now *you* know
that, don't you, Ma?'

Boris had never revealed his knowledge of this incident,

136

and had counseled young Morse to similar discretion. Thus, it remained one of the great trade secrets—only surfacing occasionally, of late, in the form of a drunken story told by Morse himself (who, after a brief period as second assistant, had become a stuntman, and finally, a hopeless boozer) and which was invariably discounted as the sort of lying fantasy that lurks in the heart of every red-blooded American.

Boris was not too susceptible to reminiscence, but now as he gazed across the table at the fabulous golden beauty, blue eyes shining, moist red lips glistening in the candlelight, he felt this odd bit of knowledge somehow gave him a curious advantage—almost as though he could *blackmail* her into a good performance. At least it thoroughly dispelled the little-match-girl aura, which at times threatened to overwhelm anyone in the vicinity—not that Boris himself had ever been duped by it, for there were other stories as well which tended to characterize her as having a slightly different charisma than the one contrived by herself and her agent, and projected by the PR department at Metropolitan. It was known, for example, that on the occasion of signing her first studio contract, after two years of bit part and extra work, she tossed the pen onto the middle of the table, with an elaborate sigh of relief, and exclaimed: 'There, that's the last kike prick *I'll* ever suck!' then dramatically raised her right hand, and her great blue eyes: '*As God is my witness!*'

Although thereby becoming a contract player, she continued to be used at her specialty—beach and surfing movies, or 'tits-and-ass flicks' as they were called—until she was further 'discovered' by Les Harrison, who, in order to get her into bed, went through a fairly conventional Hollywood courtship—lunch at the Polo Lounge, dinner at La Scala and Matteo's, and finally, a supporting role as a southern belle in a costume epic about the Civil War.

With golden, breast-length tresses, she proved to be so adorable in a lacy corset-cinching scene that Les's father, old C.D. himself (a vigorous fifty-nine at the time), decided, after seeing the rushes, to dip in for a taste, little suspecting that by now Junior was nailing her repeatedly. His own courtship, unlike his son's, was quite formal and straightforward, appearing, in fact, as a flat proposition—though not directly from him, whom she had never met, but through her agent, Abe 'Lynx' Letterman.

'He's got hot nuts for you, kid,' Abe said with cigar-hoarse enthusiasm. 'It's exactly the break we been waiting for!'

C.D.'s proposal was that the girl spend the weekend with him at the Sands Hotel in Las Vegas, in exchange for which she would play the fem lead in an upcoming romantic comedy opposite Rex McGuire, then being groomed, as everyone knew, for instant stardom.

'How can you make sure he won't welsh on it?' Angie wanted to know.

Abe shook his head firmly. 'Lissen, not *stitch one* do you take off before we got it in writing! I tole him awready, not *stitch one!*'

'Oh yeah?' Angie's perfect brow crinkled in cute petulance—already giving a hint of the wistful poignance, the deliciously bereft orphanlike countenance which was to make her a living legend in the hearts of Mr. and Mrs. U.S.A. 'What if he just wants me to suck his cock?'

'Huh?'

'Well, then he's got me, stitch one or not. I mean you don't exactly have to get undressed to suck a cock, do you?'

Abe wagged a pious finger, shaking his head, 'Uh-uh, *no touchy*. I tole him awready, "*no contract, no touchy pretty girlie!*" and *I'll* be there to see that he don't.'

'Who says he won't get me up there and then just jerk off or something?'

'So?' Abe lifted his shoulders, 'he jerks off—that's a chance we gotta take. I mean, that's a chance you take every day, right? You're in a same room with a guy, in a car, in a elevator, in a movie house, on a plane, *anywhere*, he jerks off. So? Big deal. Lissen, what I'm telling *you*, baby, is that not *stitch one* comes off without we got a deal, *in writing*,

138

which I personally will draw up, and he will sign before I leave the hotel room.'

'What if they never make the movie?'

Abe was indignant. 'What do you think, I'm a *potz*? It's *play-or-pay*, baby, *play-or-pay!* Starting October seven, rain or shine, we got ten weeks at thirty-five hundred a week! That ain't *spit*, you know.'

In the scene which had caught Dad Harrison's fancy, Angela was in her bedroom, getting dressed for a formal ball. At this stage she was still in her underwear—long ruffled pantaloons and a waist-cinch which her mother was tightening from behind, causing her to grimace in cute discomfort.

'Oh Momma,' she gasped, 'ah jus' won't be able to *breathe*, much less *dance!*' Being from Texas, she could manage a passable southern accent—too much nasal twang, but still refreshingly non-Bronx considering it was aHollywood film about the South.

The mother was played by Louise Larkin, a well-known character actress who had been under contract to the studio for many years, and whose forte was 'the ideal American mom,' Waspville apple-pie style. She was master, to an almost caricaturish degree, of the southern idiom.

'Now don't you fret youh pretty head about that, chile, you jus' mind that *in between* dances you don't stroll out onto the *veranda* with any of those boys down from Charleston! You heah?'

'Oh Momma, really!'

'Christ, look at that,' said C.D. to the film's executive producer who was sitting beside him in the projection room, 'it's a *blond* Scarlett O'Hara! That's the *real* Scarlett O'Hara! A *blonde!* A full-on *shiksa!* A *pink-nipple* ... *blonde* ... *cracker!* What the hell's her *name* anyway?'

Part of the arrangement, between C.D. and Abe was that Angela would wear the same outfit—pantaloons, cinch, and long blond hairpiece—that she had worn in the scene. And he insisted on a note, signed by the wardrobe mistress, that the garments were, in fact, the same ones worn in the scene.

'What time did you break yesterday?' C.D. demanded of the exec as soon as the segment was finished.

'Five-thirty.'

He sighed. 'Then there's no chance,' at the same time picking up the phone and signaling to cut the sound on the rushes. He called Wardrobe, then handed the phone to the exec.

'Find out if those things she was wearing were sent to the laundry yet. If not, tell them to hold it. Tell them it's *important*.'

The exec, waiting for the ring to answer, shook his head seriously. 'They'll never admit it, even if the stuff *didn't* go out yet—it's a union regulation: "All costumes cleaned after wearing." '

C.D. reached over and took the phone. 'You're right.' He hung it up. 'Okay, reshoot the scene. It's nothing, right? The set's still standing—it's a half hour's work, an hour at most.'

He leaned over and gripped the other's wrist. 'And I want *that* take used in the film. And I want *you*, Cliff, I want *you* personally to see that those things she's wearing *come straight to my office* as soon as she gets out of them. And do a few extra takes while you're at it—let her work up a little sweat, you know, a little *juice* . . . because I've got me *one hell of an idea*, buddy-boy, *one hell of an idea!*'

His 'idea,' as it turned out—at least in its most elementary and mechanical aspect—was that the two women, Angela and Louise, dressed as they were in the scene, would re-enact it in the Vegas hotel room, exactly the way it was going to appear on the screen, but this time it would be interrupted. The interruption would be a marauding, roughshod Yankee cavalry soldier—dirty and unshaven, straight out of battle, brutish, lusting with pent-up desire, and brandishing a pistol—who would burst into the room, pummel Mom aside, fling the immaculate white-pantalooned daughter onto the bed, and, still wearing his boots, would ravish her voraciously . . . pistol on the pillow, muzzle near her temple

140

to discourage outcry from either Mom or the ravished daughter.

The swashbuckling intruder, of course, was C.D. himself, who, instead of leaping through the window, Errol Flynn style, simply rushed out of the bathroom, where he had been awaiting his cue.

'She ain't going *anywhere* tonight,' he snarled, as he entered, pointing the pistol at Angela, and shouldering Louise aside, 'not before she's been *fucked half to death!*'

Both ladies gasped (as per script) in astonishment.

'Oh, Momma . . .'

'Suh, you wouldn't . . .' pleaded Louise, then to Angela, 'Scarlett, honey, don't be afraid, ah'm shuah the gentleman will listen to reason . . .'

'Shut up! One more word out of you and I'll blow your head off!' Then to Angela: 'Scarlett? Is that your name?'

Angela lowered her eyes demurely, and replied in a soft voice: 'Yessuh. Scarlett . . . Scarlett O'Hara.'

'*I'm going to fuck you, Scarlett O'Hara,*' said C.D. tersely, pushing her onto the bed, '*I'm going to fuck you hard and long!*'

'Oh please, suh,' Louise beseeched, 'that little girl is a *vuhgin!*'

'Use the *name*, damn it,' snapped C.D. in a sharp aside, 'keep using the *name!*'

'Sorry,' said Louise quickly in her normal voice, then resumed: 'Ah beg of you, suh, please don't do it to my little Scarlett! Scarlett is a *vuhgin!*'

Meanwhile, C.D. had pulled down the lacy top of the bodice, exposing her breasts.

'Oh please, suh . . .'

'All right, tell your mother what I'm—what this Yankee soldier is doing.'

'Oh Momma . . . the Yankee soljuh is . . . kissing my breast.'

'Not *kissing*,' C.D. fairly hissed.

141

'Oh Momma, he's ... this Yankee soljuh is ... *sucking* my breast!'

'Suh, ah beg of you ...' cried Louise very convincingly.

C.D. tore at the pantaloons, not pulling them down, but ripping them open at the crotch, its seam having previously been weakened by snipping a few threads inside.

'Oh Momma, he's ... he's got it *in* me ... he's doing it, Momma ... the Yankee soljuh ... he's *fucking* me!'

'Oh suh, ah beg of you ...'

'Okay,' said C.D. urgently, '*now, now!*'

'Oh Momma,' Angela wailed, 'he's making me *come* ... the Yankee soljuh is making me *come* ... ah'm goin' to *faint* ... oh Momma, he's *fucking me half to death!*'

Louise came in precisely on cue, grand old trooper that she was:

'Oh suh, how *could* you do that to my Scarlett! Ah shall report it to youh captain—'

'*Say* it, Louise,' urged C.D., 'quick, *say* it!'

'—and tell him,' she hurried, 'how *you fucked Scarlett O'Hara! And made her come!*'

And as C.D. strove into a frenetic spasm, shouting '*I'm fucking you, Scarlett! I'm fucking you, Scarlett!*' Louise picked up a Polaroid flash camera from the dresser and popped a pic.

'Hey, wait a minute!' said Angela, bolting upright in the bed, 'nobody said anything about *dirty pictures!*'

C.D. raised himself on elbow, sighed, reached for a cigar, laughed softly, and reassured her: 'Don't worry, kid, it's just for my private collection,' then shrugged, tapping the cigar, '... besides, who's ever gonna know it's you?'

It was true that neither of their faces showed clearly—just enough of Angela's top-quarter profile to give someone momentary pause when sworn to that it *was*, in fact, the famous star—after which it would be immediately dismissed as another cheap lie ... like the one told by the drunken Grover Morse.

In other respects, it was quite an arresting shot—portraying, as it did, the torn, lace-edged bodice, pulled down to just beneath the lower half of two superb breasts, and, due to its binding effect, causing them to jut out dramatically, followed by white-ruffled pantalooned-legs wrapped around bare buttocks raised in thrust, the leverage for which was being achieved by the toehold of a pair of muddy cavalry boots, spurs still intact.

Although the photograph was almost invariably discredited as *not* being of Angela Sterling, it did, for a while, enjoy a certain vogue among the smart fetishist set, the so-called Boots and Period crowd.

'You can be honest with me,' said Angela, reaching across the table for Boris's hand now and giving him her most serious look, 'you do know that, don't you?'

He smiled. In order not to smile quite too much, he raised her hand to his lips and kissed it. 'Yes, I know,' he murmured.

'Then tell me . . . do you think I have talent?'

Boris frowned and looked away for a moment. Talking to actors about their narcissism was a drain; it put one in the superior position of the psychiatrist—pointless, except on the set.

'*Everyone* has talent,' he said, 'it's just a question of using them'—he caught himself in time—'of *their* using it in the right way, at the right time, and to the right degree. Do you know what I mean?' It seemed she might not have heard.

Angela nodded silently, lowering her eyes, then raised them. 'Please tell me something,' she said, making it sound brave. 'Which one of my movies did you like best . . . no, I don't mean that, I mean which one did you think . . . well, *showed* that I could . . . or that I *might* . . .' She broke off, beseeching him with her eyes, 'You know what I mean?'

'Uh, yes, well you see, it really isn't important what *I* think was best—it's what *you* think was best, the thing *you* felt most involved in . . .'

'Oh please, Boris,' she begged, squeezing his hand, '*please* tell me one . . . one part, one scene . . .'

'Uh, well, let's see . . .' He raised his eyes as though trying to recall, and it slowly came to her that he couldn't think of *anything* of hers he liked.

'Oh God,' she said hopelessly, 'wasn't there *anything?* Surely there must have been *one scene . . . one line . . .*'

'Well, uh, the thing is, you see—'

Then she knew, and she put her face in her hands. 'Oh *no,*' she said. 'you've never even seen . . . *oh no* . . .'

'Don't be silly, of course I've seen you!'

'In what?' she demanded.

'I've seen you in trailers on TV.'

'Trailers for *what?*'

'Well, let's see . . .'

She was shattered. 'You haven't! You haven't seen *anything* I've ever done!' And then it turned to wrath. 'Would you please tell me why I'm here? Because I'm supposed to be such a good piece of ass? Is *that* the reason?' She began to weep bitterly.

Boris grasped her shoulder; it was time to be firm. 'Now stop it, Angela, you're acting like a *child!* I don't *have* to see you on screen, I know you're *exactly right* for this film! I don't want to discuss what I've seen you do, because I know that your potential has never been realized, or even approached. Now you'll just have to have confidence in me. Okay?' He handed her his handkerchief.

She dabbed her eyes and smiled at him through the tears. 'I'm sorry, that was silly.' She squeezed his hand again. 'Forgive me?'

'Here,' he said, filling her glass, 'have some brandy.'

She joined him as he raised his glass. 'To . . . *The Faces of Love,*' he said.

She nodded. 'To *The Faces of Love* . . .'

They drank, and said nothing for a moment, Boris looking at her, but his mind somewhere else.

'Do you know why the studio wasn't able to change my

image?' she asked then. 'I mean, even though I stopped doing the bikini-beach pictures and started doing nice sort of Doris Day things? And I still stayed a sex-symbol? And not only that, but it even got worse? Do you know why?'

'Why?'

'*Because*,' she went on, not without a certain bitterness, staring down at her drink, 'every man in this country likes to think that he's the Big Bad Wolf fucking Goldilocks, *that's* why.'

After holding a pouting expression for a second, she looked up at him. 'But *you're* not like that, are you . . .'

Boris shrugged. 'I don't know. Maybe I am sometimes.'

'Well, you shouldn't be,' she admonished.

He laughed. 'You're too much.'

She gave him a searching look. 'You mean *good* or *bad?*'

He shrugged and smiled, pretending to hesitate. '*Good*,' he said then, 'yeah, I'm going to have to say *good* on this one.'

'I'm glad,' she said softly, then lowered her eyes again, fingering the glass. 'Boris . . . I don't exactly know how to say this . . .'

'You mean I'm that hard to talk to?'

'Oh no, no, no, it isn't *you* . . . I mean you're *so straight* and everything . . . I mean, I don't want you to think I'm, well, you know, *out of line*, or *freaky* or something, it's just that, well, I know how some directors have to feel *close* to the actors before they can really work good together and . . . well, I mean, you're so *cool* and everything that I might not even *know* it if you wanted to . . . you know, be *close* or something . . . I mean, well gosh, I don't think you'd *come on*, you know, even if you *felt* like it . . .'

Boris saw it as a 'Monologue in Close-Up'—clocking the face . . . twitches, textures, angles, shadings, highlights . . . matching the *word*, its substance, with the substance of the *image*—or *counterpointing* them. *How*, he wondered, could it have been done better? He was thinking only of this for the moment, when he was suddenly aware—not abruptly, but with the warm, swift smoothness that accompanies a severed artery—of her hand in his, and more, that he could not imagine her 'Mon. C.U.' as having been different. Good performance.

'What I wanted to say,' she went on, almost shyly, 'was that you don't *have* to, you know, come on with me . . . I mean, I wouldn't put you through that—so if you, well, *do* have eyes . . . like the girl in the movie said, all you gotta do is, you know, *whistle*.'

Boris smiled and pressed her hand. He was not surprised that his previous strategy had been effective in preparing her for work—she would now be like a clean slate, with no hangups from the past—but here was an unexpected bonus, her offering the fabled golden fleece. He had, of course, seen many of her films, some of them more than once. God certainly looks after the man, he mused, who takes care of business first.

5

The Casbah sequence was scheduled for six days' shooting, with Angela in practically every scene—the exceptions being a montage segment of incidents and impressions from her childhood on the Virginia plantation. To play the father, they had prevailed upon the venerable and award-winning Andrew Stonington, a grand old patriarch from the Deep South of yesteryear; and, for the mother, none other, of course, than the great Louise Larkin herself. To play Angela as a young girl—in a series of scenes representing her life between eight and twelve—they had secured the services of the versatile and very pretty Jennifer Jeans, better known to close friends as 'Jenny' Jeans, and to even closer friends as

'*Creamy*' Jeans. Although she could do a passable eight, and a perfect twelve, she was actually eighteen years old. This had to be ascertained beyond any doubt before Sid would sign her.

'Morty, that fucking chick is *jail bait* if I ever seen it! I mean, she's a fucking *child*, for Christ fucking sake! Are you *one-hunnert percent sure* that broad is *eighteen?!?* I mean, I don't want to get hit with no fucking *Mann Act* and not even get *laid!* Jeez!'

'Swear to God, Sid,' said Mort, raising his hand. 'Like I tole you, I seen the birth certificate awready—and as if that ain't enough, I gotta affidavit from her folks saying she's eighteen, and how they unnerstand we're making an adult-type picture here.'

Sid put his head in his hands, keening, ' "Adult-type picture" he calls it—I think we're all going to *jail*, Morty, that's what *I* think.'

It was Tony Sanders, however, who was to have the most dramatic encounter with Miss Jeans.

'Holy fucking Christ,' he said, stumbling over to where Boris was sitting, just off the set, making notes, 'man, you really oughtta cop a taste of what's jumping off in that second trailer—there's an eight-year old kid in there twisting up hash-bombers big as cigars.' He collapsed in a chair, shaking his head. 'And it's *dyna-fucking-mite*, too, daddy, I shit you not!'

Boris laughed to see him so hopelessly stoned. 'Boy or girl?'

'Huh? The kid? Oh wow, a *chick*, man, a fantastic little eight-year-old chick—you know, she's playing Angela as a kid—well, we're supposed to work on the script, right, so I walk into the dressing room . . . *pow*, rock blasting full-out —*Jackie K. and the Plastic Hearts*—and *she's* sitting there alone, staring in the mirror and blowing this monstro joint of hash. "Want a toke?" she says, then giggles—school-girlville, but evil, dig—and says "I mean, if you're from the FBI." So I sit there and get stoned . . . *wow*.'

'But did you get laid?' asked Boris.

'No, man, but dig ... at one point I asked if there was anything to *drink*, and she said "No, baby, I don't drink," and I said, "Well, I know *you* don't drink, but I thought maybe your manager, or your *mother*, or something—" and she smiles and says, "How about if I cop your joint instead?" Eight years old, right? So I give her a big dumb *"Huh? What'd you say?"* And she runs it down for me: "Well, you know, give you some head, blow you, suck your cock, that sort of thing." Well, I'll tell you, B., it tore me up—I mean, I doubt if I've ever turned down a blow-job in my life, but *eight years old*, wow ... I don't know, maybe I'm old-fashioned ... thirteen, twelve, terrific ... maybe even eleven ... or *ten*, for Chrissake, if she's got any knockers—I mean, *any breast at all* ... but the idea of making it with a pre-knocker ... I mean, wow, who wants to fuck a chick with no tits? It must be a *fag*-trip, right? I mean, it's got to be like fucking a young *boy*, right?'

'But she just wanted to give you some head,' Boris reminded him, 'the no-knocker thing wouldn't have mattered there, would it?'

Tony clucked and sighed and covered his face with his hand, wagging his head in despair. 'I know, I know, I've been thinking about that—it was the fucking *hash*, B., I swear to God—it fucked me up ... I didn't know what I was *doing*, for Chrissake ...'

Boris, ultimate funster that he was, did a big-eyed soap-opera elevation of eyebrow, combo of surprise and indignation: 'Oh?'

But it was completely wasted, natch, on Tone the stone—who grimaced as one in pain misunderstood, shutting eyes tight, gritting teeth, shaking head, tolerance at an end: '*Man* ... don't you dig—that fucking *dope* fucked up my whole *motherfucking sense of values!*'

6

The story-line of the casbah-sequence was simplicity itself—
Angela, or 'Miss Maude' as she was called in the script, was
a fabulously wealthy and freaked-out blond American
beauty who maintained a luxurious house in Morocco, and
allowed herself to be ravished by a seemingly endless procession of husky Africans. This footage would later be inter-
cut with images from her childhood—illustrating, presumably, how she developed this insatiable taste, or perhaps
more correctly, why she had determined on this particular
method of getting a rise out of Dad.

The script called for four separate lovemaking scenes,
each complete and highly detailed. In addition—by way of
indicating the sheer scope and volume of the lady's activity
—there was to be a montage featuring approximately two
dozen more of her black lovers, in various aspects and
postures of intercourse with her. Several of these occasions
called for her to 'frolic tumultuously' with two or three at
the same time. The *dénouement*—or finale, as it were—was
a sort of *ronde extraordinaire*, which Tony had designated
'Around the Clock,' and claimed to have actually witnessed
in Hamburg. It was to feature Angela and four participants
. . . one kissing each of her breasts, another kissing her
mouth, and the fourth in full penetration of her perfect vage.
As soon as the full-pen man reached climax, they would all
shift, musical-chairs style, clockwise, to their new positions.
By the time the first arrived at vage again, his member was
once more erect at the ready—so that, theoretically at least,
the *ronde* could continue indefinitely—and the use of a
fast-dissolving montage would produce that effect to good
advantage.

'I was wondering,' said Tony, while they were working on the script in Boris's room, 'if you'd fucked Angie yet?'

Boris, sketching a setup composition, held it at arm's length, squinting at it. 'No, man, I've had too much on my mind.' He crumpled the sketch and started another one. 'Besides,' he added, 'I'm not sure I've got eyes.'

'Hmm.' Tony absently unfolded the crumpled paper and looked at it. 'I don't know whether I ever mentioned it or not,' he said casually, 'but *I* made it with her a couple of times.'

'Oh?' said Boris, expressing polite interest but continuing to work on the composition.

'Yeah, on *Marie Antoinette*, in her dressing room—once in full rig—you know, big hoop skirt, eight petticoats, high-button shoes, monstro hairpiece, the whole *schmear*, pretty weird.'

'How was it?'

'Yeah, well . . .' he seemed curiously undecided, 'well, it was *good*, man,' he said, but almost begrudgingly. 'I mean, just the *idea* of fucking Angela Sterling . . . well, that's a score going in, right? I mean, even if it's *bad*, it's *good*.'

'How do you figure that?'

'Well, at least then it's out of the way—you've fucked her, and you can forget it. Know what I mean?'

'Hmm.' Boris held up his sketch, squinting at it.

'She's got a great *body*,' Tony went on, half defensively, 'and she's, well . . . you know, quite *active* . . . I mean she gets that cooze pointed at the ceiling, and she really *throws it up there!* I mean, like *hard*, man . . . and the old scissor-lock working . . . *writhing* . . . *moaning* . . . *biting* . . . *scratching* . . . *nails digging into your back* . . . *muttering weird endearments* . . . you know, the whole passion-bit.'

Boris shrugged, 'Sounds ideal.'

'Yeah . . .' Tony muttered, lapsing then, trying to get it together. 'Well, the *first* time, the time she was in her full "Marie A." costume, she did a *rape* scene—like, you know, pretending I was raping her—and that was pretty *good* . . . I mean, I was just whacked out enough to get with it . . . I'd always had those fantasies . . . innocent blond beauty rudely pinioned to the mast, hands tied behind her, knockers thrusting out . . . you know, the whole corny "Big Bad Wolf Fucking Goldilocks" syndrome . . . Christ, I tore that costume to pieces. Les Harrison flipped out completely—we had to make up a story . . . about some extra stealing the costume, and then getting hit by a Santa Monica bus . . . or something.'

Boris chuckled. 'Beautiful. Maybe we can use it.'

'No, don't mention it to her, B., for Chrissake. I mean, I don't want to get in one of those kiss-and-tell bags.'

'That's very funny—I was *wondering* where she got that "Goldilocks and the Bad Wolf" bit. She's still using that, you know.'

Tony was shocked. 'What? You mean she actually told you about making it in the dressing room?'

'No, no, she just used the Bad Wolf thing—describing *all* men . . . except maybe me.'

'Ha-ha.'

'Well, what was the next time like?'

Tony frowned. 'It was almost a little *scary*—I mean, it was like she wasn't really all there, you dig. *Fantasy-bagville-time*, right? I mean, I got the feeling I could have slit her throat and she wouldn't have noticed . . . except maybe later, when she got too weak to manipulate her ass.'

'That's bullshit,' said Boris, head to one side, studying his comp, 'I don't think she's that . . . *pure*.'

Tony shrugged, 'Could be. Maybe she was faking the whole thing. Faking the fuck. Hmm. An age-old story, as immemorial as Woman herself. And I was just too boxed to notice. But the time in the "Marie A." rig, that was wild. I mean, you can't fault that one. I wouldn't mind trying something like that again sometime.'

'Raping Marie Antoinette?'

'No, no, something different this time.'

151

'Like getting sucked by a cute eight-year-old in pigtails?'

'*Yes*, you rat fuck! What heinous deception! How could you do that to your grand guy friend Tone? Now I'll probably *never* know the thrill of pre-teen head!'

'Listen,' said Boris, 'I don't like to bring you down, Tone, but we've got to make some decisions about the film.'

'Decisions? Oh wow.'

'Well, let's call it *choices* then.'

'*Choices*, right—that's much better.'

'Okay, do you think we ought to include a *gay* thing?'

Tony grimaced. 'Aghh.'

'Nicky thinks it's a *swell* idea.'

'I'm hip he does.'

Boris smiled. 'What, anti-fag, Tone?'

Tone shrugged. 'Well . . . aside from that—*if* true, which I doubt—I just don't think it makes it erotically.'

'We had the lez sequence.'

'And that was great. Lez, I dig—two chicks fucking, or whatever they're doing—beautiful. I mean, that turns me on—but two *guys*, hairy legs, hairy ass-holes, hairy cock and balls—forget it.'

'What if they're beautiful . . . young, beautiful . . . *Arab* boys, fourteen or fifteen, slender as reeds, smooth olive skin, big doe-brown eyes . . .'

'You mean, like *chicks?*'

Boris regarded him curiously. 'No man, I mean we've got an opportunity here, *and* a responsibility, to lay it *all* down —and I just don't think we should blow it. I mean, I don't want to cop out on some aspect of eroticism simply because I don't happen to dig it personally.'

'Yeah?' Tony snorted, '. . . okay, why don't we do some full-on S. M.? You know, burning off nipples, tearing out clits, that sort of thing. . . . Or how about some *coprophilia?* How about that, B.? We'll do *the definitive cinematic treatment of shit-eating*. I mean, there *are* certain people who claim that's the greatest.'

Boris cocked his head to one side, smiling, slit-eyed,

doing his Edward G. Robinson: 'I like the way you handle yourself kid—how'd you like to fight for *money?*'

Tony drank, shaking his head in true despondence. 'I really don't know, man ... I mean, I *know* I couldn't write a good nipple-burning scene, or a good shit-eating scene ... and I don't *think* I could write a fag-fuck scene ... I mean, not a *good* one—not like, say, *Genêt* could ...'

Boris considered it, preoccupied, moving the felt-tip pen silently back and forth across the page, slowly obliterating what he had drawn. 'Have you ever *had* any homosexual experiences?'

Tony made a face, shaking his head. 'No, man ... well, I mean like not since I was eleven or twelve.'

'What happened then?'

'What *happened?* Well, we just fooled around with each other's cocks, that's all—I mean, we got hard-ons, and then we ... Christ, now I can't remember what the fuck we *did* do. ...' His brow darkened, trying to recall, and he sighed, 'Oh yeah, now it comes back ... wow, ha ... well, what we used to do—my friend and I ... Jason, his name ... Jason Edwards—we'd be in this tree house we built, and we'd jerk off together ... sort of competitively, you know, like see who could come *first*, or *most* ... or *farthest*—that was the best, we'd stand up for that one, like in a spitting contest. And, dig, he was about six months older than me, or anyway a little more hip than me because he had this *sister*—she was fifteen—and he'd get these diagrams out of her box of Tampax, these drawings of Tampax being pushed up into the vage, with one finger, and he'd show them to me, and he'd say: "Look, *this* is where you put your thing, *right in there*." Fantastic! I mean in these drawings, these profile cross-section diagrams—of uterus, womb, tubes etcetera—the artist, for some weird reason, always gave the figure a ... *marvelously rounded, pert, provocative, Jane Fonda type ass!* Well, I think that's how we made the association ... I mean, the idea of the *ass*—his and mine—being some kind of possible substitute for the cooze ... or at least for jerking

153

off, which was where we were at at that moment. Anyway, we tried it a couple of times—but it didn't particularly grab me ... I don't even remember if I came ... I mean, the thing I was into then was watching his sister undress—we would watch her through the bathroom window, and she would stand in front of the mirror and massage her breasts, and that was pretty wild—and I began to use her as a jerk-off image ... my *first jerk-off image*—I mean, aside from the Tampax-girl diagram, which didn't really count because she was *faceless* ... even *headless* and *shoulderless*, for Chrissake! And *legless! Absurd.* The point is, those couple of times I fucked Jason in the ass I was actually pretending it was his *sister* I was fucking.' He looked up at Boris then, and chuckled dryly as though aware he might be taking himself too seriously. 'Pretty healthy imagery, eh, Doctor? None of your proverbial "cocksucking queer" in that kind of relationship, right?'

Boris smiled, and went into his Strangelove accent. 'Iz true you hafe tole zee *abzolute trut?* No suck? *Nicht kommen ven cornhole?*'

'Nope,' Tony shook his head sadly, 'that was it.'

'Rather a sheltered existence ... for one who hopes to capture the elusive feelings ... fears ... hopes of the legendary *Everyman*.'

'Yeah, well, the thing is I've got a good imagination ... you dig? And all I'm trying to say about using a fag sequence for the movie is that we would end up using *chick values* ... or rather, non-gay values toward chicks. I mean if you try to romanticize fucking a young, supple, smooth-skin boy in the ass, then what you're really talking about is fucking a *chick*. Right?'

'In the ass?'

'Oh wow ... in the *ass*, in the *cunt*, in the *armpit*—I mean, *someplace* ... but it's still a chick ... a soft, warm, cuddly, smooth-skinned *chick*—not some *bony, hairy asshole!*'

Boris nodded thoughtfully. 'I just wanted to give it a fair

154

shake before we dumped it ... you know, kick it around, run it up the pole and see if anybody salutes ...'

'*Or*,' said Tony, 'as the great S. K. Krassman would say, "Stroke it a while and see if we get any jissem." '

'Right,' said B.

Tony sighed. 'And now we know.' He took a drink. 'I thought I was about to get the ax.'

'And I thought you were about to walk.'

'Never, maestro.'

'Well, what we've got to decide is how many episodes—four of twenty-three, or five of eighteen. Now it's going to be very tough, maybe impossible, to keep the lez and the nympho segments under twenty-five minutes each—there's just too much happening in them—so that leaves us with forty minutes, ideally, for the rest of the picture. Okay, we've still got "*Idyllic*," "*Profane*," and "*Incestuous*." I just wonder if there's time to do all three. Now I feel pretty strongly about the "*Profane*" one—you know, "The Nun and the Gambler," "The Priest and the Hooker," something along those lines—could even be *funny*. A little of the proverbial "comic relief," eh, Tone? Ha.'

'We'll have to keep it in taste.'

'No toilet jokes about the priest.'

'Right.'

'Now let me ask you this—what about the biggie? How's that shaping up in your great gourd? Mother–son? Father–daughter? Brother–sister? I think we've got to follow our most personal impulses on this one. Now tell me, had you rather fuck your *daughter*, or your *mom* ... assuming, natch, that your mom is a trim thirty-two or thirty-three?'

'*Thirty-two* or *thirty-three?* Christ, is that *possible?* I mean, how old does that make me?'

'Sixteen or seventeen.'

'Hmm,' Tony raised his brows, obviously intrigued, 'a trim thirty-two or thirty-three, eh? Red hair?'

'Could be.'

'Wait a minute, I think I've got an idea—let's talk about

the "*Idyllic*" . . . you know, I said before when I was fucking Jason I'd pretend that it was his *sister?* Well, that wasn't quite true—I mean, I'd pretend that it was *her* all right, the same girl, but I'd pretend that she was *my* sister . . . dig? See, I never *had* a sister, and I used to construct these great fantasies about having a beautiful sister and being very close, like a *twin* maybe, having this fantastic rapport with her, and then *making it*. I mean, what could be more *romantic* . . . more *idyllic?* I think I could write a *beautiful* sequence about that, B., I really do.'

'Hmm, that's pretty wild—combining the "*Incestuous*" and the "*Idyllic*." Now we're going to run *short*, for Chrissake.'

'I can get twenty-five minutes out of that—Christ, I could get twenty-five *hours* out of it.'

'What age would they be?'

'*Young*, but mature—I mean, not thirteen or fourteen, but sixteen or seventeen, maybe eighteen, old enough anyway to know what they're doing.'

'Okay, groovy. Start writing it. How about if we get Dave and Debbie to play the kids?'

David and Deborah Roberts were actor and actress, very young and beautiful, brother and sister, siblings *extraordinaire*.

'Wow . . . that'll be *sen-fucking-sational!*'

FOUR

The mark-inside *was coming up on the Rube . . . and that's a rumble* nobody *can cool.*

> BURROUGHS
> *Naked Lunch*

1

Angela Sterling, lithe and rounded in her famous wrapper of blue brocade—a gift from Hans Heming—which she wore during most of her movie-mag interviews (hence its fame), strode across the Casbah boudoir set to where Boris and Lazlo were working out the first shot. Grips laying cable and gaffers driving nails stopped work like the freeze-frame in a movie, all heads turning as though swiveled by a single wire, every gaze riveting the fabulous face for an instant before dropping abruptly to a region below hip-line, where the blue wrapper parted with each long-limbed stride, flashing a stretch of famous bare thigh like a stabbing knife.

'We'll open with those stock exteriors,' Boris was saying to Lazlo, 'beginning with the long, wide aerial, to establish that it's Morocco, and we'll stay with that, down, down, down, right to this window, and then we'll pick it up inside, dig?' With his view-finder to his eye, he backed slowly away from the window, continuing: 'We'll pick it up right at the window, like a *perfect reverse*, and we'll keep the camera moving at exactly the same pace that it came down, pulling back from the window very slowly, avoiding the bed for the moment, going for details of the room—exploring, lingering—and this could be quite long, because we might use it behind titles . . . then finally, of course, we end up on the bed, where they're making love. . . .' He lowered the view-finder, and looked at the cameraman, 'And you've got to work out the move, Laz, so that it's *logical* and *inevitable* we end on the bed—*not* just because there happen to be a couple of people *fucking* on it, but because the directional symmetry of the camera movement *requires* it. It's got to be *inherent* in the move—so we better make it generally a left—

right move, and vaguely clockwise ... I think that will work. Okay?'

'Okay,' said Laz, already studying it with his view-finder, retracing the move Boris had indicated.

Boris turned to Angela, sitting on the edge of the bed, watching and listening in much the way she had sat on the edge of her chair at Actors Workshop.

'Sorry,' he said, taking her hand, 'we were right in the middle of something.'

She smiled up at him, shaking her head, eyes glistening—her adoration radiant. 'No,' she said softly, 'it was wonderful—it's such a ... *privilege* to be, well, you know, sort of "behind the scenes"—I mean, *creatively*, with someone like *you*.'

He smiled and sat down on the bed beside her. 'Have you read the script?'

'Oh it's *beautiful*,' she sighed. 'I'm not sure I understand it, but I *do* know poetry when I see it, and I *love* poetry.'

The 'script,' as he called it, was scarcely more than an outline, an incoherent mishmash of sensual scenes inter-cut with childhood impressions—which he and Tony had thrown together the night before, solely for her benefit.

'I thought the childhood scenes were so *marvelous*,' she exclaimed, then with dark concern: 'Do you think Jen can handle it?'

Boris patted her hand. 'She'll be perfect.' He looked at her for a long moment, head to the side, as though calculating a risk. 'Tony says you've been talking about a *double*.'

'You mean for the lovemaking scenes.'

'Hmm.'

'Well, I just naturally *assumed* ... I mean, if they're going to actually *make love* ...'

He laughed in a chiding way. 'But *you've* been studying at the *Workshop*—didn't they even teach you how to make love?'

'Oh Boris, really,' she turned aside as if she could some-how dodge the painful remark, but then she had to face it.

160

'You mean, when you show ... well, show it *going in* and everything, you want me to actually be *doing* it?'

'Arabella did.'

She was very impressed. '*Arabella? Really?*'

'*And* Pamela Dickensen.'

She was *not* impressed. 'Oh well, *Pam* ... *she* would.' She tossed her head haughtily, '*She's* still working for two-fifty a picture, isn't she? *I* know, we have the same agent.'

'She wasn't doing it for *money*, Angie,' Boris said gravely. 'She did it because she *believed* in the *film*.'

'Hey, wait a minute,' said Angela, her brow crinkling, 'I thought they were doing the thing about *lesbians*.'

'So?'

'So, where does the *lovemaking* come in?'

'*They* make love, in their own way.'

'You mean *kissing* each other? Oh come *on*, Boris, there's a big difference between *that* and being *fucked on camera!*'

Just off the set, not far from where they were sitting, a curious assembly was in progress. Under the supervision of Freddie the First, about twenty-five Senegalese were being lined up and sorted about. Having been recruited by able Morty Kanowitz from the African quarter of Paris and off the streets of Morocco itself, they were of various ages and various shapes, though all of them—either by girth of by height—seemed larger than life; and, collectively and singly they were the color of anthracite coal: the purest of black, highlighted, or so it seemed, by glints of blue.

'You're not *anti-spade*, by any chance, are you?' asked Boris.

'Huh?' Angela, who had been staring at the milling group with a sort of dumb consternation, turned to face him again. 'No, of course not.'

'Have you ever made it with a black?'

She adjusted her wrapper, so that at the part, where it had been swinging open, one side now carefully over-lapped the other. 'What difference does that make?' she asked coldly.

161

Boris shrugged. 'I was just curious.'

'Well, as it so happens, I *haven't*. For one thing, there's just never been any ... *occasion*. I mean, I don't think I even *know* any Neg— spades, blacks, whatever it is you call them now.' She looked back at the assemblage. 'My God, they're really *black* though, aren't they!?! Christ, I've never *seen* any like that before!'

'Does it turn you on at all?'

She looked at him again, eyes going up in a gesture of exasperation. 'No,' she said evenly, 'I can't say that it does.'

'You think you'll be able to *play* it?'

She was breathless with her reassurances. 'Of *course*, darling, I'll be able to play it! It's just that I couldn't actually *do* it—I mean, if I had to actually *do* it, I *wouldn't* be able to play it. Don't you see?'

Boris nodded. 'That makes sense,' he said. 'Okay, we'll try it your way.'

She squeezed his arm, beaming gratefully. 'Oh thank you, Boris, you won't regret it.'

He returned the squeeze with a smile. He had never, of course, expected her to do the full-pen scenes without a double; but, through his insistence on it, he had managed to put her on the defensive—and *that* was a score, natch.

2

KRASSMAN
HOTEL IMPERIAL
VADUZ, LIECHTENSTEIN
ARRIVING 1700 HOURS THURSDAY 26TH. PLEASE
HAVE SCRIPT AND SHOOTING SCHEDULE MY ROOM
PENTHOUSE SUITE HOTEL IMPERIAL BEFORE
THAT TIME.

REGARDS
L. HARRISON

Sid paced up and down the office, waving the cable about frantically. 'Well, boys, the shit is about to hit the fan!' He He turned imploringly to Boris. 'B., what the hell are we going to *do* when the Rat Prick sees what's happening here?'

Boris sat slumped in a chair, his head resting in one hand, eyes closed. 'I don't care what you do—just keep him away from the set. I don't want him on the set, and I don't want him looking at any footage.'

Sid threw up his arms. 'Oh sure—and just how am I going to do that?'

'By force. We've got two guards—hire two more.'

Sid gave a sign to Mort, who immediately left the room to take care of it.

'And listen, Sid,' Boris continued, without raising his head, 'keep him away from Angie—I don't want him fucking up her head at this point.'

Sid rolled his eyes in despair. 'Oh great, "Keep him away from Angie," he says. She under *contract* to him, she's in *default* of contract—Christ, that's the first place he'll go.'

Boris shook his head. 'We're going to have trouble with her if they start rapping—she's shaky enough as it is.' He opened his eyes and looked up wearily at Sid. 'Didn't you see her this morning? Christ, she's *scared shitless* of all those black cocks. A couple of times I didn't think she was going to make it through the scene.' He stretched and yawned. 'It's very simple, Sid—just don't let them be alone together.'

Sid became quite irate. 'Then *you're* going to have to start *fucking* her, damn it!' He paced about, wringing his hands, his face twisted with anguish and apprehension. 'I mean, she's here four or five days awready, the most beautiful girl in the world, and *nobody's fucking her!* How do you think that makes *her* feel?!?'

Boris laughed. 'Well, we thought you had it covered, Sid.'

Sid grimaced. 'Okay, look, it's outta my league, right? I mean, Christ, I'd give *five years of my life* to fuck Angela Sterling . . . but it's outta my league, okay, I *know* that . . . but *you* and *Tony* . . . I mean, what the hell's the *matter* with

163

you guys? You into some kind of *fag bag* awready? What're you guys, on *dope* or something?' He paused and wagged a severely accusing finger at Boris. 'I mean, *one* of you guys better start taking care of business, and *fucking that broad!*'

Boris shook his head, blinking his eyes. 'Wow, am I tired . . . Christ, I don't think I could get it *up*, Sid. Listen, why don't you just give her some head?'

But Sid was adamant. 'I'm *serious*, B.—I tell you, the *first thing* Les Harrison is going to wantta do is *get laid* . . . relax his tension after the trip, right? Okay, who's he going to hit on? *Angie*, right? Well, if she's not getting it from one of *you* guys, then she'll get it from *him*, for Chrissake! I mean, broads feel . . . *insecure* when that hold is *empty*— believe me, I know!'

Boris shrugged, half asleep now. 'Okay, suppose *both* of us are fucking her—Tony and me—and *you're* giving her head, right? How does that keep her from *still* being nailed by Les?'

Sid's fat hands flailed the air with his objections. 'No, no, no, what I'm talking about is an *affair* . . . this is a *romantic lady*—she'd have an *affair* with one of you guys, and when Les hits on her she'd be *faithful* for Christ-fucking-sake, she'd tell him to get lost . . . Jeez, don't you know anything about a woman's *love* and *faithfulness?!?* Well, I mean it's only for *two or three fucking days*, for Chrissake!'

He looked at his watch. 'It's ten-thirty—she's probably still awake. But it don't matter she's awake or not—you just go in there, she'll be glad to see you, believe me, I know—if she's not glad to see you, it's just because she's sleepy . . . it don't matter, knock her down and take it off her . . . a big solid piece of it! B., she'll thank you later, believe me, I know.'

But B. was asleep.

'Oh Christ, Christ, Christ,' Sid wailed, 'what a terrible business!'

Film-making is a fragmented and tedious process, and the day's shooting that had so exhausted Boris had begun in the most ordinary way—with neither ide nor omen to suggest any departure from the norm.

When the lighting for the first shot was finally right, and the camera had been walked through its move several times, Angela demurely stepped out of her blue wrapper, handed it to Helen Vrobel, and lay down on the bed. Between her legs was a flesh-colored strip of rubberized canvas, the same length and width as a sanitary napkin, secured by tape just above the pubic hair, and again beneath each cheek of her buttocks. From the side, of course, neither canvas nor tape could be seen.

About half of the Senegalese spoke English, or at least understood enough of it to take direction—so to play the first scene with Angela, Boris had selected one he considered to appear somewhat less menacing than the others, perhaps more intelligent, and who seemed to understand English perfectly. His name was Feral, a tall, straight blue-black, whose mouth was open in a constant pearl-tooth smile.

'We ought to lose that smile,' said Lazlo to Boris. 'That's going to look pretty *weird*, isn't it—balling a chick and smiling like that?'

'Let's do one *with* the smile, and one *without*.'

'Right.'

'And stop being against something just because it looks "weird." '

'Right.'

After introducing him to Angela, Boris explained the scene to the loinclothed Feral. 'Now, you understand what's happening, Feral—it's a simple love scene. You are making love to Miss Sterling here, and she is responding to your caresses ... to your lovemaking.'

Feral nodded, grinning. 'Make *real* love?'

'Make real love, yes. *Intercourse*, right? *Zig-zig*, right? *Fuck-fuck*, right? Well, I mean that's how it's going to *look*, you understand. You don't *actually* make love, but you *pretend* you're making love—we want it to *look like* you're making love. Understand?'

'Yes, understand, yes, yes.'

'And while you're making love, I want you to keep kissing her ...' he reached over, pointing, 'here, here, here, and so on,' touching her mouth, throat, shoulders, and breasts. 'Keep your head *moving*, right? Don't cover her *face* from the *camera*, understand?' He indicated the camera lens and traced a direct line from there to the pillow where Angie's head lay, her great blue eyes somewhat wider than usual.

Feral agreed eagerly. 'Yes, yes, understand.'

'Okay, let's try it—take off your Tarzan suit and climb aboard Miss Sterling.'

Boris turned to go to the camera, but was stopped short by a shriek, '*Oh Christ!*' unmistakably from Angie. He wheeled about to see that Feral, having dropped his loincloth, was standing by the bed, grinning insanely, and sporting a monstrous erection—thrusting straight out, throbbing up and down like a metronome, and, either by chance or design, pointing directly at Angie.

'What the hell does he think he's *doing!?!*' she demanded, sitting up in the bed, folding her arms protectively across her breasts. Helen Vrobel rushed forward and draped the wrapper over her shoulders.

Boris slowly returned to the bed. 'Uh, listen, Feral,' he said, nodding at the offending member, 'you won't *need* that ... I mean, not in *this* scene—in *this* scene, you just *pretend* to make love ... later on, in a *different* scene, you can *really* make love, but right now, *no* ... it's just *playlike*, understand?'

166

Feral nodded enthusiastically. 'Oh yes, understand, understand.' He looked down at his organ, shook his head, as grinning as ever. 'I no *try* to make like that! Just happen! I no try! *No real zig-zig! I understand, no real zig-zig!*' He shrugged to indicate his helplessness.

'Hmmm.' Boris scratched his head, considering it, then crossed over to the smoldering Angela. 'Pretty weird, huh?' he said, managing a weak smile.

She didn't return it. 'I thought you said he could understand *English*.'

'Uh yeah, well, the thing is he actually *does* understand that he's not really going to make love to you.'

She seemed quite skeptical. 'Oh yeah? Then why the oil derrick?'

'He says he couldn't help it, it just *happened*.'

She glowered past him toward her co-actor. 'Well, tell him to just *unhappen* it!'

Boris sighed and looked over at Feral, standing as he had left him, grinning idiotically, and no sign of abatement member-wise.

'You couldn't, uh, play the scene like that, I guess,' he asked, coming back to Angela, 'I mean even if he *does* know it's not going to be for real . . .'

She took a sharp breath between clenched teeth. 'I'd rather *die*,' she hissed.

Tony, who had been writing on the other side of the set, joined them at the bed, walking past Feral as he did, and glancing back at him briefly. 'Wow, that's some *whacker* that guy's got on him, isn't it?!? Jesus Christ, a girl could *choke* to death on a piece of that, couldn't she, Ange?'

Angela turned her head away with a snort of disgust.

'Angie says she won't do the scene with him like that.'

'Oh?' Tony frowned down at her pelvic area. 'You look pretty secure in that rig,' he playfully reached out and gently snapped it, '*and* perfectly adorable. I can't say I blame the savage black.'

She struck at his hand, 'Will you get out of here!' She

167

turned to Boris. 'Will you please tell him to get out of here!'

'All right now, let's just cool it. We've got a problem—'

Angela's impatience was mounting. '*Some* problem—why doesn't he *jerk off*, for Chrissake!?! Just send him over to a dark corner and have him *jerk off!*'

Boris scowled at her. 'You can't ask a man like that to jerk off . . . they're a proud—'

'*Then get him laid, for Chrissake!*' she fairly shouted.

'Why don't you use a different guy?' asked Tony.

'No, I like this guy—that *grin* of his, that could be pretty strange . . .'

'Okay,' said Tony, 'how about sticking his cock in an *ice bucket!*'

'Great,' said Boris, '*that's it*, for Chrissake! We'll stick it in an ice bucket, bring it down, then we'll spray it with novocaine! *Terrific!*' He signaled to Props. 'Joe, get an ice bucket up here—half ice, half water. And *keep* it here, ha, we may need it again.'

'Better make it a *big* one, Joe,' Tony shouted after him, then smiled down at Angie, 'Right, Ange?' and gave her a big wink. But she just glowered, took a deep breath, and turned away in smoldering indignation—an abrupt movement which had the incongruous effect of causing her perfect breasts, seen from above through the parted wrapper, to jiggle briefly, almost comically, before settling down, and into—or so it seemed, with the nipples poking out like angry little mushrooms—a permanent pout.

The ice-novo combo had proved wondrously effective, and Angie was so relieved to notice that Feral's org ('like some kind of terrible black *club*,' she'd said earlier) had finally subsided to a shrivel of innocence that she went all out in the scene, allowing him to hunch against her rising mons with apparent wild vigor and abandon—though, in actual fact, quite flaccidly—while she, in turn, sobbed, twisted, writhed, moaned, scratched, screamed, swooned, in a superbly feigned display of outlandish passion.

'Print *all* of it,' said Boris when they'd finished, and then to Angie, after Feral had gone: 'Wow, that was *fantastic!*' He sat down on the bed by her, while she slipped into her Helen-held wrapper. He laughed, shaking his head. 'And you said they didn't turn you on. Ha.'

She lit a cigarette. 'That's right, honey,' and when Helen Vrobel left them alone, she had a quick surreptitious glance around the set, then took his hand in hers and discreetly guided it through the parted wrapper, between her legs and beneath the strip of rubberized canvas covering the mons, pressing one of his fingers inside the lips of her vage— while her smile glittered up at him fanatically. '*Dry as a bone . . . right, B.?*'

4

Sid, with chauffeur in the big Merk, met Les Harrison's plane at the airstrip, and, as they started for the hotel, he opened the refrigeration compartment and took out a bottle of champagne.

'All the comforts of home,' he said with a chuckle which did not quite camouflage the anxiety beneath it.

Les shook his head grimly. 'It's a little early in the day for me,' then continued in terse tones, 'How's Angie taking all this?'

'Huh? You mean the *picture?* Oh she's fine, fine.'

'No, I didn't mean the *picture*—whatever the hell *that* may be—I meant the twelve-million-dollar breach-of-contract suit we're contemplating against her.'

'Uh, well . . . Jeez, I don't know, Les . . . I mean, I don't think she's mentioned that.'

Les sighed, wagging his head. 'The girl is *sick*, really *sick*. First, that New York acting-school nonsense, and now *this* . . .' He closed his eyes, lowered his head, massaged his temples with thumb and forefinger.

'Hey, wait a minute, Les,' Sid went into his effusive style, 'don't *knock* it! This could be the hottest thing since *Funny Girl!* I mean, you guys have got an investment here *too*, you know! Don't knock your own picture, Les!'

Les opened his eyes, and turned his dead-blue killer's gaze on Sid. 'We "have an investment here too," ' he repeated with maniacal calm, Rod Steiger style, '*we* have an investment . . . in *Angela Sterling*, we have a *big* investment in Angela Sterling.' Then he leaned forward to continue, almost whispering, as in mock confidence: 'Let me tell you something, Sid—Angela Sterling's last two pictures grossed *eight million* apiece. All right, she's good for another five years, maybe six. At four pictures a year, you figure it out . . .' From the extreme deliberation with which he resumed, patiently gesturing with his fingers, as though explaining something to a child, it was apparent that his inner turmoil was threatening to get out of control. The pressure on the floodgates was mounting. '*Four . . . times . . . eight . . . is thirty-two. Six . . . times . . . thirty-two . . . is one hundred and ninety-two . . . and you . . . you say we have an investment here? An investment? AN INVESTMENT? YOU'RE TALKING ABOUT TWO HUNDRED MILLION FUCKING DOLLARS! IS THAT AN INVESTMENT!?!*'

As the floodgates burst, and Les was leaning forward and screaming at the top of his voice, he seemed on the verge of actually lunging at Sid's throat—but, with the crescendo, he stopped, visibly trembling, then slumped back down in the seat. And when he spoke again, it was with quiet, consummate control. 'The girl is *sick*, Sid. She's in *desperate* need of psychiatric attention.'

Angie's vage, 'dry as a bone' though it may have been, had begun sweetening noticeably at the exact introduction of Boris's middle finger—which he then, for want of better, proceeded to agitate gently ... and the girl, still gazing up at him with a nightmare grimace of hilarity, had responded by contracting her sphincter muscle with increasing speed and severity.

'Say,' said Boris, somewhat nonplussed by these unexpected developments on the set, 'that's, uh, well, that's, uh some *control* you've got there.'

Without altering her expression, which was like something frozen at the peak of manic hysteria, she said, 'You know what they call that back in Texas?'

She had used a pure southwestern accent, and for the moment he assumed she was kidding. He smiled. 'No,' he said, what do they call it?'

'*Snapping-turtle* pussy.'

He nodded his understanding.

'It's supposed to be the best kind,' she added quite ingenuously.

'I can believe that.'

Twice they had to cool it because Nicky or Fred the First came to inquire about something.

'Why don't we go to my dressing room?' she suggested after the second interruption.

'Hmm.' Boris's mind clocked the contingencies like a low-hurdle runner in a very short race: (1) there was still an hour of shooting time before breaking for lunch, (2) as yet he felt neither hint nor promise of an erection. Loathe to squander shooting time under *any* conditions, the notion of doing so without getting laid—and/or, moreover, at the risk of alienating his principal actor—gave him certain pause, certain ambivalence.

'You know something,' Angie suddenly said, attempting to look mischievous, but succeeding, rather, in looking extremely weird, lifting her eyebrows and casting a theatrically eccentric glance at his trouser fly, 'Ah jest bet yore tally's stiff 'n' hard as a dang ole hickory limb right about now!' And her vage layed a seizure on his middle finger so strong that, in combination with its full-on slick wetness, the finger was actually expelled for an instant, just as in a postcoital coughing spasm.

'Oops,' she said, her smile a caricature of a toothpaste ad, *'naughty, naughty!'*

It was just about then he realized she was on *speed*—not speed alone, but in some curious combination which would account for her reverting so completely to the language of her childhood—not just its *accent* but its *substance* . . . 'a dang ole hickory limb.' Well, well, he thought, if that's what it takes to get a performance out of her . . . *solid*.

'Let's do another scene first,' he said softly, 'we don't want to lose what you've got going now—it's too precious.'

'*You're* the doctor—I mean, *director*,' she said, beaming frantically.

6

'Wow,' he said to Tony at lunch, 'she's really hot today. Two beautiful scenes. Beautiful.'

Tony looked over to where she was sitting at a table with Nicky and Helen Vrobel, who were joined in animated conversation, while Angela observed them, as if fascinated, her gaze switching from one to the other as each spoke, like she

172

was watching the flight of some odd physical thing between them.

'She's *boxed*, for Chrissake,' said Tony, sounding half surprised and half annoyed, as though envious, returning to his steak and taking a huge bite. 'Wonder what she's on?'

'I don't know,' Boris said, 'but, man, she's *smokin'*.' He laughed softly, shaking his head. 'Never thought I'd see the day.'

'Well, B., you bring out the best in people, I've told you that all along.'

'Listen, see if you can find out what she's on, and *keep* her on it. It's some kind of speed.'

Tony looked at her again, chewing thoughtfully. 'Christ, man, it's more than just *speed*—she's *spaced*.'

Boris emptied his wineglass, touched the napkin to his lips, and stood up from the table. 'I'll just bet you're *right*, Tone,' and he gave him a smile and a wink before leaving for the set, calling back over his shoulder in an absurd cracker drawl: 'Ah done ast you to find out what it *is*, you heah?'

Because she was working this well, spaced or no, Boris decided to shoot the so-called Around the Clock sequence that afternoon. This was the scene where she was being made love to by four men simultaneously—one in full vage-pen, and three fondling her various.

With great tenderness and patience, he explained to her how in this sequence, or at least part of it—namely, the medium, or master-shot, which was to show the whole group—it would be necessary for *some* of the men to have erections, but was quick to reassure that it would *not* include the one between her legs, and that none of them—the erections—would actually touch her.

'Just *ignore* them,' he advised, 'just *don't look*—then it won't bug you. Okay?'

She nodded, and closed her eyes. '*I love you*,' she said with hushed urgency.

173

In addition to the already established Feral, the four Senegalese who were to be her partners included a giant man name Hadj—six-feet-seven, weighing two-eighty-five, and with a Mr. Universe build.

The action, as it was now conceived, called for Feral to be at full-pen as the scene opened, with Hadj *on deck*, so to speak—or, more precisely, at left breast, ready to take over full-pen on the shift.

'So, you dig,' Tony explained, 'camera holds on Hadj, *before* he's fucking her, while he's *waiting* to fuck her—that way we get a taste of what's in *store* for her, what's *coming up* ... this *incredible stud*, with his *monstro, black, throbbing, animal cock! Full of fantastic pent-up black lust for the beautiful blonde, and a gallon of black jissem!*'

'Tone, you're getting carried away,' said Boris.

'I know,' he had to admit, 'it's just too *fan-fucking-tastic!*'

'That almost gave me a hard-on.'

'Yeah, me too. You know how I'd like to fuck her now? I just realized—if I could get into a *spade bag* ... like if I could pretend to be a spade ... yeah, that's it, *spade-rape bag*. You think she'd lie still for some *burnt cork*, B.?'

'I'll sound her for you, Tone. How about *you* finding out about that *dope* she's on, like I done tole you to do.'

7

A curious and unforeseen complication arose in connection with filming the sequence. While Feral was again required to have his unruly member plunged into ice water and sprayed with novocaine, neither Hadj nor one of the other one quasi-lovers (the 'mouth man') could achieve erection.

'I don't fucking *believe* it,' said Tony.

Boris shrugged. 'I guess they just can't make that kind of *vicariousness*. I sort of dig them for that.'

Tony was growing very apprehensive. 'But what about the *scene?* I mean, we've *got* to have her being fucked by one guy, and surrounded by *three big hard cocks!* Sticking up like ... *flowers!* I mean, dig the image—*she's being fucked in a garden of cock!*'

'I'm with *you*, Tone—how do we get it up for them?'

'Why don't you ask Angie to touch it ... just *touch* it.'

'Uh-uh, she's liable to wig out any minute as it is.'

'Okay, what about those *funeral-car chicks*—you know, those two hookers who met me at the airstrip?'

'*Terrific*,' said Boris. He called the Freddie over, sent him to locate Mort or Lips Malone and apprise them of the situation.

'It doesn't have to be the *same* two girls,' he called after him, 'but we need them right away. And if you see Mr. Krassman, tell him production has ground to a halt.'

'Say,' Tony mused, 'I wonder if *Helen Vrobel* would do a little stroking—she's a good company-girl.'

Boris guffawed. 'Christ, she couldn't get it up for the *Boston Strangler!*'

'I don't know,' said Tony, sounding serious, 'I have an idea that these guys would *prefer* fucking her to Angie.'

'Are you out of your skull? *Why* in God's name would they prefer fucking *her* to *Angie?*'

Tony did a little two-step, rolled his eyes back, and went into his minstrel delivery: ' 'Cause she done been white ... *long-ah!* Yak-yak-yak!'

Before Boris could hit him with his rolled-up script, they were joined by the smiling Feral, who kept nodding, Japanese style, to express apology at the intrusion.

'Excuse, excuse. I may speak, yes?'

'Of course, Feral,' said Boris, 'you make speak.'

'You have trouble, yes? You have trouble with Hadj and with Achmed. Here, yes?' He pointed down at his loincloth.

'That's right,' said Boris, speaking carefully, 'and now we

175

are going to bring in *two pretty girls*, and see if that will help. Understand?'

'Understand, yes. Pretty girl very good for *Achmed*,' then he shook his head, beaming ecstatically,' but for *Hadj—no*. Girl *no good* for Hadj.'

Boris groaned, putting his hand to his head, 'Oh, my God . . .'

'I don't fucking *believe* it,' said Tony, '*a fruit!* A monstro black *fruit!*'

Feral resumed his joyous nodding. 'Hadj *no like* girl, yes?'

'Yes,' said Boris wearily, 'Hadj like *men*, right?'

'Yes, Hadj like men.'

'Well, well,' Boris could not recall a similar quandary in his film-making experience. 'This presents quite a problem. Tell me, Feral, just, uh, what *kind* of man does he like? I mean, how about some of the other Senegalese on the picture—does he like any of them?'

'No, no, Hadj no like. Hadj like *white* man.'

'*Strong* white man, yes?'

'No, no, *weak* white man . . . like *woman*, but *man*, yes?'

'Hmm.' Boris was genuinely disturbed. 'Christ, Tony, I think we're in a lot of trouble. I mean, where the hell—'

But Tony snapped his fingers, face suddenly alight. 'I've *got* it! Ho-ho, B., baby, just call me Mr. fucking match-maker! Are you ready for *this?*'

'Lay it on me, Tone,' said Boris patiently.

'Then, dig . . . *Nicky Sanchez!*'

8

When producer Sid Krassman arrived at the stage that afternoon, he was taken aback by a succession of untoward events. The first occurred when, in looking for Boris, he stopped at the trailer sometimes used as an office, opened the door, only to find Tony Sanders lying on the couch, his member being kissed and fondled by an unfamiliar girl in black panties and bra. Sid quickly shut the door, and moved on toward the set, looking back at the trailer several times, before he practically *stumbled* over another such coupling— now featuring a black-panty-and-bra girl, rendering avid fellatio to giant Achmed. As he stepped around them, muttering something incoherent, his glance happened to cross the set, where, in the shadow of the camera itself, he could clearly see his art director, on hands and knees, voraciously sucking the organ of yet another huge black, the great Hadj.

'*What in the name of Christ is going on here!?!*' he roared at Fred the First.

Had these incidents occurred on the set—that is to say, *on* camera, it would have been understandable, but for them to be occurring *off* the set—*and* at three in the afternoon— was incomprehensible. An orgy! A bacchanal! And to Sid it could signal only one thing—total collapse of the organizational discipline so absolutely vital to efficient production.

'Where the hell is your *director?!?*' he demanded. 'Christ, I've never seen so much *cocksucking* going on in my life!'

Fred the First explained the problem, and how it was being dealt with.

'Oh yeah?' Sid was dubious. 'What about *Tony Sanders?* I *know he* don't have trouble getting it up! Besides that, he aint even in the picture!'

'Yeah,' said Fred, 'well, I think he and Mr. Adrian just figured that seeing she was already here and paid for, there was no sense to waste it.'

'*Waste*, my ass! That's *not* going to be charged against the picture! Now where the hell is *Boris*—off somewhere getting blowed too?'

'No sir, he went to the john.'

'How many shots you get since lunch?'

'Well, uh, we're still working on the first one, because of that unexpected development . . .'

'You mean to tell me you haven't got *one* shot since lunch?' He frowned furiously at his wristwatch. 'Holy Christ, man, we're supposed to be making a *picture!* And *you're* supposed to keep things *moving* around here!'

'Yessir, well, we were all set up, and then that unexpected development—'

' "Unexpected development"! You call casting a *fag* in the role of a . . . a *whatever* the hell he is . . . you call that an "unexpected development"?!?' He glanced over to where Nicky and Hadj were still locked in fervent embrace, then turned back, with an expression of acute distaste. 'Christ, that's *disgusting!* Nicky Sanchez! You know, if I hadn't seen it with my own eyes, I wouldn't of believed it.'

Fred the First shrugged. 'Well, I guess *somebody* had to do it.'

'*Had* to do it! Christ, he *loves* it! Just *look* at him, for Chrissake!'

'Yeah, well, what I mean is maybe we're lucky that he *does*—because we were in real trouble before.'

' "*Trouble before*"!' Sid blustered, forcibly tapping his watch, then the first assistant's chest. '*Three-fifteen*, and you haven't got the first shot! You're in trouble *now*, buster!'

Only Boris's arrival kept the admonishment from becoming more severe. 'Lay off, Sid, it's not Freddie's fault.'

'Awright, awright, can we please get the first shot now?'

'We have to wait a few more minutes.'

'*Wait?* For *what?*'

'For Hadj,' he nodded, in that direction, 'the big one with Nicky.'

'You mean it's not working?'

'Oh yeah, it was working great. A little *too* great, I guess.' Sid's brow furrowed. 'You mean . . .'

Boris nodded. 'Didn't stop in time . . . I guess Nicky just got carried away.'

'Why that . . . that dirty little . . . *cocksucker!*' Sid was raging. 'Of all the . . . *rotten* . . . *selfish* . . . why, I'll *kill* the little bastard!' and he moved as if to actually rush toward them, but Boris restrained him.

178

'Just take it easy, Sid—he'll have it up again in a minute.'

Tony joined them, looking relaxed and affable. 'Hello, Sidney, how's the boy?'

Sid glowered at him. 'Where the hell have *you* been?'

'What? Oh, I was over in one of the trailers, uh, working on the script.'

'Like hell you were! You were in there getting your *cock sucked!* Ha! I saw you!'

'How *was* that, by the way?' asked Boris.

'Oh . . . I think I'd rate it good to excellent.'

Sid was not amused. 'Ha! And how would you rate the work you've done on the *script* today?'

Tony gave Boris a quizzical look. 'What's with him?'

'He's a little uptight about the schedule.'

'*Plus*,' Sid added, '*plus* the fact that Les Harrison is liable to drop in here *any minute*—and we're two days behind schedule, and no script to show him! What if he had walked in *today?* Huh? Not *one shot* since lunch, and a lot of *crazy cocksucking* going on all over the place!'

'That reminds me,' said Boris, looking around, 'I better check on Nicky.' He started to go over, then stopped short, seeing that they were no longer embraced but were walking to the set, hand in hand. 'Well, I guess we can shoot,' he said, and signaled the first assistant to get everyone ready.

'Holy Christ,' muttered Sid, 'look at the whang on that coon!'

Boris left them to go to the camera, and Sid glanced at his watch. 'Three-thirty—I hope to Christ he can finish that scene today.' He seemed much more at ease now that work was about to resume. He and Tony walked slowly along the row of trailers, approaching the one Boris sometimes used as an office. At the window the silhouette of the girl inside could be seen moving about.

Sid coughed a couple of times, and looked at his watch again, before speaking: 'You say that broad gives pretty good head, huh, Tone?'

179

9

The afternoon's work had extended into evening, but it had gone extremely well—the Around the Clock sequence was completed, and another begun. In addition, the three 'finalists' for the job of doubling for Angela were auditioned, and a decision reached. The 'audition' had consisted merely of scrutinizing each girl's anatomy in the appropriate areas to determine which of them mostly closely matched Angie's, and finally, in ascertaining that she was fully and realistically aware of what she would be required to do in the 'scene'. As in the case of the double for Arabella, it was Lips Malone who had once more prowled mean streets and delivered the goods—scoring on this occasion, not from Paris, but from the infamous port city of Hamburg, where he had succeeded in procuring half a dozen extraordinary, although somewhat cynical, nifties.

Ordinarily, it would be necessary to employ only *one* double, but because of the strenuous nature of this particular role, Boris had asked for *two*—and Sid was even *more* cautious. 'Christ, let's take *all* of them—those fucking boogs may turn *cannibal* any minute! Then we'd *really* be up shit creek!'

So the three were engaged—but Sid's problems on this count were not at an end. He was flabbergasted, then furious, when the doctor who represented the insurance firm the company was using, upon seeing the horde of giant blacks, and being informed of the details of the sequence, had flatly refused to insure the girls at all. 'Why, the fucking *quack!*' Sid stamped about the set in a rage which turned to apprehension. 'Christ Almighty, if Les Harrison finds out we're working uninsured actors, he'll blow his stack! Holy Christ, man, he could even shut us down!'

'We just won't *tell* him,' said Boris.

'Okay, but if something *does* happen to one of the broads? I mean, suppose one of those big boogs flips his wig, and does something screwy?'

'Listen,' said Tony, sounding serious and confidential, 'why don't you get the First to wear a *pistol?* Clyde Beatty style, right? Animal-trainer time. One of the boogs blows his stack, goes for a broad—*pow*, you blast him!'

The mere image seemed to excite Sid terrifically. 'Christ, that's it! Where the hell is he?' And he rushed off to find Fred, while Boris and Tone enjoyed a hearty guffaw.

10

During the past two days, in another part of the studio, a second unit had been shooting the 'Maude, as a child' footage with Jennifer Jeans—supported, of course, by the two great veteran thesps, Louise Larkin and Andrew Stonington, as Mom and Dad—neither of whom had any real notion of what was taking place on the neighboring set. The footage being prepared here was thoroughly conventional, even wholesome—including the occasional pseudo-artistic use of a partially smeared lens to render the image in an impressionistic style of things dreamed or remembered. Visiting this set gave Sid a warm, nostalgic feeling and a comfortable reassurance, suggesting as it did, with its cliché treatment of extremely genteel material, a certain normalcy of film-making. He even took a sympathetic interest in the material itself, feeling that, after all, this was just the sort of childhood *he* would have liked—with its huge, white-pillared manse, servants in livery, and a back-projection of countless rolling acres. So he visited the set often. 'An island of sanity and decency,' he called it, and only once was this appraisal briefly shaken—when he happened to notice, sitting on top of a lens case, a small jar of Vaseline, and his face contorted in anger and confusion, while his eyes raced frantically around the set. '*What the hell's going on here!?!*' he demanded, with feverish urgency, of the unit director, thinking that somehow the weirdness and corruption of Boris's set had spread plaguelike to his own sanctuary—but then was enormously relieved to realize that the jar of Vaseline was, of course, merely being used, *and* in almost infinitesimal quantity, to haze the camera lens and soften even more the already very romantic image.

'Frankie, my boy,' Sid had grown fond of saying to the unit director, 'let's do another *take*,' and he would snap his fingers with what he assumed to be the *largesse* of the *grand seigneur*, 'better safe than sorry, eh Frankie? Ha-ha,' while the crew looked on in irate wonder, some of them knowing him from Hollywood days as 'Mr. Shorts,' a reference to penury and avarice based on his use of 'short ends' of film— that is to say, the last bit of film remaining on the spool after the shot is finished, generally discarded as of no use, but often snipped by lab assistants, prior to processing, and sold for little or naught. One of the less apocryphal of the Bev Hills afterdinner anecdotes was the story of how Sid Krassman had tried to structure an entire shooting script on the use of 'short ends.' But, unbeknownst to the grips and gaffers, scowling in confusion, was that this apparent foible of Krassman's—this absurdly tremendous *overshooting*— was, in fact, boss relevant ... because it was *this* footage which they intended to show to Les Harrison, or, for that matter, to anyone else who might suddenly drop by, and insist on seeing 'just what the heck kind of motion picture they were sinking their hard-ready into!'

And now, of course, he *had* arrived. Tony was up all the night before, writing some fairly conventional—and wholly arbitrary—scenes and dialogue, supposedly representing Angela's Casbah sequence. For the purposes of this subterfuge, the locale had been retained, since a tour of the handsome Casbah set was planned as part of Les Harrison's diversion. What had been changed, quite basically, were the characters in the sequence: the protagonist was no longer a decadent, drug-crazy nymphomaniac, but a sort of Eva Marie Saint type Peace Corps worker, who had come to the dark continent in search of 'inner values,' or—'and I hope this doesn't sound too darn pretentious,' Tony had written in a marginal note—'what I like to think of as "the eternal verities," ' while, for the dozen or so black ravishers, he had substituted a single lover—an ofay Frenchie Pepe le Moko type. Les perused it with considerable interest, even making an occasional suggestion.

'I think we can play this love scene pretty *hot*,' he would say, boldly thumping the script at an open page, 'you know, the whole bare-tits bit—naturally, we'll do a cover-shot on it, so there won't be any hassle about a TV sale. Too bad, though, we couldn't get Belmondo—what'd you say this other kid's name is?'

'Uh, Lamont,' said Sid, 'yeah, André Lamont . . . I mean, when we couldn't get Jean-Paul, we decided what the hell, let's go with an unknown . . . get a fresh face up there—right, Les?'

Les nodded wisely. ' " If you can't get the *best*, go with the unknown every time!" Dad told me that when I was nine years old, Sid, and I remember it like it was yesterday.' He glanced at his watch. 'Hey, sun's over the yardarm—you know, I wouldn't mind *having* that drink about now.'

Sid beamed. 'Coming up, Les!' and he poured out the bubbly.

'And I'll tell you something else, Sid,' Les hit the script again, hard but curiously affectionate, slapping it the way a businessman might smack a good-natured whore on the ass, or like the football players do each other, 'you know, this is *pretty damn good* . . . I mean, I don't say it's Stan Shapiro, but, Christ, when Tony's *hot*, he can really wrap up the old ball game, right?'

Sid had to cough for a second, but quickly recovered. 'Yeah, oh yeah, he's ... well, he's ... well, I mean, *you* know how *he* is ... right?'

Then he took him to see some footage—six hours of Jennifer Jeans, playing Angie as a child.

There was a moment when Jen—as an eight-year-old with pigtails and innocently short schoolgirl hemline—back to camera, slowly bent over to tie her shoe.

'Say,' said Les, next to Sid in the darkened projection room, 'how *is* Jen, anyway?'

'Oh she's fine, Les, just fine—she'll sure be glad to see *you*, I bet.'

'Hmm,' said Les, returning his scrutiny to the cineramic stretch of back-of-calf, back-of-knee, back-of-thigh, right up to back-of-straight-edged-simple-snow-white-young-girl-panties, 'uh, you know, she might be just right for ... well, uh, see if you can get her up to my room, Sid, in, say, half an hour after we finish here.'

'Take it off your mind, Les,' Sid assured him, 'she'll be *there*.'

'That's beautiful, Sid, and, uh, have her in that *same outfit*, okay? "*Little Miss Marker*" ... I mean, we're thinking about doing remakes of the whole Shirley Temple series. Be a hell of a break for the girl who's right for it—know what I mean?'

Sid nodded vigorously. 'I'm with *you*, Les.'

By the time they came out of the screening room, it was about seven o'clock.

'What I see,' said Les, tight-lipped, nodding his head firmly, 'I *like*. I like the *look* of it. Dad used to say, "Show me eight frames of film, and I'll tell you what your picture's going to look like!" ' He repeated his wise firm nod. '*This* I like the look of.'

Sid's spirits were soaring, and his heavy gait took on the sort of prancing bounce which, on good days, he had used to saunter in and out of the executive dining room at the

Metro commissary, every step reflecting outrageous confidence. He glanced at his watch. 'Say, tell you what, Les—Jenny will be up to your room at eight . . . that gives you about half an hour to kill, why don't you have a look at the terrific Casbah set we had Nicky Sanchez do for Angela's sequence?'

Les nodded. 'The kid's a genius. I've said so for years. Dad discovered him, you know.'

Although it was Saturday, Sid knew that they had been shooting—but he also knew they had wrapped at five-thirty, because at about that time he had seen Helen Vrobel and a couple of the technicians come into the hotel bar when he went there to pick up Les. He was somewhat surprised, therefore, to find the heavy soundstage door unlocked, and then inside, to see light from a distant set.

'What the hell,' snapped Les, looking at his watch and frowning, 'don't tell me you're into *overtime* already!'

'Uh, no, no,' Sid assured him, falteringly, straining rather wild-eyed to see what was happening on the set beyond, 'it's probably the, uh, *cleaning women* . . .'

'Cleaning women, my ass—*that* set is *lit!*' He looked furiously at his watch again, 'Christ, man, it's seven-ten Saturday night—that's *one hour and forty minutes golden time!* What kind of operation *is* this, anyway?!?'

Then there was the unmistakable echoing snap of the clapboard, and the indistinct murmurs of: 'Turning' . . . 'Speed' . . . 'Action' . . . and Les surged forward toward the set, only to be slammed back by the sheer visual impact of what confronted him there. It was the 'double work' in progress, and all three girls were being used—or, more properly, *ravished*—by a dozen schwartzo-starkers in a spanking new 'orgy version' of the so-called Around the Clock number, as devised by Boris and Tone that very afternoon. Three cameras were turning—the big Mitchell on the medium master-shot, taking in the entire scene, while the two Arries moved about freely, from one crotch and full-pen shot to the next . . . in and out, so to speak.

185

Boris, Lazlo, and a man holding a 'sun-gun,' high-intensity portable light, were laying on their stomachs, about two feet from one of the most dramatic crotch actions occurring—Laz filming it with an Arrie, the sun-gun man lighting it from various angles, and Boris, like some mad scientist, peering through his view-finder, point-blank at the close-range crotch, and tersely whispering directions: 'Slower, Simba, *slower* . . . raise your left leg, Gretchen . . . your *left* leg—oh Christ, get the translator out here. And bring the glycerin spray up, too—we're not getting any refraction.' So that, with the German translator and the glycerin man from Makeup, there were now *five* men lying on their stomachs, peering intently at the crotch and full-pen action two feet away—while the glycerin man, at an occasional nudge from Boris, would dart a tiny burst of spray at the member when it reached full mast, poised at the very top of its downthrust, piston-style—and the translator would repeat Boris's whispers to the girl in an impassive, guttural growl.

Above, attacking each breast, was a ravenously sucking, apparently *chewing* great black mouth—while the lips of the girl (who appeared, of course, to be Angela herself) were eagerly wide in accepting the fourth member of this '*ensemble macabre*,' as Nicky had dubbed it.

This same, rather bizarre spectacle—give or take a degree of shock value—was being staged simultaneously on three parts of the set—so that the total graphic effect, specially for someone just coming down from six hours of *Heidi-time*, was considerable. Les reeled away from the scene as though taking a solid right to the jaw, and, as if that weren't enough—like Archie Moore going down from Rocky's monstro right and then getting the gratuitous coals-to-Newcastle left hook before he hit the canvas—even so, was Les smashed again, since, as in reeling, his eyes swept the scene, desperately searching for some explanation, only to strike, well off the periphery of the set, his Academy Award-winning art director, Nicholas Sanchez, stark naked, on

186

hands and knees, in turbulent sexual consort with two giant
blacks—avidly sucking the one in front, while writhing in
catlike ecstasy from the unrelenting, full anal-pen of the one
behind. It didn't quite snap Les's mind, but it was enough to
bring forth the ultimate from his vast reservoir of righteous
indignation—that, of course, being quasi-British: 'WHAT
THE BLOODY HELL!?!' he roared. But this only alerted
the two heavies nearby—the extra 'guards' they had hired,
already derelict, having left the gate to catch some of the
weirdness at hand, and now beset by extreme chagrin and
remorse at being found out (since such jobs were not readily
come by)—hence, the immediate backlash of monumental
overcomp, rushing against Les, as they did, pummeling him
wildly about the head and shoulders, even *before* Boris had
looked up in dark annoyance at the interruption, recognized
Les, and shouted impatiently: *'Get that creep out of here!'*
nudging the translator, whose own relay was perhaps even
more caustic, certainly more inflammatory, because then
they fell upon Les in very real earnest indeed—with such
vigor that it was probably only Sid's intervention that spared
him mortal injury.

'Don't hurt him!' Sid kept repeating, frantically, as they
hustled toward the door amidst a sustained flurry of rabbit,
kidney, karate, and weird Liechtensteinian knee-groin shots,
'he's okay, I tell you! I mean, Jeez, it's . . . it's all his money!'

11

Morty Kanowitz had taken the semiconscious Les to a
private mental hospital in the big Merk, chauffeured on
this special occasion by Lips Malone. Before they were halfway there, Les had started coming around, and had to be
given his first morphine injection. ('Okay, he's quiet,' Sid
had told them, 'let's *keep* him quiet.')

'Slow down, for Chrissake,' Mort shouted, his hypo flailing the air, 'I can't hit him, you driving like a maniac!'

Lips, who was not without a certain Jersey-flats type criminal outlook on life, was indeed driving as though from a Hollywood bank robbery, burning rubber on every curve.

'Don't *mainline* him, for Chrissake,' he, too, shouting at the top of his voice, 'we'll have a fucking *stiff* on our hands!'

'Will you *shut up!* You think I don't know what I'm doing? I was a *medic* with the *Big Red* in *Normandy*, for Chrissake!'

Lips, who had spent that time in prison—on various book-making and morals raps—was impressed. 'Jeez ,that's great, Mort—I didn't even know you *been* in the service!'

'You *kiddin'*?' demanded Mort in high dudgeon, 'I give enough fixes in the Army I could be a *first-class dope pusher* awready!'

Posing as Les's personal physician, Mort was able to remain at his bedside and to keep him under quite heavy, in fact, speechless, sedation for the next forty-eight hours. By way of additional security, Mort and Lips deemed it wise to wrap Les in surgical gauze, quite snugly, from head to toe—so that he now very much resembled a mummy, or a cocoon—a big, oblong packet of white gauze being fed intravenously. Mort maintained a bedside vigil, and every two hours or so, just as Les was about to come around, he would hit him with five grains of the Big M. And during this time, Boris managed to shoot two more superb scenes with Angela—one of which was fairly extraordinary in its implications. It opened with her on top, sitting astride a single lover; when this had been exploited to full advantage, including several first-rate (thesp-wise) multiple orgasms on Angie's part, they were joined by a second hulking black who stood directly facing her, so that she, still sitting upright, could receive his full thrust orally. Quite before the novelty of this image—which was also being shot in the canopy's mirrored reflection—could grow stale, yet two more lovers began to partake . . . standing behind her, for full, slow, and majestically sensual penetration of armpit, one on each. 'The Human Cock Cushion' was how Tony referred to the scene.

Since Angie had steadfastly refused to work in direct contact with erections, it was necessary to shoot the scene—beginning with the arrival of the second lover—entirely from the rear, so that it would not be apparent that the members were, indeed, flaccid. For the actor with whom she was to simulate full-mouth pen, she had insisted upon gay Hadj as being the least likely to offend, by even so much as the merest phallic tremor beneath his stout restraint—for he was, in fact, required to wear a genital rig, not altogether unlike her own . . . a piece of heavy cloth over his member, so that she could press her face against the area in question without actually touching bare org, flaccid or no. When edited, of course, this footage would be indiscernibly intercut with the actual org-pen close-ups—one in vage, one in mouth, and one under each arm—all four going at the same time . . . moving in harmony, and in counterpoint, at varying speeds, and at different rhythms. 'Like one of those Scandinavian *industrials*,' Boris explained, 'you know, very abstract and lyrical . . . where you see pistons and things moving in close-up . . . so close sometimes you don't even know what it is, you lose perspective. Beautiful.'

Also during the period of Les's confinement, there had been a veritable spate of phone calls from the coast, and then a deluge of enigmatic cablegrams ('Red wing imperative potato time nil repeat nil,' that sort of thing) . . . enigmatic until realized that they were in code from C. D. Harrison himself.

For Sid it was panicville again. 'Now *that* cocksucker will be on our backs!' He paced about rereading the gibberish.

Tony chuckled. 'You've got to *break the code*, Sid—it's our only chance. You and Lips get to work on it—I'd help you, but I've got to get laid.'

Sid shook the handful of cables dramatically. 'You think

you're *kidding*, right? Well, I got news for you—we don't send some kind of answer, he's going to *be here* in twenty-four hours! Believe me, I know.'

Tony assumed a 'last plane out of Lisbon' seriousness, and glanced hurriedly about the room. 'There is only one man who can give you that code. I won't speak his name, but ... here, I'll write it on this paper.' He tore off half a page of the script and scrawled on the back: *'The Rat-Prick Man,'* and handed it to Sid, who glowered at it, then crumpled it and flung it on the floor. 'You know what you should of been?' he demanded, pointing angrily at Tony. 'A *gag*-writer, that's what—on *some lousy TV show!*' He paced about, muttering, ' "The Rat-Prick Man"! Jeez, you still think you're *kidding*, right? Well, it just *so happens* that we *tried that* awready!'

'Wouldn't crack, huh? What'd you do, the fingernail bit? Electrodes to the prostate? I never said the "Prick" didn't have moxie—'

'What we *did*,' Sid interrupted firmly, 'in case you are interested—and you fucking well *ought* to be, because I think we're in some *real trouble* ... okay, what we *did*, was to give him a shot of sodium whatever the hell it is—you know, the *truth* stuff.'

'Sodium pentothal?'

'That's it, the truth serum, right?'

'What happened?'

Sid shrugged. 'Well, seems like it don't *mix* with morphine, so ...' he shrugged again, *'nothing* happened ... well, I mean he got kind of *sick*, or something. Started turning *blue*, I don't know ...'

Tony shook his head and gave a low whistle, 'Wow, you guys must be *crazy*—don't you know you could *kill* somebody like that?'

'Mort knows what he's doing.'

'Mort? Morty Kanowitz? What the hell does *he* know?'

'He was a *medic* with the First Division in Normandy, *that*'s what.'

190

Tony sighed, 'Oh wow.'

Boris came in from the set, and flopped down in a chair, groaning with fatigue. 'Man, I never thought I'd get tired of watching people *fuck*—it's really exhausting.'

'Sidney here just nearly killed Les Harrison with an O.D.,' said Tony.

'Now hold it, hold it,' Sid protested stoutly, pointing his accusing finger again at Tone. 'In the first place it wasn't *me*, it was Lips and Morty, and it wasn't *my idea* to begin with, it was *Morty's*. And in the second place, nobody said anything about being *killed*.'

'We got a problem,' said Boris quietly.

'Look,' Tony continued irately to Sid, 'if he's *already* so stoned on morphine that he can't even *talk*, then you shoot him full of something else, and he starts turning *blue*, why that's an *overdose*, for Chrissake! And people die like that every day!'

'Awright, awright. I told you awready I wasn't even there!'

'We've got a problem,' Boris persisted, eyes closed.

'Oh bullshit, a minute ago you were trying to take *credit* for it, for Chrissake!'

'Okay, okay, let's forget it,' and he turned to Boris, brandishing the cablegrams. 'What're we going to do about *this*, B.? C.D. hits this town, we're in real *trouble*—believe me, I know.'

Boris sighed wearily. 'That's what I'm trying to tell you . . . *he's here*.'

12

By informing C.D. that his coded cables went unanswered because Les had departed three days ago for Paris in the hope of persuading Belmondo to do the role opposite Angie, it was made to appear that they were quite deliberately trying to cover for him.

'Why that's a *damn lie*,' snapped C.D. 'Belmondo's in *Australia*, and he knows it! He went to *Paris* all right, but he went there with some *slut tramp of an extra!* Isn't that true, Sidney?'

'Well, C.D.,' Sid replied, waxing expansive in the manner he thought appropriate to conversing with the head of a major studio, 'you know what the *French* always say,' and he gave the old man a salacious grin and wink. ' "*Cherchez la femme!*" '

'He's sick in the *head*,' said C.D., 'he's got pussy-on-the-brain—*that's* what's wrong with him—the little *son of a bitch!*'

For the moment, Sid was able to distract C.D. with the meaningless script and irrelevant footage, and, ironically enough, with the same Jenny Jeans whom Les had failed to nail, due to his untimely detour. Sid was required to explain to her, just before she left the set, still in her eight-year-old braids, her short, starched pinafore, her Mary Jane shoes, and her white ankle-socks, and her little-girl, white-cotton panties. 'No, listen, Jen, you misunderstood—it wasn't *Les* Harrison, it was *C. D.* Harrison—he practically *owns* the studio, for Chrissake. I mean, he can really do *big things* for you!'

'Well, I waited a couple of *hours*, for Chrissake.'

'Yeah, I know—he got hung up at this very important meeting—I mean, he feels *terrible* about it, so don't mention it. Okay? And, you know, just sort of be *nice* to him.'

'You mean, like *drop* on him?' she asked acidly.

Sid didn't crack. 'Yeah, well, that would be *swell*, Jen.' He started to leave, then added, 'And keep the dress and pigtails, okay, Jen?'

She glared at him, iceville. 'You want me to bring a *lollipop* too, Sid?'

But Sid was not to be put on, now that the chips (big, blue) were down. 'Whatever you think, Jen,' he said with

192

apparent innocence, 'I mean, you *know* how much emphasis everybody puts on *youth* these days ... including major producers. You just hang in there.' And he gave her a serious wink and walked slowly away, leaving her to glower after him, furious in pigtails and pinafore, her expression one of contempt for all mankind.

13

One of the more curious aspects of C.D.'s presence was his surprising camaraderie with Lips Malone. Two people with less apparently in common would be difficult to imagine; yet they were together constantly, and it was fairly obvious —from their hushed tones and the occasional guarded exchange of confidential looks between them—that they were involved in something clandestine, or at the very least, secret from the others. Sid, especially, found it annoying; he knew that C.D. had not previously known Lips, so that whatever was happening between them could only have begun after his arrival. And Lips, of course, was scarcely more than a chauffeur, a runner, a flunky; to see him in hushed converse with the head of the world's largest motion-picture studio was almost more than Sid could bear. 'What the hell are they *talking* about?' he would demand of Morty, 'I mean, Jeez, Lips Malone don't know his ass from a hole in the ground—and there he's yakking away to *C. D. Harrison*, for Chrissake! What the hell's going on!?!'

Mort shrugged. 'Who knows? Some kind of *procurement*, right? I mean, what else? He's *procuring* something for the old man.'

Sid snorted. 'Well, he ain't come through with much, is he? I ain't seen a broad *yet* with them two!'

Mort raised his brows. 'So? Maybe the old man's into a *new bag* . . . who knows?'

'Are you *kiddin*'?' Sid was growing irate. 'That old man's got a *cunt* for a *brain*, for Chrissake! Believe me, I know! What else could it *be*, for Chrissake? *Dope?*'

But wise Mort only shrugged. 'With those two? Who knows?'

Sid's concern, aside from the purely abstract annoyance and confusion (spiced with a dash of envy) at seeing Lips and C.D. together like that, was based on the very real fear that Lips would blow the 'Les in Paris' cover story.

'He'd *never* do it,' said Morty. 'Lips may be a lot of things, but one thing is sure, he ain't no *fink*.'

Sid doubted it. 'Oh yeah? The money's *right*, Lips Malone is a *fink*—believe me, I know the type.'

'I'll tell you where you're wrong, Sid—*principle*. With guys like Lips, it's *principle*. I mean, I know the neighborhood he grew up in . . . well, that neighborhood, there was a lot of things he didn't learn, but *one thing he knew:* "If you *fink*, you're *dead*." '

'Okay, Mort,' Sid cautioned, his finger wagging sternly, 'but you just better make sure you're right—because if he blows the whistle on us . . . I mean, if that old man finds out we got his kid stashed in a nut house, shooting him full of dope every two hours, it'll be *us* who's *dead!* That's a fucking *federal rap*, buster—*kidnapping*, they call it!'

Mort began to perceive the grotesquely serious possibilities and was quick to don his trouble-shooter's hat. 'Right, Sid,' he said tersely, 'I'll check it out.'

Meanwhile, everyone—except, perhaps, Jenny Jeans— was pleasantly surprised that C.D. had not made a thorough nuisance of himself. Instead, he had been quite content, thus far, to look at some of the 'Maude, as a child' footage, making only a single comment throughout the screening, though Sid sat alongside, with a yellow-padded clipboard and ball point poised, ready to take any note or critique required. His one comment occurred during a sun-lit exterior, when Maude (Jenny) at age eight, pigtails and short, starched pinafore, in a full-figure medium-close shot, turned away from camera to lean over and pick up a kitten from the grass—a movement which filled the screen with the back of her limbs, beginning at the white ankle socks above the patent-leather Mary Jane shoes, and going up the back of calves, back of knees, back of thighs to the pert bottom—gift-wrapped, as it were, in her little-girl, plain-edged, white-cotton, Fruit-of-the-Loom panties.

'Uh, make sure she wears those same underclothes, all right, Sidney?'

'*Check*' Sid replied at once, Mr. Efficiency, reflexively snapping on the light at the top of the clipboard, then realizing it wasn't the sort of note he need—or, in fact, should—take, so he went into a small coughing spasm instead, and switched off the light. 'Take it off your mind, C.D.,' he said, jovial and brisk, trying to get back in the ball game, 'I've got it covered.'

But C.D., as he continued staring expressionless at the same shot, just nodded and grunted.

About then Lips arrived to pick him up. Sid was surprised because he had scheduled an hour screening and it wasn't finished. He looked at his watch—still fifteen minutes to go. 'You're a little early, Lips.'

Lips, who, after a hushed exchange with C.D., was now helping him with his coat, looked at Sid, but avoided his eyes. 'No, I don't think so, Sid. I mean, you know, not really.'

'It'll keep, Sid,' said C.D., gripping Sid's shoulder as they left the projection room, rather hurriedly it seemed, while yet another take of the fabulous 'Maude bends over to pick up the kitten' shot filled the silver screen behind them.

But the boss surprise for Sid was yet to come—and did, indeed, at the next day's screening, during one of the most engaging sequences of the assembled footage—or so Sid felt,

195

being as it was the scene in which 'Momma' (Louise Larkin) explains to Maude the concept of *noblesse oblige* as it pertains to a young lady of the South. During this scene—and Sid was pleased to observe, out of the corner of his eye, that C.D. seemed to be enjoying it—the door of the projection room again opened with a stab of light, just long enough for someone to enter. Lips Malone. He bent over C.D. and whispered—completely unintelligible, except for one word which sounded like 'warm,' but Sid couldn't be sure; in any case, C.D. responded with the serious alacrity usually reserved for rushing to a mother's deathbed.

'I'll see this later, Sidney, it's beautiful,' he said hoarsely as he left, carrying his coat, and this time Lips didn't say anything at all, or even look at Sid—just hurried after the old man, in his hand the chamois-skin bag Sid had seen before.

14

It did not take the able Mort Kanovitz long to learn the true nature of the odd friendship between Lips Malone and old C.D.—albeit more by chance than design that he did. It was on the second day of C.D.'s screening—when, as it happened, the interruption coincided with the very time Mort was required to leave the bedside of his 'patient,' for a trip to the local chemist to replenish his waning supply of morphine, now being consumed in ever increasing dosages.

Having completed the transaction, he emerged from the apothecary and was alarmed to see the big studio Merk swerve past him, Lips at the wheel, driving insanely, while old C.D. crouched hawklike in the back seat, looking sinister indeed in his jet-black shades and clutching his chamois-skin bag in a taloned grasp. Mort reflexively drew back into the doorway, his first thought being that Lips had spilled, and they had followed him to the dope connection; he looked wildly about, fully expecting, also, to see some cop-type with them, or behind—and was greatly relieved when he did not, and again, when the huge car continued past the apothecary to turn the corner, one building farther along. His relief, however, gave way to surprise and curiosity when the car stopped, as he could tell by the sound, a few seconds later. With rather obtrusive stealth, he walked to the corner and peered around it. There was the great Merk, parked near the rear of the building, empty. This was the building next to the apothecary—and, from the looks of things, they had left the car, and gone in the rear entrance. *What the hell's going on?* Mort wondered, and he stepped back to study the front of the small building, trying to determine what it was. There was something strangely familiar about it, but it escaped him for the moment. Then he did remember—this was where they had rented the hearse; it was the mortuary. This realization almost staggered him with panic; it could mean only one thing—Les Harrison had died of an overdose. Yet how was that possible? He was all right fifteen minutes earlier, and that had been when he was more than half an hour into his fix, whereas, the symptoms of M-overdose are instantaneous. He must have died from something else, Mort decided. In any case, he must find out at once. 'If those guys think *I'm* taking the rap for it,' he muttered, 'they're *nuts!*' He checked his watch—he could be out of the country in twenty-five minutes.

The front of the mortuary was dark, its shades drawn, the door locked. He walked around to the side, down to the Merk, and then into the narrow alleyway where the rear entrance was located. Three wooden steps led up to a door and a window beside it; Mort cautiously ascended. The window was partially open, but its shade was drawn, and the door was shut. At the bottom of the windowshade, however, was a slit of light, and he found that by leaning down so that his eyes were on that level, he could see, quite clearly,

197

into the room. Standing close together, in the center of the room, were three distinct figures, two of whom he recognized immediately to be Lips and C.D. The third man, he then recalled, was the man from whom they had rented the hearse, and he appeared to be counting small packets of currency as they were handed to him from Lips, while C.D., holding his chamois-skin bag in one hand, stood alongside them, trancelike, staring down at the fourth occupant of the room, lying on a narrow table—a figure which Morty had overlooked before, but which he now saw very plainly—a dark-haired woman of indeterminate age, half covered by a sheet, and quite obviously a corpse.

'Hurry it up!' he heard C.D. whisper tersely, as he took off his jacket.

Lips and the mortician completed the count, and started for the door. 'I'll wait in the car,' Lips muttered.

Morty jumped off the steps, and ducked behind, on the side away from the street—so that when the two men reached the bottom of the steps, they turned in the opposite direction from where he was hiding.

He waited for a minute after they had rounded the corner, then he came out, tiptoed up the steps again, and looked in beneath the shade.

'*Holy Christ*,' he muttered, his mouth dropping open.

Inside the room, standing naked by the table, C.D. was in the process of strapping an odd, dildolike extension device, which appeared to be made of plastic, onto his already erect member, giving it a startling even caricaturish length and girth. From the chamois-skin bag, which now lay open on the floor, he extracted a jar of what was, presumably, a lubricant and began applying it vigorously to the device.

Standing naked, wearing only the device and his dark glasses, he presented a bizarre spectacle indeed as he massaged lubricant onto the absurdly exaggerated phallus, with serious mien.

While Mort looked on in astonishment, he removed the sheet from the corpse with a flourish, arranged the legs, pulling up the knees to a coital position, placed himself between them, and maneuvered the device to penetration.

Morty, who had begun to feel somewhat dizzy, half turned away to descend the stairs, but stopped short at the sound of what he recognized to be C.D.'s voice. He leaned down again, peering intently, cocking his ear to one side, straining to decipher the husky tones. Then he made it out, being delivered in a theatrical stage-whisper, expressing an almost frightening urgency: '*You slut, tell me you can't feel it! I dare you! Tell me you can't feel it, you dirty slut!*'

15

'Now then,' Boris was explaining to Angie, 'the obligation of this scene, as I see it, is to *establish beyond any doubt* exactly where Maude's *head* is at this particular moment—that is to say, the full extent of her mania, which takes her, in fact, to the very edge of madness. Right?'

She stared at him, eyes glistening with adoration. '*You're so wonderful*,' she said softly.

The drug she was on, as far as Tony had been able to determine, was a combination of methedrine and liquid opium, presumably tinctured with something to stabilize the mixture. In any case, its effect was that of a mammoth tranquilizer, embodying as it did both *boss-upper* and *boss-down dream*. It had arrived in her studio fanmail about a month earlier—a small carton containing twelve large capsules, each in a separate compartment. The accompanying letter read:

DEAR MISS STERLING:

I am a graduate student at Berkeley, where I study Advanced Chemistry.

199

Needless to say, I am also a fan of yours, and the other day I read (in *Silver Screen*) that you were 'sometimes blue.' The next time you are, try one of the enclosed capsules.

With best wishes for your continued success,

HOWARD K. LAWTON

The inside flap of the carton was marked: '*For Little Girl Blue.*'

She had promptly put the carton aside and forgotten about it, only to come across it again when packing and hurriedly toss it in with her many other medicines. Then, on an impulse, when she was having such trouble with the first scene, she had taken one—and the rest was cinematic history, or hopefully soon to be.

Tony had learned the nature of the concoction by stealth and ruse—rooting about in her things until he found her 'medicine box'—followed by a lengthy, highly impressionistic process of trial and error. He identified the meth by its effect, and the liquid O by its taste and blackness. He showed up at the set absolutely zonked. 'This is it,' he said, handing Boris a sample. 'I advise you to take one immediately.'

'What is it?' asked Boris, scrutinizing the capsule.

'Well, it's *something else*, whatever it is. "Blue" it's called, "Little Girl Blue." '

'How many does she have?'

'Uh, seven . . . no, six . . . well, *five*, if you don't count that one.'

'Well, put it back,' he said firmly, returning it, 'and don't *you* take any more. *She needs them.*'

The strength of the scene in question appeared to lie more in its *intensity*, if fully realized, than in anything novel or erotic about the action per se—which was fairly straightforward, portraying, as it did, Maude and a single lover, engaged in the conventional, or classic, 'sixty-nine,' with cunnilingus and fellatio being simultaneously rendered.

'I think the beauty of this,' Boris continued, his voice soft and serious, his hands moving in tentative gestures, 'will arise out of its total . . . *purity*.'

'*You're* the one who's beautiful,' breathed Angie, '. . . and *pure*. You're *everything* that's *beautiful* and *pure*.'

'Hmm.' He regarded her with certain concern. She looked so whacked out he was beginning to doubt she could do the scene. On another level, however, he was wondering, somewhat wistfully, if perhaps now, under the spell of this rather obviously spellbinding sense-deranger, she might not just possibly be persuaded at last to do a full-pen without double. No, he immediately thought, it was madness—Angela Sterling would never stand still (so to speak) for being 'fucked on camera' . . . she had said as much herself.

'Okay, Laz,' he said wearily, turning away from Angie, 'I guess what we'll do here, we'll shoot toward the cut-away . . . setting it up for the old, pardon the expression, "*insert*," eh? Ha-ha,' his laugh like a death rattle.

'Listen,' he went on after a pause, head down, eyes closed, rubbing his temples with thumb and forefinger—much in the manner of the late, great Lester H., 'I think we're in trouble on this one . . . "*sixty-nine*" . . . wow, well, I mean that's full-on *clichéville*, right? To do a *serious* . . . *non-contrived* . . . *relevant* . . .' and he opened his eyes and looked at Laz—who was waiting with a soft, benevolent expression that seemed to say: '*You lay it down, B., and we'll pick it up!*'—and then he resumed: 'I think we'd better go for *anal-tongue* on this one, Laz. Otherwise we're in trouble,' he put his head down again, hand to brow, thoroughly wasted physically, and at the same time getting some sort of curious debilitating contact-high through Ange and Tone, '. . . otherwise,' he repeated, in a disturbed and oddly plaintive way, 'this scene is just going to curl up and *die*—D. H. Lawrence style. I mean, we've got to get some *generation-gap stoppage* going for us in here, you dig?'

16

'Now then, Feral,' Boris was explaining with great care and deliberation, 'in this scene you will be kissing Miss Sterling's ... how do you say, "*pom-pom*"?'

'*Pom-pom*,' Feral nodded, grinning wildly, 'yes, *pom-pom!* But not *real* kiss, yes? Only make-believe kiss, yes?'

'Uh, yes, well, that's what I want to talk to you about. Now, she's wearing that *thing*, right? That piece of cloth ... over her *pom-pom*, yes?'

'Yes, yes, cloth-piece over *pom-pom!*'

'Right. Well, what I'd like you to try to do, Feral, is get your *tongue*—' he stopped long enough to stick out his tongue—'*tongue*, yes? To get your tongue *under* the cloth ... and *into her pom-pom*. You understand?' Speaking with his tongue thrust out, and twisting it down and around to demonstrate the maneuver, caused his speech to be fairly garbled, so he had to repeat it a couple of times—but, even so, Feral was quick to grasp.

'Yes, yes, Feral-tongue in *pom-pom!* She *know*? Missy Sterling *know*?'

'Yes, well, that's the thing, you see. We've got to do it very ... *carefully* ... just a little at a time ... very *slowly* ...' he wasn't sure of what words to use, so he did a brief pantomime with his hands, 'like the *lion* and the ... *antelope*, yes?' and his hands moved in a meticulous simulation of the stealth of the hunt. Feral nodded vigorously to show understanding.

'She *like*?' he wanted to know, 'Missy Sterling *like* Feral-tongue in *pom-pom*?'

'Hmm. Well, I think she just might at that. Anyway,

nothing ventured, nothing gained,' he patted him on the back. 'Right, Feral? Ha. But remember, *easy does it.*'

'Yes, yes,' Feral's head bobbed in hearty agreement, 'yes, yes. We hunt like the lion! We hunt the *pom-pom!*'

17

The 'C.D. at the mortuary' incident had so unnerved Morty that, after fleeing the scene—down the alley, in opposite direction of the Merk—he had stopped at the first bar he reached and went inside for a few quick belts to steady himself. But he must have required more than he'd anticipated, because by the time he'd finished lushing it up and got back to the hospital, his 'patient' had flown the coop, leaving coiled through the corridors behind him, like the discarding of an extraordinary white snakeskin, a seemingly endless trail of the gauze in which he had been so carefully swaddled. To judge from appearances, he must have been moving through the corridors with terrific speed and determination at the time.

18

Philip Fraser, a young London film-editor, who had worked with Boris before, was brought over shortly after they started shooting—and, under Boris's supervision, worked continuously on a rough assembly of all that had been shot to date. He had completed the Arabella-Pamela Dickensen sequence—*'Première Amour'*—which, in terms of the 'aesthetic eroticism' Boris had been trying for, exceeded all expectations.

Sid, whose Hollywood conditioning had given him a rather Pavlovian reflex to screenings—that is to say, blind, boundless enthusiasm—and especially when he himself was holding a piece of the action, let this be no exception. The nature of the material, however, did require a certain change in the *substance* of his praise so that, instead of the usual weeping or guffawing to express appreciation when the lights went up, he was shouting: 'I swear to Christ, B., I never got such a terrific bone-on in my life! Like a fucking *rock*, I swear to Christ,' over and over, litany style, before catching himself, genuinely embarrassed, '. . . Jeez, I didn't mean to say it like *that*—I got carried away, I guess.' But he was quick to see the positive side of it—'Just goes to show what a *powerful picture* it is! I mean, listen, you guys, I think we got a fucking *hit* on our hands, for Chrissake!'

The Angela footage was also being edited and assembled as it was shot, including the flashback intercuts, and, since they were shooting pretty much in sequence, it was possible to keep the continuity of the assemblage almost up to date. So far, however, only Boris, Tony, and the editor had seen it.

'I can't fucking believe it,' said Tony softly, 'it's just too much.'

'Hmm,' Boris thought about it, 'you know, it reminds me of something . . . a fairy-tale . . .'

'*Beauty and the Beast?*' Tony suggested with a coarse chuckle.

'No, no, something with a more strange, dreamlike quality . . . *Midsummer Night's Dream*. I mean, the whole thing could be a *dream*, couldn't it—a sort of never-land sexual fantasy the girl is having . . .'

'Wow, I don't know—it look pretty *real* to me. You know, if you guys hadn't been here, I think I'd have *stroked* on that one. Like I had my handkerchief all ready and everything.'

'What'd you think of it, Phil?' Boris asked the editor.

'Well . . .' Philip began, head tilting back, eyes closing for a second, voice in the nasal upper register that always successfully betrayed his Etonian-Oxford background, 'I mean, it really is quite extraordinary, isn't it? I mean, I don't know that there *exists* anything one might judge it *against* . . . well, of course there simply *doesn't*, does there? I mean, it *is* quite unique, isn't it?'

'Did you find it *exciting?*' Boris asked, '. . . you know, sexually exciting?'

'Oh yes, indeed—extremely so. In actual fact, I found myself wondering just how one would go about *restraining* the audience in such a case. Well, I mean to say, aren't they likely to become *so* sexually excited that some sort of . . . of *orgy* will develop and disrupt the entire showing?' He found the image amusing. 'Perhaps if the seats were *enclosed*,' he went on, 'each member of the audience in his own little glass box . . . in that way, one might reasonably hope to avoid sexual pandemonium. Eh? Ha-ha.'

Boris considered it. 'Hmm. You know, I'm not sure that *women* are much affected by things like that . . . *visual* things. However, that's something we shall find out—right, Tone?'

'Right, B.!' exclaimed Tone with exaggerated enthusiasm, then turned to an imaginary audience, Billy Graham style, 'and to you out there tonight, I put forward the solemn pledge that, God willing, we shall cause the cherished, the sacred, the immaculately white panties of the incredibly cute and lovely "Miss Average Movie-Goer" to become absolutely *sopping* . . . yea, be they white, pink, yellow, blue, black, beige, red, flesh, or sepia . . . be they frothy lace-edged or sweet scalloped-edged . . . latex or spandex . . . bikini, brief, or full-fashioned . . . nylon tricot, Danskin, or acetate . . . size four, five, or six . . . yea, I say unto you, even so shall they be sopping . . . and, in truth, the darling girl shall literally *drown* in her own precious love-juice as it surges up about here—by the end of the fan-fucking-tastic . . . *show-stopping* . . . *SECOND REEL!*' He paused for breath, and added in soft, swift urgency: '*As God is my witness!*'

19

Lying on their sides, head to foot, on the big pink satin bed beneath the rose-mirrored canopy, Feral's head was snugly encased between Angie's thighs, while his hands firmly cupped her buttocks, and his tongue moved cautiously for *pompom*—unbeknownst to the *pom-pom* girl herself, who was similarly situated, cheek pressing against the cloth of his organ restrainer, while the 'long-ago-and-far-away' glitter in her eyes reflected the double dose of liquid O–meth she had dropped for the occasion.

The first shot was from behind, with the camera on Angie's bare back. Feral's hands, gripping her bottom, covered the adhesive strips which secured her chastity rig, while his head moved rhythmically up and down in a tenderly voracious tongue-over-clit simulation—not yet going for full-tongue pen, nor for clit nibble-and-suck. Angie, in turn, writhed about in a quite adequate representation of increasing excitement.

For the reverse of the shot, that is to say, with the camera on Feral's back, Boris planned to come in very tight on Angela—an extreme close-up of just her eyes and mouth. For the purpose of this shot he had persuaded her to caress an artificial penis, made of dark firm rubber. The action called for her to hold it in one hand, just at the base, while licking, kissing, and finally sucking it with growing ardour. The shot would be cropped so as not to go below her hand; in this way, it would be indiscernible that the member was, in fact, not attached to Feral's body.

Boris was not entirely satisfied. 'Christ,' he said, staring through the camera, 'I can't tell whether it looks like a *real* cock or not.' 'Perhaps,' Nicky Sanchez coolly observed, 'that's merely because *you* happen to *know* it isn't real.'

'Hmm. You may be right. Look okay to you, does it?'

'Oh heavens yes,' Nicky murmured, peering through the lens himself, 'simply *delectable.*'

So that the two organs—Feral's and the artificial one— would match as closely as possible, Boris had insisted that the artificial one be made from an actual mold of Feral's penis.

Nicky, of course, had personally supervised the entire process, first taking a plaster-of-Paris impression of Feral's organ at full rigidity, then casting it in molten Latex with a flexible metal rod at its center. It was remarkably detailed, the surface seeming to pulsate with veins and taut sinews.

'I'll tell you where it doesn't work,' said Boris after considering it further, 'at the *foreskin* . . . now watch what happens when she comes all the way up on it . . . Angie, dear, just bring your mouth all the way up, okay . . . that's it . . . now back down, slowly . . .' He turned to Nicky again, 'You see, since he's not circumcized it should pull the foreskin *up* just a little when her mouth reaches the end, then it should push it *down* a little when she takes it back in. But the trouble is, the foreskin doesn't *move* on a mold. You get the *contour*, the *definition* of the foreskin, but you don't get any *movement*. I mean, I had an idea for a beautiful image— where she puts her tongue *under* the foreskin and slowly moves it around the head. Get the picture?'

'Uh, yes,' said Nicky, huskily, 'yes, I do indeed.'

'Well, we can't do it with a mold—there's nothing for her tongue to go *under*.' He sighed in frustration. 'Why the hell won't she just *suck his cock* for a minute or two? What's so terrible about that?'

'I simply *cannot* imagine,' said Nicky arching his brows in great hauteur, '. . . the silly little goose!'

Meanwhile, Feral's tongue was far from idle; in fact, as Boris and Nicky could see, it had breached the periphery of the chastity rig and even now was snaking along the labes, clitoral-bound like a heat-seeking missile. As yet, Angie didn't seem to have noticed.

'Try to ease that thing off of her,' Boris whispered to Nicky, referring to the strip of cloth, 'and if that works, then we'll take *his* off . . . and see what happens.'

The ruse was thwarted however by the excited arrival of Sid and Morty, bringing the news of Les Harrison's escape.

'Well, just keep him out of here,' said Boris, highly annoyed at the interruption. 'Listen, did you get me off the set just for that?' he demanded of Sid.

'No, B.,' said Sid gravely, 'there's something else . . . it's about C.D.'

'Well, what *is* it, for Chrissake? I'm trying to shoot a scene!' He kept glancing over at the set to see what was happening.

'Tell him, Mort.'

Mort shook his head. 'No, you tell him, Sid.'

Sid cleared his throat. 'B.,' he said, in his most serious tones, 'he was . . . having *sexual relations . . . with the dead . . . sexual intercourse . . . with a dead corpse.*'

'What the hell are you talking about?'

'Morty seen him. Right, Mort?'

'Right.'

'Look,' said Boris impatiently, 'will you guys please get out of here?'

'But he *seen* him, B.! I tell you, Mort seen C. D. Harrison humping a fucking *corpse*, for Chrissake!'

'And I'm telling *you*,' Boris yelled, '*I don't give a shit! Now just get out of here!*' And he turned on his heel (so to speak), and strode back to the set, leaving Sid and Morty to stare dumbly after him. Sid wagged his head, clucking sadly. 'Jeez,' he muttered, 'seems like nobody cares about nothing anymore.'

20

The arrival of Dave and Debbie Roberts was not without certain fanfare—mainly due to their agent, the erstwhile Abe 'Lynx' Letterman—the very same—having leaked it, rather profusely, to all media, so that on hand for their touchdown was a strong contingent, fairly representative, of their youthful and highly dedicated following. Most of them were French students, or drop-outs, who had hitchhiked from Paris, or from neighboring hippie communes—and a veritable potpourri of types they were: the men, some bearded, were wearing shades and Levis, while others, with shoulder-length hair, sported extravagantly foppish attire, flower-child and neo-Edwardian style; and the cutie-pie girls, meanwhile, were doing their thing, in the Carnaby Street and Kings Road manner of no-bra, see-through blouses, bell-bottom jeans, microminis, stumble-length maxis, bare feet, granny spectacles, and garlands of daisies in their hair. Flying above them was a huge tricolor star flag of the Viet Cong, and a number of placards on sticks, variously inscribed in both French and English: 'LEGALIZE ACID NOW!', 'WAR SUCKS!', 'TURN ON A FRIEND TODAY!', 'FREE KIM AGNEW!', etc., etc., decidedly not the clean-cut turnout Lynx Letterman had hoped for—imagining, as he did, that youthful movie fans the world over were still like those of the Andy Hardy days.

So, while Debbie lay stretched across one seat, a purple sleep mask covering her eyes, Dave and Lynx sat in the seat opposite, gazing out the window at the crowd, as the plane taxied toward the Merk.

'Holy Christ, Dave,' Lynx muttered, 'can't you tell 'em to get rid of that Viet Cong *flag?* The press is gonna *clobber* us for that!'

The young man shook his head lethargically. 'I can't tell 'em *nothing*, daddy-O,' he mumbled. 'I'm their *boy*. Besides, I kinda dig those V.C. cats—they sure hang in there, don't they?'

Lynx looked anxiously around the plane to make certain no one had overheard. 'Now, for God's sake, Dave, just please don't *ever* say that again—not even as a joke.'

The young man smiled wearily. 'That's what you told me about *pot*,' he reminded him, 'remember?'

Lynx grimaced. 'Okay, okay, so I was wrong about *pot*. we're getting some terrific PR mileage out of pot, I admit it. But that's a fucking *Viet Cong flag* they've got out there! We're at *war* with those gooks, for Chrissake!'

Dave shrugged. 'I'm always for the *underdog*—you know, like David in "David and Goliath"? I mean, I dig underdogs ... I used to be one, Lynx—remember?'

The plane made a rather abrupt left turn, and stopped. 'You ain't *kiddin*', I remember!' said Lynx, leaning across the aisle to wake Debbie, with excessive gentleness, while managing to cop quite a bit of no-bra cashmered knocker and sleeping nip, without pausing in his admonition to Dave: 'A year ago I couldn't *pay* a studio to use you! Now you're at the *top*, and that's where I want to *keep* you!'

They started getting up, and the boy laughed softly, shaking his head. 'Not *you*, daddy-O ...' he jerked his thumb toward the crowd outside, '*they're* the ones who'll keep me at the top.'

Lynx shrugged, and nodded his head. 'Okay, tiger, it's *your* red wagon.'

'Hip,' said the young man, smiling and nodding agreement. And when they stepped out of the plane, he stood for a moment, one hand raised in the peace sign as he slowly turned, dispensing it toward the crowd like a papal blessing. Apart from the main group was another, smaller, more eccentric cluster of so-called Crazies, about twenty in all, flying the black flag of anarchy, and flaunting two posters: 'DOWN WITH PANTS!' and 'OEDIPUS SUCKS!' They were dressed

210

colorfully, and a few were wearing crash helmets as though prepared for a riot; several of the girls were topless. Every few minutes the entire group would shriek out a series of Indian type war-whoops—like the women in *Battle of Algiers*—then they would jump up and down in a terrific frenzy, pogostyle, raise their clenched fists in Panther salute, and remain perfectly still, until the next outburst.

'What's with them?' asked Lynx, his face twisted in anguished consternation.

'Doing their thing, man,' said Dave softly, and nodded to show perfect understanding.

Lynx also nodded, somewhat differently, and after just staring at the young man's face for a second, looked away, his expression one of weary contempt. Actually, his true and heartfelt concern at the moment (and practically every other moment as well) was not with young Dave and Debbie, but with his boss, flat-top, million-a-pic client, *Angela Sterling*—she who had forbade him, 'unconditionally,' to come to Liechtenstein, thus forcing him into this shabby, almost flagrant ruse of pretending to be there on behalf of Dave and Debbie Roberts . . . 'a couple of snot-nose brats,' as he was wont to say, and—except for the odd attempt now and again to get into Debbie's pants—he rarely thought of them at all, so convinced was he that 'all this *youth* crap' was merely a passing fad and a quick buck, the whole thing a Madison Avenue fabrication. But his *Angie*, on the other hand, was like an institution—and his constant nightmare was, of course, that she would elope with a new agent at any moment—a move whereby Lynx would suffer grievously, both prestige-wise, and to the sprightly tune of about four hundred thou a year in commissions. She had defied his advice before, but never so blatantly; and she had *never* started work without a contract. What was even worse was their present position vis-à-vis the studio . . . in default of contract, and doubtless vulnerable to monstro court action should C.D. and the others so deign. He found himself wistfully speculating as to how much it would have strengthened their hand (his and Angie's) if she hadn't already been to bed with all of them. Surely, he thought, there must be *one ... single ... major ... stockholder ... who hasn't fucked her yet ...* and he sighed and sank back to begin the tedious tabulation, while the big Merk rolled toward the hotel, and Debbie Roberts, with the bright-eyed eternal astonishment which was her mark, exclaimed to her brother: 'Gosh, Davey, won't it be just too terrif seeing Angie again!'

Dave shrugged, super-cool. 'Hope she's got it all together,' he murmured, 'hope she's doing her thing.'

'Well, I just hope she's *there!*' Debbie exclaimed, and turned to the agent. 'Are you sure she's still there, Lynx?'

Lynx shook his head, smiling sadly. 'Seems like you can't be sure about *anything* these days, kid. But we'll soon see, won't we?' And, saying this, he felt a genuine chill. An inveterate horse-player, with a compulsive faith in hunches, he was alarmed to feel his apprehension increasing with every turn of the Merk's big wheels. But now it was beyond apprehension, it was a dire foreboding.

21

When C.D. had returned to the Merk from his extraordinary assignation, he collapsed in the back seat like a burned-out long-distance runner—but one couldn't say if he'd won or lost.

'Where to, Chief?' asked the unruffled Lips Malone.

'Just drive around for a while, Lips,' said the other, eyes not telling behind black shades, 'I've got some production problems that need thinking through.'

After an hour or so, he designated the hotel as next stop— so he could 'freshen up before dinner,' as he put it.

As he stepped from the car, he turned to Lips, who was holding the door, and tucked two carefully folded five-hundred-dollar bills into the breast pocket of Lips's jacket.

'In the meantime,' he added, in tones of terse confidence, 'you know where to find me . . . *in case anything important comes up.*'

'Right, Chief,' said Lips, expressionless, then raised two fingers to an imaginary cap, just the way he'd seen the British chauffeurs do in the movies.

Meanwhile, back at the *pom-pom* hunt, all was not well. Things had proceeded for a while exactly as Boris had projected they might. Under the sublime influence of the exotic speed-opiate, '*Blue*,' Angie had been oblivious to the advance of Feral's tongue, which first achieved clit—and, after a decent interval—full vage-pen. Whatever sensations this produced in the girl, she apparently attributed to the general euphoria induced by the drug itself, because she carried on, thesp-wise, as though nothing were amiss—her closed-eyed writhing and moaning exactly as before, while, at the same time, she continued to caress, kiss, and suck the artificial member, with a show of sustained and mounting passion.

When Boris saw that Feral's tongue had scored full-pen, he whispered to Nicky: 'Okay, get that thing out of the shot,' whereupon the Art Director very delicately inched off the tape securing the chastity rig, just above and below Angie's pubis, and then gently eased the piece of cloth away, thus giving Feral-tongue immediate and profound access to the fabled *pom*.

'Now stay on that, Laz,' Boris whispered to the cameraman, who was shooting with a hand-held Arriflex, '. . . and then try to get her face in the same shot.'

'See if he's got a hard-on,' he said to Nicky after a minute, not wanting to leave the camera himself. 'Oh, I'd be *delighted* to,' the other trilled in extreme camp, gliding balletlike to that side of the bed, and having ascertained it, arched his brows as in exaggerated astonishment: '*Oh, Mary, has he ever!*'

'Okay, Laz,' said Boris, 'let's try this side.'

They quickly moved around the bed to where closed-eyed Angie was sucking the rubber org. At a sign from Boris, Nicky deftly unfastened Feral's restraint, allowing his erect member to bob up, jack-in-the-box style.

'Yummy, yummy, yummy,' Nicky cooed.

'Okay, Laz,' Boris whispered, 'be ready, because this may not last long.' Then he bent over and whispered to Angie: 'Don't open your eyes, Angie, we're still shooting . . . it's beautiful . . . I just want to try a different one for a minute . . . I think it may be better . . .' and while he spoke he held the artificial org with one hand, and Feral's with the other, easing the one out and the other in, even before he finished— in an extremely graceful transition which caused Angie, still closed-eyed to go: '*Hmmm . . .*' as in sleepy contentment.

'There, isn't that better?' asked Boris softly, at the same time stepping back out of the shot and forcefully gesturing for Laz to get a move on.

'Umm-hmm,' she murmured, '. . . *warmer,*' and snuggled a bit, like a cat settling down to a saucer of cream.

Tony, who had arrived on the set just in time to see the 'great cock-switch,' as he later dubbed it, watched in disturbed fascination. 'Now, you can't tell me she doesn't know that's a *real cock* she's got there!'

'I wonder,' said Boris, 'but I bet it's going to look pretty wild up on the big screen. Dig that *face*—it's *angelic,* for Chrissake! We've got to get her a *halo!* And he looked about wildly for one of the lighting crew.

Whether it was the drug causing her to be unaware of what was really happening, while at the same time she *pretended* that it *was* happening, or whether it was the drug enabling her to *accept* the transition from pretense to reality, it was not yet possible to discern. What it was most like was the kind of *dream* wherein the dreamer, aware that

214

it *is*, in fact, a dream, and therefore harmless, allows it, even encourages it, to go on.

While Nicky and the lighting crew were working to get a halo effect, Lazlo moved around to shoot at the other (Feral-tongue) end. 'Listen,' he asked Boris, continuing to shoot, hardly moving his lips, 'what about that *ass-hole* stuff you mentioned?'

'Fantastic,' said Boris. 'We'll get *anal-tongue and halo* in the same composition! *Beautiful*.' And he was just about to convey this *pom-pom*-to-derrière move to Feral himself when he caught a fleeting telltale look in his eyes that suggested he was on the brink of an orgasm. 'No, no, Feral,' he pleaded, 'not yet, please! No *boom-boom!* Please, no *boom-boom* yet!' Frantically pushing Lazlo in front of him, he rushed to the other (Angie-head) end of the set, as though he could somehow prevent it at the source. But naught could avail, as was all too evident from the moaning wail of ecstatic release that rose from Feral's lips, and the convulsive shudder that seized his body and limbs. As for Angela Sterling, at the initial instant of spasm, it seemed she still felt it was all part of a romantic dream, a sexual pretense, and that she could go along with it, even repeating her murmured '*hmmm . . .*' —as in pleasure, or anticipation of same, as a kitten about to get comfy and snuggle down for some more warm cream. But with the first spurt came the rude awakening, and she snatched the member from her mouth, regarding it with wide-eyed incredulity, a tiny trickle of semen glistening down from the corner of her lips, while in her firm grasp the stout org began to unleash its main salvo . . . but now straight into Angie's *smart, new, studio coif*. She simply *could not* believe it, or so it seemed—she, who was frozen, mesmerizmo-ville, holding it as though it were a spitting cobra, at the same time turning away, so that the great bulk of the discharge went point-blank into her golden tresses from right profile, causing, as Helen Vrobel later described it, the 'most godawful icky mess you can imagine!'

However, the *immediate* effect of Feral's massive emission into Angela's golden tresses was fairly traumatic, heightened perhaps by the devilish meth. In any case, she flew from the set, completely naked (devoid of rig) and shrieking like a madwoman, with Helen Vrobel closing in pursuit, blue brocade wrapper extended and flying.

Boris, in a state of extreme agitation, stamped around the cameras. 'What did you *get*, Laz? What did you *get?*'

Laz shrugged. 'Well, we *got* it . . . I mean, I'm not sure what it was, but we *got* it.'

'Wow,' Tony said, 'that sure was a bossload of *jissem*— those guys must be *oversexed* or something. Hey, did you hear about old man Harrison, fucking a stiff?'

Boris sighed, looking at his watch—four-thirty—they'd never get her back today. 'Okay, Freddie,' he called, 'wrap-wrap.'

'No kidding,' Tony continued, as they started walking toward the trailer, 'right here in town, a couple of hours ago—Morty Kanowitz *watched* him do it. Can you *imagine* that? Fucking a fucking *corpse*, for Chrissake? Man, that must really be *weird*.'

'Hmm,' Boris was thinking that he might have just made his first serious miscalculation. The question was, had the scene actually been that much better than it would have been using inserts, to justify the risk of permanently alienating the actor? His mind's eye began to re-create it, image by image . . . yes, he decided (or, at least, so rationalized), her *sucking* toward the end . . . her *face*, the angelic quality . . . it could *only* have been gotten the way they had gotten it—by doing it for real. And that image alone, he felt, had made it worth the risk. Moreover, if Feral hadn't *come* so soon, who knows what other extraordinary things they might have gotten? It was just bad luck.

As they reached the trailer, they were overtaken by Feral himself, now wearing his loincloth, and, for once, not smiling—in fact, looking pretty depressed.

216

'Very sorry,' he said. 'Feral no try *boom-boom*. Just happen. Feral very sorry.'

Boris patted his shoulder. 'That's okay, Feral. It happens to all of us.'

'And Missy Sterling? She angry, yes?'

'Don't worry, she'll be all right. You did *good pom-pom* work, Feral.'

'Yes?' That set him smiling again. 'Good. *Pom-pom* very good *taste*. Feel very *good* to Feral-tongue.'

'Well, I'm glad you liked it, Feral.'

The latter nodded enthusiastically. 'You tell Missy Sterling, yes? Feral say her *pom-pom* very good! Feral say her *pom-pom* best ever!'

'Yeah, I'll do that, Feral. See you tomorrow.'

22

Boris and Tone were having a 'pre-sundowner' in the trailer and considering the ironic vagaries of art and existence; at that same moment, a meeting of certain import was going forward in the penthouse suite of the Imperial Hotel in downtown Vaduz—a 'gathering of eagles,' so to speak . . . C.D., Les, and Lynx Letterman. Les, quite disheveled, still wearing his gray nuthouse bathrobe, and totally strung-out in coming off the big M, had been trying to brief them as to the true nature of the movie they were producing.

'Dad, I swear to God, it's a *stag* film!'

But Dad wasn't buying. Never one to be easily convinced —certainly, not by some strung-out disheveled person in a nut-robe, and, above all, not by his own son—he was quick to take the offensive. 'You've got pussy-on-the-brain, boy,' he said sternly, 'now go in the bathroom and get cleaned up!'

After Les, sullen and slightly staggering, had left the

room, C.D. sighed and poured a couple of large ones.

'I don't know,' he wagged his head in pious despair, 'young people today—*they just don't seem able to take care of fundamentals.* You know what I mean, Lynx?'

Lynx was now deep into his intuitive bag. 'I know what you mean, Mr. Harrison,' he said with a sympathetic nod, but he had already decided that it was probably true . . . what Les had said about the film. And *that* was bad news indeed; for Lynx to contemplate any changes in Angie's image was like contemplating a series of needless amputations on his own body.

'Is that the only footage you've seen, Mr. Harrison—the stuff with Jenny Jeans?'

'Beautiful,' said C.D., 'beautiful footage—reminds me of Selznick.'

'Nothing with Angie?'

'Eh? No, no, nothing with Angie yet—something came up, you see, during the screening . . .'

'Don't you think you'd better find out what sort of movie Angie's making over here, Mr. Harrison?'

The old man winked and smiled mischievously, 'Lynx, my lad, that's *exactly* why I'm here.'

The instant Angela went into her freak-out, Fred the First had summoned the company physician, Dr. Werner, who hurried to the dressing room, arriving only seconds after Angie—with a strong assist from Helen Vrobel—had stumbled in, still hysterical, and collapsed on the bed.

Since no one except Tony knew what drug she was on, Dr. Werner could not administer a specific antidote, but he did inject her with a strong sedative, which put her to sleep at once, whereupon he listened to her heart with his stethoscope for a minute, then opened her wrapper and gave her a once-over-lightly from shoulder to knee. 'Just to make sure, uh, there are no broken bones, eh?' he explained. 'Better safe than sorry in matters of this sort, heh-heh.'

'*She didn't fall,*' Helen Vrobel observed coldly.

218

'Hmm? Oh yes, of course,' said Dr. Werner, closing her wrapper and carefully adjusting it. 'What's this in her hair? Where it's wet here?'

'I can manage that, Doctor.'

He touched it, rubbing his thumb and forefinger together, noting its texture, smelled it, tasted it. 'Hmm, curious,' he murmured, standing, staring down at her for a moment, as in a reverie. 'Right,' he said then, coming out of it. 'You stay with her until she wakes up. She should be fine by then ... if she isn't, call me.' As he spoke, he absently picked up a box from the dressing table. 'Ah, perhaps this is what she was taking.' He raised the lid to reveal twelve small compartments, all empty. 'Oh well,' he said with a shrug, dropping the box into the wastebasket, 'whatever it was, it looks like she's finished with it now.'

23

The sequence Tony had written for Dave and Debbie Roberts was simple and romantic, even sentimental. It was a story of sibling love between two beautiful, sensitive children—brother and sister—who, because of their situation as the only children on a ducal estate were constantly together, and, in their aloneness, turning ever closer to one another, until, when they were sixteen, their rapport reached its moment of ultimate consummation. The opening of the sequence called for a montage of shots to establish their idyllic life and their happiness in doing things together—skiing, sailing, riding, swimming, tennis—all in joyous camaraderie. There was also a scene in which they look at photographs in a family album; these further establish their closeness, progressively, from their infancy to the present. The climactic love scene was to occur in a conventionally romantic setting; caught in the woods during a rainstorm, they take shelter in an abandoned cabin. Soaking wet and freezing, they build a fire; they take off their clothes to dry, wrapping themselves in two blankets they've found. The storm continues, and they have to spend the night in the cabin. It becomes increasingly cold, and they snuggle together for warmth beneath the blankets. Their embrace, which, in its childish beginning, was one simply of warmth, laughter, and deep affection, is gradually infused with sexuality. And they make love, in a pure and innocent way, on the blankets in the firelit cabin. In the subsequent lovemaking scenes, their passion would become much stronger, *growing*, as would their love and understanding, and the intensity of their attachment to each other. They would neither express, nor feel, any form of guilt or taboo-violation regarding their relationship, but they would be circumspect about it since they were aware of society's attitude. And because of this attitude, there would be one scene wherein each has just returned from making love to someone else, in an experimental attempt to at least soften the intensity of their involvement. However, it hasn't worked, and they fall into each other's arms and make love more passionately than ever. Thus, it ends in uncertainty as to what the future holds, and the last images in the sequence are of their lovemaking and their happiness together.

'Wow,' said Dave softly, when Boris had finished telling him, 'that's pretty far out, man ... I mean, like that's a *heavy line* ... that's a groove and a gas.'

'Have you ever had any, uh, experiences, or feelings like that?'

'You mean with Deb? Naw, not really—well, maybe some kid stuff, a long time ago, like looking through the bathroom window, that kind of thing. But I guess I was always too dumb maybe. Anyhow, we were usually away at different schools. I mean, it just never happened.'

'Well, how would you feel about doing it now?'

'You mean actually *balling* her? Deb?'

'Uh-huh.'

'Yeah, well, like wow, man, I mean, for one thing I don't know how that would go down with my old lady . . .'

'I didn't know you were married.'

'Yeah, well we decided it's not exactly the best PR right now, so we're just sort of cooling it—but the thing is, she's pretty uptight *in front* about Debbie, so the idea of my actually *balling* her might just snap her wig . . . you dig? Hey, rhyme-time! "*Her wig, you dig*"!'

'Well, we could tell her we used *inserts*—that the actual balling parts were somebody else.'

'Hmm,' he seemed dubious, but not really caring too much, 'yeah, that might work . . . anyway, she's been a pain in the ass lately.' He shrugged. 'Well, man, if it's cool with Deb, I'm ready.'

'But you're not particularly turned on by it . . .'

'Yeah, well, I mean it's like this, man, sex is not such a heavy groove for me any more—I'm into more like a *spiritual* bag, you dig? I mean, like I've been making some heavy trips, and, well, balling has gotten to be, you know, like kind of . . . "*irrelevant?*" Is that the word?'

'But you can stay off trips for a little while, can't you?'

Dave laughed. 'You mean like long enough to fuck my sister?'

'Well, yeah, but also to dig doing it.'

'Sure, man—I mean, if *she* can get it up for me, *I'll* stick it in.'

'Fair enough,' said B.

'Yeah, well, you know, like I'm not here to *rumble*, man, I'm here to *groove* . . . I mean, I dig all those heavy lines you've been laying down, and, well, you know, like I'm *loose*, you dig?'

'Beautiful,' said B.

Dr. Werner having advised that Angie have a day's rest, it was decided to begin the Dave and Debbie sequence the next morning.

Pert Debbie Roberts was America's perennial cute-as-a-button favorite teen-ager, who had, in fact, reached Hollywood by route of the coveted 'Miss American Teen' crown, and now was star of the TV series *The Girl Next Door*. This prime-time show—a classic in the 'Gosh-Golly-Gee Whiz' tradition—enjoyed a very favorable rating among older viewers, whereas, due to its canned laughter and never-land content, it was anathema to anyone under forty. Like Angela Sterling, Debbie was keen for a change of image. Ironically, however, despite her vast notoriety as a libertine and '*swinger extraordinaire*' in her personal life, she had acquired, during her two years as 'Barbie' (the Girl Next Door), a striking number of that character's inanely cute mannerisms and expressions, so that her remarks at the initial script conference with Boris, Tony, and Dave assumed a curious incongruity.

'Gosh,' she exclaimed in wide-eyed surprise, though not without interest, 'you mean he's really going to (gulp) *screw* me? *Davey?*'

'Big deal, huh, Sis?' Dave stretched lazily. 'We'd have to cool it with Trix though—might put her pretty uptight.'

'*Trix?* Good grief, what about *Mother?!?*'

'No, what we'd do,' Boris explained, 'we'd say it was *inserts*—I mean, the actual lovemaking shots—we'd say we used doubles there.'

She looked from one man to another, cute, puzzled: 'Well, can't we just *do* it that way?'

Boris shook his head. 'Somehow it doesn't have the same overall quality—it doesn't have the same . . . *aesthetic tone*. It seems false.'

'Also,' Tony added, 'with doubles, you can't *pan*—you have to cut away each time.'

'Dig?' asked her brother.

Still wide-eyed, she nodded at each of them to show understanding. 'I guess so. I mean Mother's going to have conniptions about this whole thing anyway . . . no matter *how* we do it.'

'Not when you get an *Oscar* for it, Debbie,' suggested Tone.

She clapped her hands, then gripped Dave's arm, beaming with delight. 'Oh, wouldn't that be just too *terrif!*'

So, by mid-morning they were shooting Debbie undressing ('First things first, eh, B.?' Tone had quipped) in the foreground, while her brother knelt, his back to camera (and to Debbie) building the fire.

'Gosh, even my *underclothes* are wet,' went the line, when she was down to her white panties and bra.

'Well, take 'em off,' he said, 'you don't want to catch *pneumonia*,' and, as he reached his hand over his shoulder behind him, he added teasingly, 'Don't worry, I won't look.'

'Silly,' she said, laughing, and handed him the small garments, which he held up in front of him for a second—first, the bra, stretched horizontally between the thumb and forefinger of each hand, and he gave a mock wolf-whistle; then, the panties, holding them the same way. 'Hey, you can see the fire right through them! Ha, bet those sure keep you warm, all right!'

'You *nut*,' she said, and laughed again, while he arranged them alongside her other clothes on the firescreen, and she enveloped herself in one of the blankets, and sat down beside him, shaking her hair loose and leaning toward the fire to dry it.

'Now, your turn,' he said, getting up to stand behind her and take off his clothes, handing them to her one at a time, while she accepted them, hand back over shoulder, just as he had done, then draped them across the other end of the fire-screen.

'Wow,' Tony whispered to Boris, even before Debbie stepped out of her panties, 'she must have one of the cutest asses in the industry.'

Boris nodded accord. 'Nice little knockers, too.'

'*Perfect* little knockers,' Tony agreed. 'You know anyone who's fucked her?'

223

Boris, squinting through his view-finder, muttered half-heartedly, 'Oh . . . one or two, I guess . . . maybe three.'

'Yeah, what'd they say?'

'Great,' said Boris.

'I'm hip it is,' said Tony, not taking his eyes off it. 'Did they say it was *freaky?*'

'*Freaky?*' Boris shrugged. 'No,' he said, absorbed in the view-finder still to his eye, 'just your average . . . *nice, wet, tight, hot, cheer-leading, baton-twirling, teen-age American pussy*. Ha, how does *that* grab you, Tone?'

'Wow,' said Tone, grooved by the image, 'can't beat that!'

However, while Boris and Tone were thus engaged in innocent badinage, sinister things were afoot in another quarter of the town—penthouse-time, Hotel Imperial—where the resourceful Lynx Letterman was presiding over an exclusive, audience-of-two-*soirée-cinégra-phique*—projecting color slides onto a screen in the darkened room . . . slides he maintained were single frames of 35-mm. motion-picture film, snipped from the work-print of Angela's sequence in *The Faces of Love*.

The audience was composed of C.D. and Les Harrison, and the slides were, in fact, exactly what Lynx had represented them to be, featuring, as they did, Angela in every conceivable situation—indeed, 'position'—of stardom compromise.

Old C.D. was sobbing quite openly, while the vindicated Les attempted to share the grief, tears streaming down his upturned face, one arm around his dad, occasionally gripping his shoulder, whimpering and wincing as he did, in some curious (perhaps due to his recent M-run) Pavlovian-like *reversal*, as though each grip of reassurance on dad's shoulder was an *injection* of recognition and security into his own. Finally the old man actually pulled away, as if wanting to do his thing alone—or, quite possibly, out of sheer annoyance.

In any case, when the lights went up, it was *Les*,

presumably anticipating an emotional finale from dad, and wishing to prolong their shared experience, who forced his own grief to a crescendo, burst into tears anew, and groped blindly for his father's shoulder, as though at last they would weep together and be the closer for it . . . or, at least in terms of corporate structure.

But the only effect it appeared to have on C.D. was one of embarrassment—an embarrassment which then seemed to call forth a certain inner strength, or dignity—*iron-in-the-soul* style—from the old man.

'Get hold of yourself, boy!' he admonished, shaking his son with one hand, wiping tears from his own cheek with the other. 'Do you really think that this . . . this little *nobody* . . . is going to make *one iota* of difference to the profit-and-loss sheet of Metropolitan Pictures?!? One year from now?!? Two at the most? With all the . . .' he fumbled a bit, clearly improvising, 'the . . . *new stuff* that's coming up —new *ideas*, new *material*, new *faces* . . . the era of the super-star is *over*, son . . . the economics of film-making today simply are *not* compatible with budget allocations of exorbitant fees for the actors.' He grasped his son's shoulder, Caesar style. 'It's a *responsibility*, . . . a *responsibility* we have to the *stockholders*.' And then, in a tender fatherly way, he handed him his handkerchief. 'Here, son,' he said softly.

'Thanks, Dad,' said Les, equally soft, touching the handkerchief gingerly to his eyes, then unfolding it and blowing his nose—an action which caused C.D. to grimace in annoyance. 'Goddamn it, boy, that's *one-hundred-year-old Irish linen!*' He snatched it from him. 'You just don't have any sense of *style*, that's the goddamn trouble with you!' He looked at the disarrayed handkerchief, shaking his head in concern, then crumpled it and stuffed it into his side coat-pocket.

'Sorry, Dad,' Les mumbled, eyes averted, going the full S-M route now.

The old man coughed and chortled, slapping Les on the back reassuringly. 'Well, what the Sam Hill, son—it's only

money. Just like that little *nobody, no-talent, no-heart, sleep-anywhere tramp of an extra, Angela Sterling* . . . only money.'
He wagged his head sadly, put his arm over his son's shoulder, and continued in tones of fatherly confidence, 'Well, that's *not* what makes this old world go around, my boy . . .' and he looked up to Lynx Letterman—he who had been sitting there, eyes without expression, waiting with reptile patience—'Right, Lynx? I mean, no offense, I'm sorry to have to say those things about the girl, I know you were very close, but—' He broke off, shrugged, eyes filling with tears again, 'What else can we do?'

Lynx coughed, cleared his throat, waited a second, and made his pitch: 'What you can do, Mr. Harrison, I'll tell you what you can do. You *and* your son—as vice-president in charge of production—what you *can* do, and what you *should* do, and *must* do . . . out of respect for the vast majority of Metropol *stockholders* who have *trusted* you, and who have put their *confidence* in you both—*you and your son*—what you must do now is *repay that confidence!* And by that I mean that we—that is to say, *you* and *Les*—have got to persuade *Angie to kill the picture* . . . I mean, I found out she hasn't *signed* yet . . . no contract . . . no release . . . *nothing*—just a lousy letter of agreement that wouldn't hold up in a Tijuana post office.'

As Lynx spoke, his listeners' eyes began to clear, then to harden, with remarkable similarity.

'If you show her these *pictures*,' he continued, indicating the slides in a gesture of distaste, 'and if you *tell* her that she will be absolutely *destroyed* by this film, that you will *personally* see to it that she *never works again*, and that what's more you are suing her for *twelve million dollars*. Well, if *you* do that, and then *I* say it's all true . . . I'll just bet my sweet ass she *walks*.'

24

'I've been thinking about that *"Profane"* sequence,' Tony was saying to Boris at lunch. 'You remember you mentioned "a nun and a gambler," or "a hooker and a priest"? Well, dig—suppose we got to the priest route ... but instead of a *hooker*, the chick is some kind of *nut*—I mean, not just *sexually*, but like *physically weird*, and he *still* wants to fuck her. But we don't know that yet, right? I mean, it could open in a very conventional way—church, Sunday morning, he's in the pulpit, doing his thing, she's third-row center, digging him over her hymn book—but *demurely*, because she's boss *respectable, wholesome, clean* ... knee-length dress, white gloves, Easter bonnet, beige pumps, seamless stockings, the full fifties schmear, right? Padded-bra and garter-belt time, right? Quarter pound of deodorant and six ounces of Listerine ... very *clean* woman ... "Mrs. Midwest Front Porch Swing," toast of the Great Silent Majority, queen of artifice. Okay, he's got eyes ... goes over to her place after church ... for a little "spiritual counseling," right? ... makes his move, shoots his best shot —I thought that might be a fun title, incidentally—*His Sunday Shot*, ha. Anyway, he gives her a big, wet, soul, tongue kiss—and, because she responds so warmly, he takes the liberty of forcing her hand down to grasp his divine joint, which he has had the presumption to expose during the soul kiss. Naturally, our heroine is plenty keen for some of this hot Presbyterian cock straight from the pulpit, but *not* before she has taught him the fundamental precepts of *existentialism*, you dig? So with "Preacher Malone"—I thought we might actually get Lips to play it—trousers off now, his rude donkey-cock extended grotesquely in front of him, chasing our heroine about the room, grabbing at her—and during this, by the way, there occurs what you might call a "running dialogue," right? Ha. Anyway, so she's telling him about the "historical irresponsibility of the Church," and how the "concept of *faith* has merely served as a convenient receptacle for Man wishing to shirk his own responsibilities to Man," and so on, you know, lay out the whole Jean-Paul store . . . and all the time she's telling him this, he's in what you might call "hot pursuit," trying to nail her, finally getting all her clothes off—you know, all the weird American middle-class *harness* stuff—so then he thinks he's got her, but on the next grab, part of her *body* comes off . . . like a wig, or a leg, or a breast—'

'It's *fantass*,' said B. 'And I know exactly who to play it.'

'I'm hip,' said Tone, 'but dig—so then it gets really *weird*, like *surrealistic*, where it turns out that *everything* about her is false. Even her *cunt* is false—she has a *false cunt*. So in other words, this gradual dismantling finally reduces her to *absolutely nothing*—like, in the end, there's *nothing REAL left of her to fuck*. So he puts back on his white collar—and his trousers—and goes home.'

'All a dream?'

'Maybe.'

'That's *heavy*, Tone.'

'Well, that's what you *pay* old Tone for, eh? Heh-heh.'

'Heavy . . . but not very *erotic*, Tone.'

'I thought you wanted some comic relief here.'

'Yeah, but . . . couldn't she suck his cock or something? I mean, aside from the funny parts?'

' "Suck his cock"!?! Christ, man, there's so much *cocksucking* going on already in the picture that it's liable to get blasted as some kind of weird *fag-cocksuck* film or something.'

'Okay, not suck his cock, but . . . *something*. I mean, we can't just suddenly do some kind of . . . *Three Stooges* bit right in the middle of the picture.'

Tone was irate. ' "*Three Stooges*"?!? Are you *kidding?*
That's *Beckett*, for Chrissake!'

'Okay, okay, but we've got to have *something* . . . less
esoteric . . . less *highbrow* . . . something people can relate to.'

'How about that "anal-tongue" bit you mentioned?'

'Hmm . . . wait, I know what we'll do—we'll let *her* think
of something when she gets here.'

'Beautiful.'

So they put in a call to Malibu, to the inimitable Teeny
Marie.

25

It was not until about an hour before wrap time—after a
great deal of hemming and hawing (and then only because
she couldn't bear being thought of as 'square')—that Debbie
had finally agreed to try the love scene with Dave, or at
least had agreed that they would get under the blankets
together, naked, and hold each other close . . . which they
did, and, after a bit of nervous giggling, tickling one another,
and kidding in general, they had just about settled down
enough to try a take.

'Well, Dave,' Boris asked, 'how does it feel?'

'Groovy,' said Dave.

'Debbie?'

'It feels *nice*,' she said, 'nice and warm,' and she snuggled
up a little closer.

'Well, I think the way it should happen,' Boris went on,
'is that after you lie there for a minute, embraced, and
you're no longer cold, you begin to feel, you know, sexually
aware of each other's presence—and so, Dave, you slowly
take the blanket off, to look at Debbie's body, which you've
never really done before—I mean like *deliberately*.'

'But isn't it supposed to be *cold* in the room?' the girl wanted to know, instinctively grasping at straws.

'Not anymore. Remember, the scene opens with you both asleep, under separate blankets ... the fire is very low, the room is cold—Dave wakes up, shivers, puts some more wood on the fire, sits in front of it, huddled in his blanket ... then *you* wake up and ask him what's wrong. "I'm freezing," he says. "So am I," you say. He moves closer, still shivering, a genuine chill, teeth chattering, that kind of thing, so you say "Maybe we should get under *both* blankets ... until the room is warmer." And that's what you do. I know it may be cheating a little, timewise, but we've got to lose blankets—I mean, we can't put the camera *under* the blankets. Dig?'

'Dig,' said Dave, and then to Debbie. 'Okay, Sis?'

'Well, gosh ...' she sighed, 'I guess so.'

'Everything's cool, Sis,' he went on, 'just stay loose,' and then to Boris, 'About how slow with the blanket, B.—like this?' And he moved it down, gradually uncovering her. '*Wow*, Sis,' he admitted softly, 'that *is* a pretty wild body you've got going. Yeah, I think I'm going to dig this.'

She giggled, grasping the top of the blanket just as it passed her navel, 'Well, you don't have to pull it down all the way *now!* I mean, they're not even shooting!'

'That's perfect, Dave,' said Boris, 'just take it a fraction slower—we'll get a little *tantalization time* going for us.'

'Dig,' said the young man.

'Mr. Adrian,' Debbie called, now demurely holding the blanket just below her chin, 'when we make the shot, do you think it would be possible to get just a *few* of these people off the set?'

Boris smiled. 'Somehow I *thought* you might get around to asking that. Yes, of course,' telling Fred the First to clear all but essential personnel from the set.

And it was just then that Angela arrived, looking very distraught indeed.

'I've got to talk to you,' she said, looking everywhere but at him, 'there's something I've got to tell you.'

Because they were nearly ready to shoot, his first impulse was to give her a momentary brush, but she appeared so seriously upset that he decided against it.

'Okay, let's go to my trailer,' he suggested, since that happened to be the place of privacy most convenient to the new set. 'You go on,' he added, 'I just have to speak to Tony for a second.' While she went ahead, he stopped by the set, and took Tony aside. 'Listen, I'm going to talk to Angie for a minute, she seems to be flipping out. But we've got to keep this thing going between Debbie and Dave—if we work it right, I think they'll actually *do* it—so why don't you go over the lines with them, try to get them excited, tell them about your own sister-fucking fantasies. Okay? Besides, it'll give you a few shots at Debbie's perfect cooze and knockers. Right?'

' "Full rehearsal," I'll tell them.'

'Well, as long as they don't actually *make* it—I mean, we've got to save that for the camera . . . it might be a *one-shot*. Ha.'

When he reached the trailer, he found Angela sitting on the edge of one of the chairs, hands clasped in her lap, staring down at the floor.

'What's wrong, Ange?'

'I can't be in the picture.'

Boris silently counted to *eight*—a number which he (sometimes) considered of occult significance. 'Why do you say that?'

'Well . . . Mr. Harrison, who's head of the studio, and his son, whose vice-president in charge of production, they're over here now, and so is my agent, Mr. Letterman . . . and they explained to me how it would destroy my career completely, and how I could never work again, ever, if I went through with it—and they showed me a bunch of stills from the picture, and I could see what they mean, how a lot of people might not understand that it was *art*—'

231

'*Stills?*' said Boris, frowning. 'What are you talking about?'

'You know, color slides—from some of the scenes we did.'

'Those dirty *bastards*,' he muttered, 'they must have bribed someone at the lab . . .'

'And then they told me that they were ready to sue me for twelve million dollars if I didn't do what they said—and I don't think I even *have* twelve million dollars. So you see, I just don't have any choice.'

Boris leaned back, staring at the ceiling without expression; then he took a deep breath, and slowly expelled it. 'Listen,' he said softly, 'you know what those people *are*, don't you?'

'Huh?' she looked at him as if he were obviously crazy. 'Are you *kidding?* Well, of *course* I know what they are!' She gave a snort of contempt. 'I bet I know them one *helluva* lot better than *you* do! C.D. is head of the studio, and Les is vice-president in char—'

'No, no, I mean what they *really* are. Angie, they're *parasites . . . leeches . . . vultures*. They *feed* on other people's talent . . . they're *merchants* . . . merchants of *crap*. They have no interest in *art* . . . or in *truth* . . . or in *beauty*—their notion of *beauty* doesn't go beyond a Vegas chorus line. They have one interest, Angie . . . *power. Power* through *money*. And that's it—that's how simple they are.'

She shook her head, like she might not have been listening. 'They told me not to come here, or talk to you any more . . . they told me you'd say all that—all those things you're saying right this minute, about *art* and so on. But they said it didn't make any difference, it's an *exploitation* film no matter how you slice it.'

Boris gave a short laugh. 'That's very funny. Tell me something, Angie . . . why do you think they've kept you doing those tits-and-ass movies all this time? Why do you think you're still known as the "queen of the tits-and-ass flicks"? Don't you understand? *They're* the ones who do

232

the "*exploiting*." Christ, Angie, I thought you wanted to *change* that image.'

She looked at him with a terrible frown. 'Oh yeah? Well, I got news for you . . .' What had begun as a merely defensive, almost apologetic attitude, was transforming—through the miraculous alchemy of guilt and adrenaline—into a cornered-cat viciousness: '. . . we talked about *that* part of it too—I mean, just how the hell is me getting *fucked*, on camera, by a bunch of . . . *stupid* . . . *dumb-ass* . . . *nigger extras going to help my image?!?*'

Boris sighed, and after a minute, he got up and walked to the door, where he stood looking down at his hand on the knob. 'Okay, Angie,' he finally said, 'I guess I was wrong about you . . . I thought you had . . .'—he broke off with a shrug—'well, never mind, I've got to get back to the set . . . so, you know, do whatever you have to.' He opened the door, and started to step out; then he turned and looked at her again. 'Maybe you're right,' he said, with a soft smile, 'about fucking "nigger extras"—maybe you should have stuck to seventeen-year-old "seconds".' And he left, closing the door behind him.

'Deb got too horny,' Dave jokingly explained, when he reached the set, and found them under separate blankets.

She squealed with delight. '*You're* the one who got too horny!'

'Listen, B.,' said Tony, 'we worked out a great scene. We actually ran through it—well, right up to the nitty-gritty part, and it's beautiful. Dig this: first, he uncovers her, looks at her body, then he touches it—you know, like "wondrously," first her face, then slowly moves his hand down . . . over her throat, her shoulder, her breast, the curve of her waist, her hip, along her thigh, moving to the back of it, behind the knee, along the calf . . . then slowly up again, stopping on cooze, and at the same time bringing his lips forward to her breast. Right? Okay, meanwhile, *she's* started moving *her* hand over *him*, beginning the same way, but beginning *after* he did, so by the time he gets back up to the cooze, she's arriving at his—pardon the expression, Debbie—*cock*, which by now, needless to say, is plenty erect.'

'You ain't just a' jivin'!' Dave interjected, and Debbie giggled and squirmed in her blanket.

'Now, dig,' Tony continued to Boris, 'all this is happening with no dialogue ... just exploring each other's body, with an innocent sense of wonder, not even kissing ... I think if we save the kiss for the climax—save the kiss until they're actually *coming* ... *together* ... it could be *fantastic*—it would really be a *kiss* then, wouldn't it? I mean, they've never *kissed* before—except, you know, brother and sister style, on the cheek, or lightly on the lips—so that when they finally do this full-on, open-mouth, lots-of-tongue, hot, wet, soul kiss, while they're *coming* ... well, *that* will be like the real taboo-breaker, the *kiss*, even more than the fuck. Dig?' He looked from one to the other.

'Gosh,' said Debbie.

'Heavy,' said Dave.

'Let's shoot it,' said Boris.

What had ensued was quite remarkable. Apparently, Tony's fantasy as to the intense sexual potential between siblings was not without certain psychological basis. The relationship (and the action) between Dave and Debbie progressed almost exactly as he always dreamed (and then written) it might. It was as though they were filming at the Masters-Johnson clinic—that is to say, an authentic love-making couple ... but, instead of *clinical*, it was *beautiful*—beautiful *people*, beautiful *lighting*, beautiful *photography* ... only the credibility of the sexual experience was the same—except, with Dave and Debbie, it had an *intensity* quite beyond anything previously documented.

For Dave, aside from whatever extraordinary psychic impact the relationship itself ('fucking his sister,' so to speak) may have had, the pure *sexual fact* of it—for some-

234

one coming off an extensive drug-and-celibacy trip—was like a child's rediscovery of a forgotten toy.

The first time he *came*, even though it was very dramatic, and obviously complete, he continued, hungrily, compulsively striving, as though he could never possibly get enough of it—while the fabulous Debbie held on, it seemed, for dear life—great eyes closed, wet red mouth open, not moaning or sighing, just sort of gulping and swallowing, as though coming with each breath—these being about one eighth of a second apart—with her perfect 'Miss All-American Teen' face transfixed by an unaltering expression of *nirvana toto*.

It was going so well that Boris decided to do a little overtime for a second take. There was a serious consideration at this point as to whether to reshoot the same scene, or to shoot it as though it were a different scene, one occurring later on in their relationship—in which case, certain variations could be introduced . . . different positions, and so on. While Boris and Tony were quietly discussing the pros and cons of doing a segment with Debbie on top—and Boris was suggesting that Tony might have ulterior motives, just wanting to observe Debbie's incredible derrière in motion—they both suddenly noticed Sid, standing with Morty near the stage door, acting very strangely, his clenched fist raised against his forehead, striking it from time to time as though to express some unspeakable grief.

'What's with him?' said Tony.

'Looks like he just got the news.'

'What news?'

'Angie . . . I think she's walking.'

Tony looked at him in bewilderment. 'What the fuck are you talking about?'

Boris shrugged. 'Well, that's what she said . . .' He sighed. 'The old man got to her . . . and Les . . . all of them.'

'Wow,' Tony shook his head, '. . . what about the stuff that's already been shot?'

Boris grimaced. 'I don't know, man. All I know is *I've* got a print of it. If *they* don't want to show it anywhere . . . well that's *their* problem.'

Tony shrugged. 'That's one way to look at it.' He continued to stare at Sid, who was now grasping Morty by the shoulders and shaking his own head as though in tears. 'Wow, dig Sid, he's really flipping out.'

Boris stared at him too. 'Yeah . . . Sid's very sensitive,' he said, as though his thoughts were elsewhere, '. . . about some things.' He looked back at the set, where Dave and Debbie lay propped on their elbows, talking quietly, and, he noticed, holding hands. 'Okay,' he said. 'I think they can probably make it again now. Maybe the best thing is to see how *they* feel about it. I mean, I'll tell them about your idea of her being on top, but maybe they'll want to do something else . . .'

'Get him to fuck her in the ass,' Tony suggested, 'we haven't done that yet.'

'Oh sure, we've got that with *Angie* . . . well, you know, an *insert*.'

'You mean, you *used* to have it with Angie—before she bolted . . . anyway, inserts aren't like the real thing, are they?'

'Hmm. Listen, why don't *you* go talk to Angie? Maybe you can get her to change her mind. No kidding, she might listen to you . . . tell her your story about C.D. and the corpse—maybe she'll decide he isn't such a swell guy after all.'

'Man, that isn't *my* story . . .' Tony sighed in annoyance, 'that really happened.'

'Yeah, well, tell her that . . . or anything else,' he turned to go back to the set. 'Use all your ploys, Sanders—tongue, finger, clit-manip, whatever is required. Okay?'

Tony shrugged. 'I'll give it a whirl.'

When Boris got back to the set, Dave and Debbie still under respective blankets, heads together, hands clasped, talking in hushed tones, he felt like an intruder; by this time, they were way out on a reminiscence excursion, into far-flung childhood, summer vacations when they were eight, measles when they were seven—the whole trip.

'Time to go to work, huh?' Dave asked, after a minute of Boris just standing there looking at them, then quickly added, with a pseudo-lewd grin, 'and "*nice* work if you can get it," huh B.?' causing Debbie to squeeze his hand and giggle.

'You *nut*,' she said affectionately—a line right out of the script, it was too weird. *Wow*, thought Boris, *talk about quick studies . . . psychodrama-time*, it was spooky.

'Now then,' he began, 'let me ask you this—what would you like to do next?'

Dave looked at Debbie, then back to Boris. 'I think we'd dig just rapping for a while.'

Boris smiled. 'Uh, yeah, well, I was thinking more in terms of the *picture* . . .'

'You mean like *balling* again?'

'Yeah . . . only different somehow—you know, to repre-sent another phase in the relationship . . . like a different time, a different place . . .'

'You got another set?'

'Well, we'll do the establishing shots later—this will all be *tight* . . . just the two of you, very close. We've already set up a *bed* . . . well, I mean, a bed is a bed, right? So this time it's a bed instead of the floor, it'll be like it's a different place.'

'Hey, did you dig I came *twice?*'

'It was beautiful,' said Boris.

'It was *fantastic*,' said Dave, with near manic enthusiasm, then looking at Debbie, 'Wasn't it *fantastic*, Sis?' while she, averting her eyes, blushing like a virgin bride, nodded happily.

'Uh, what would you think . . .' Boris began, by way of getting the show on the road—seeing as how they were set up, ready to shoot, and about thirty-two people standing around waiting—'what would you think of Debbie being on top for this one?'

Dave wagged and nodded his head, brows arching. 'Outta *sight*, man ... wow, yeah, that would be a ... groove, ha-ha, I almost said "ball," ' he nudged Debbie 'get it, Sis?'

'You *nut*' she giggled.

'Yeah man,' Dave went on to Boris, 'I mean like I'm hip it would be a boss trip ... and let's get a *mirror*, I really groove on a mirror with the chick on top—and so do a lot of chicks ... I mean, it's like *narcissusville*, you dig?' He turned to Debbie again, 'How about it, Sis, is that part of your bag—I mean, like can you *come* on top?'

She smirked self-consciously and gave him a playful elbow jab to the ribs, 'You silly-billy,' she chided in her anomalous 'Barbie' manner, '*I* can come on *card tricks!*'

'Too *much*, man,' said Dave, shaking his head and glowing with admiration. 'Where have you been all my life?'

'Beautiful,' said Boris,' let's, uh, shoot it.'

Within half an hour, they were pretty well set to shoot. Nicky had thrown up a new wall with a large mirror on it alongside the bed, the actors were adequately 'primed,' so to speak, and ready to go ... then, a last-minute hitch—certain ambivalence with Boris and Nicky as to whether the room should be a hotel room or a room at their home, the only difference, for the purpose of this shot, being the night stand next to the bed—a rather picayune consideration, but one which could have troublesome consequences later on.

'Where is Tony?' Boris demanded of Fred the First and then remembered he had sent him to see Angela, but even as he was remembering, he saw him, standing, arms folded, leaning back against one of the trailers, looking somewhat spaced. 'Hey, Tone,' Boris yelled, 'come here a minute,' and when he got there, Boris said: 'You look stoned ... never mind, do you think this scene will work better as a hotel room, or as a room in the chateau—like hers or his—just

238

for the night table, it's a question of *walnut* or *mahogany*, nothing else works in this shot, just the bed and the night table and the mirror, all very tight on them, we'll establish the room in detail later, I just want to get these *tight fuck-shots* while the kids are still cooking . . . well, what do you think, Tone—hotel or chateau? walnut or mahogany?'

'Something I should tell you, B.'

Boris frowned. 'Later, man, we've got to get this shot.'

'Too heavy for later.'

Boris looked around the set, where everything seemed to be hanging, precariously, in mid-air. He gave a short, humorless laugh. 'It sure as fuck *better* be heavy.'

'The heaviest, B.—it's about *Angie* . . . she did that famous Big Sleep routine. Know the one I mean? Made it, too.'

Boris just stared at him for a long minute, then shook his head and looked away. '*Oh Christ* . . .' he said softly.

'It must have been right after you left her—she must have gone straight to her trailer . . . and did it up.'

Boris nodded, staring at the floor, as though the camera of his mind was already turning. '*How?*'

'Well, a couple of ways—both pretty far-out—first, she ate a lot of the *lead-base makeup* she always used. Then . . . ready for this? . . . she *electrocuted* herself . . . with her *hair drier*, in the bathtub. Weird, huh?'

Boris sighed, closed his eyes, and let the sequence flow.

Tony took a swig from a styrofoam cup he was holding, and gave a dry laugh. '*Electrocution*—how about that? She must have committed some kind of . . . *capital offense.*'

What had happened—more or less—was that when Tony left to find Angela, he had encountered Sid, wailing and pounding his forehead in anguish—he, who upon seeing Tone, had pointed an accusing finger, cried, '*Murderer!*' and rushed away, as though the sight of him was abhorrent beyond enduring.

'What the fuck's with him?' Tony had demanded of

239

Morty Kanowitz, who, in turn, unfolded the gruesome tale.

As for Sid's curious behavior toward Tony, that was based on the simple misapprehension that Angie killed herself because of drugs, and that Tony was the one who had given the drugs to her.

Enhancing the personal trauma of it was the fact that it had been Sid himself who found her ... in the overflowing bath, dressed in her famous wrapper, the hair drier—a complex and heavy metal device from West Germany—over her head like a grotesque diving helmet, which when raised revealed the horror clown ... the lower part of her face, from nose to chin a multicolored smudge of the heavy red, white, and blue oil-paste makeup she had eaten—while scattered around the floor lay the crushed tubes, like so many spent rifle cartridges ... and beneath the dressing table an overflowing wastebasket with an empty carton at the very top, its lid dangling in a random way, inside out, and upside down, so that one would have to twist his head way around, just as Sid had done—to make out the words 'FOR LITTLE GIRL BLUE.'

'How long were you standing there?' Boris asked Tony, looking at him curiously.

'Not long,' he said, but said it in such a way it could have meant from two to twenty.

'Why did you wait to tell me?'

'I don't know ... I guess I thought you should get the shot first.'

Boris frowned. 'Then why *did* you tell me? I still don't have the shot.'

Tony shrugged. 'Well, I never said I was perfect.'

'Ha,' Boris snorted, then glanced back at the set where Dave and Debbie were waiting. 'Okay, we'll do just that—so cool it around Dave and Debbie till we get the shot.' He sighed, shaking his head. 'Wow,' he murmured, 'what a drag. Is she ... still in there?'

'I don't know. Sid wasn't sure how to handle it ...

because of the bad press. I think he's trying to get in touch with somebody on the Coast—Eddie Rhinebeck in studio publicity. I told him he ought to call the cops first.'

'Christ,' Boris muttered, in weary disgust. 'Well, come on, let's go see her.'

When they reached Angela's trailer, they were met by Lips Malone, dapper in pearl-gray pinstripe and shades.

'Is she still in there, Lips?' Boris asked.

Lips nodded, expressionless. 'Yeah.' In the past week Lips had acquired, aside from his new demeanor, a new mode of dress as well, remarkably like that of George Raft in the films of the forties—dark-shirt-and-white-silk-tie time —not without certain sinister connotations. Now, when he said 'Yeah,' Boris moved to go inside, and Lips detained him, grasping his arm with one heavy hand. 'Not yet, Mr. Adrian, you'll have to wait a few minutes.'

Boris jerked his arm out of the other's grip. 'What the fuck are you talking about?' he demanded.

Lips moved back a step, looking from one to the other. 'Mr. Harrison's with her—he's paying his last respects.'

Tony shook his head, '*Wow*,' he said softly.

'You'd better get out of the way, Lips,' said Boris, menacingly calm.

Lips repeated his previous move, stepping back slightly, looking from one to the other, as if calculating both their distance from him and their intentions toward him, but this time his right hand went up and just inside the left lapel of his jacket, and to the now quite obvious shoulder holster beneath it. 'I wouldn't do it if I was you. Mr. Adrian—no offense intended, but I got my orders—Mr. Harrison don't want to be disturbed.'

Boris was flabbergasted; disbelief vied with indignation. 'Why you . . . you fucking *moron!* Are you threatening me with a fucking *gun!?!*' At the same time, he made a tentative move forward, but was restrained by Tony.

'You call it what you want, Mr. Adrian,' Lips went on, 'I can't let you go in. Like I said, no offense intended, you always been decent with me, but I got my orders from Mr. Harrison himself.'

Boris scoffed. '*Mr. Harrison*, my ass, you're supposed to be working for *me!*'

'Well, the way I figure, Mr. Harrison is head of the studio, so it's like we're *all* working for him. Anyway I never crossed you on that other job—grabbing the kid, and so on—I never cracked to him about that.'

'Ha. You mean not yet!'

Lips shrugged. 'Okay, remember *you* said it, Mr. Adrian, not *me*.'

'You know what he's *doing* in there, don't you?' Tony asked.

'That I wouldn't know, Mr. Sanders,' said Lips, watching them both carefully. 'Like I said, Mr. Harrison is paying his last respects, and don't want to be disturbed—how he pays 'em is not my business.'

'*Jesus Christ* . . .' Boris began to seethe again, and Tony gripped his arm. 'Forget it, man,' he said softly, 'moron with gun, very bad combo. Besides you're going to blow the whole Dave and Debbie thing if you don't get back to the set. Come on, B.,' he pulled him gently, but firmly, 'let's go finish your movie.'

And Boris, shaking his head and muttering, allowed himself to be led away by Tone.

'No offense intended, Mr. Adrian,' Lips called out ingenuously behind them, 'like I said, I just been acting on orders . . . from above.'

242

FIUE

*He who laughs
has not yet tuned in
the 'Honky-Brinkly Report.'*

Anon.

1

Ever since Sid's initial ('hookers-in-the-hearse') confrontation with Cardinal von Kopf, the latter had conspired against him, with a determination increasingly diabolic—so that even as the last droplet of her brother's turbulent seed was being carefully dabbed from Debbie's perfect inner thigh by Helen Vrobel, and it was a wrap, even then was the outlandish Card mounting his *monstro coup*, in congress with certain eminent personages from the Eternal City itself. Only a brief deliberation had been required of their full committee meeting—or 'Council of the Exalted' as it was called—to 'unanimously condemn' the subject in question (namely, the film in progress, *The Faces of Love*) on the basis of Cardinal von Kopf's testimony. Their subsequent proclamation deemed the work to be 'a blasphemous outrage' and 'a social menace,' and when the civil authorities had failed to act upon their advice, they felt obliged to take matters into their own hands—'in God's great name, for the general weal, and upon the authority vested in this body by Our Lord and Savior, Jesus Christ.'

So it was that on a dark and starless Wednesday night, just at the hour of ten, the gross Cardinal Hans von Kopf—personally leading up a veritable *posse of Vatican toughs*—did, by stealth, ruse, bribery, and more than a little bit of roughhouse, manage to cross the moat of the chateau, to breach the great gate itself, and to stream into the maze of stone-vaulted corridors like a drug-frenzied horde of ravaging Goths, possessed with the zeal known only to those driven by a sense of absolute righteousness.

At one end of the maze was the cutting room where the film was edited, and at the other end was the projection room where it was shown; and, in fact, at this very time a screening was in progress—a rough assemblage, comprising a selection from the sequences already completed, was being presented to all principals involved in the production: Boris, Sid, Tony, Nicky, Lazlo, Morty, Lips, Phil Fraser, Helen Vrobel, and Dave and Debbie, who had stayed over to see it. In addition to this stellar gathering was the grotesque triumvirate: C.D., Les, and Lynx Letterman; the reason for their otherwise questionable presence was that, after due consideration, they had decided to support the production, instead of the dead star. This attitude, on the part of C.D. and Les, merely reflected what was now in the best interest of the studio and the stockholders and was quite understandable as such. The sustaining interest of the redoubtable Lynx Letterman, however, was another matter; to secure his full cooperation, PR-wise, they had, following a certain amount of negotiation, assigned to him Angie's share, which had been determined in this case to be two and a half points of the gross action.

Sid, despite his *professed*, indeed almost *professional*, cynicism, was somewhat shocked when he first learned of the matter-of-fact disposition of this part of Angie's estate, indeed of Angie herself. Mort Kanowitz, however, was quick to reassure him. 'Okay, Sid, so she was a great star—one thing is sure, no matter how you slice it, nobody makes money on a *stiff*. Right?'

Other than the aforementioned members of the audience, also in attendance was the almost legendary Tina Marie Holt—known to most as 'Teeny Marie,' she who had jetted in from the film capital that very day, and was now squealing with unbridled delight as she watched the exquisite Arabella writhing beneath the rude hunching embrace of big Sid Krassman.

'*Put the wood to her, Sid!*' she screeched. '*The uppity frog dyke!*'

It was at just about this moment that the first '*Hey. Rube!*' reverberated through the vaulted corridors from the direction of the cutting room, scene of the initial strike of the assault party's lead-element flying wedge. Sid, Morty, and Lips—in each of whose past was a phase of carnival life—were quick to harken to the alert, mouths dropping agape, eyes rolling back, 'What the fuck!?!' muttered almost in unison. Sid and Morty bolted from the projection room and into the corridor, while Lips, heeding the beat of a different drummer now, clocked C.D. once, then stepped into the shadow near the door, loosened his jacket, and allowed his fingers to trail lightly over the contour of the heat beneath.

In the corridor outside, pandemonium was rife, and the passageway echoed with strident shouts in German and Italian.

Two men from the cutting room, clothes torn and awry, looking very much under duress, suddenly rounded the corner.

Sid grabbed one of them as he tried to rush past. 'Eddie, what the hell's going on?' he demanded.

'Run for it!' the other shouted, 'it's the *goons!*' He wrenched free from Sid's grasp and bolted away.

Sid wheeled and forcibly detained the second man. 'Harry, what's he talking about? *What* goons, for Chrissake?'

'Beats me,' said Harry, breathing hard and looking over his shoulder. 'Eddie thinks it's a *union* beef . . . thinks they sent a goon squad to break up the joint . . . I don't know, look like straight *hoods* to me . . . Mafia types . . . some kind of shakedown operation, I guess.'

Sid couldn't believe it. 'You mean they . . . broke into the *cutting room?*'

Harry nodded. 'They grabbed the out-takes and the second dupe . . . I think they're after the *negative.*'

The last word hit Sid like a twisting knife. '*Holy Christ!*' He turned to Morty in panic, 'Morty, quick, *get the gorillas!*'

'Right!' said Mort, and disappeared into the maze, with Harry close behind.

At that instant, from the opposite direction, appeared an

advance echelon of the raiding party, intent upon storming the projection room, with Card at the fore.

'Holy Christ,' Sid muttered, 'I should of guessed it!' And he rushed out to confront him. 'Hold it, buster,' he said firmly, 'where do you think you're going?'

'*We have come for the film,*' the Cardinal replied, equally firm, and in an accent reminiscent of Eric von Stroheim.

Sid looked uneasily over his antagonist's shoulder to the ruffian band behind him, many of them dressed in what appeared to be the cloth of the Church.

'Now, step aside,' the Cardinal ordered, and he pointed a huge golden cross at Sid, flourishing it the way one might to banish a vampire—but because of its size, it was not without threat of a more tangible nature.

'Wait a minute,' said Sid, 'you mean that you ... you would take the law into your own hands like that?'

'Ha!' the Cardinal bellowed, 'and why not? *You did it with Eichmann!*'

'Huh?'

'Now get out of the way!' And he brandished his cross again.

'Go fuck yourself, buster!' Sid roared, gave him a straight shot to the snoz, whirled around, and darted into the projection room and up to the stage, switching on the lights as he did and yelling at the top of his voice, Paul Revere style: 'IT'S THE FUCKING WOPS! THEY'RE AFTER THE NEGATIVE!'

The 'audience' poured out into the corridor, just as the marauders finished ransacking the projection booth and emerged, carrying six cans of film, and trailing it behind them like a Les Harrison bandage.

What ensued was one of the most extraordinary occurrences in the history of group conflict. The maze of corridors was choked with scenes of strangeness as the Hollywood weirdies joined in pitched battle with the freaks from the Holy See, and the halls rang with a conglomeration of earthy obscenities and curious biblical anathema.

The tide of battle seemed to shift almost momentarily, usually related to the arrival of reinforcements for one faction or the other. First, it was the timely appearance of the grips and gaffers, led by Freddie the First and stout Morty himself, plunging into the melee to set the churchmen reeling. But this was soon more than counterbalanced by the advent of another of their own fanatic contingents, black robes flying.

Meanwhile, on the individual level, instances of prowess and valor were not uncommon. Nicky Sanchez and Teeny Marie worked together as a hard-hitting little team, confounding the adversary with their pesky windmill flurries of scratches and bites.

Sid and Mort used their street-fighting heritage to good advantage, laying about them with great gusto, constantly looking for some heavy object to wield. 'Where is *Lips* and that fucking *gun?!?*' Sid kept shouting. But Lips remained aloof, content to do his own thing, which now consisted of protecting old C.D.—one of the first to fall—and he managed this by dragging him to one side of the raging fray, and then merely waving the gun about—a smart .38 Police Special—whenever anyone ventured too near.

'Use the *gun*, Lips!' Sid had shouted once when things seemed at their most dire, 'For Chrissake, use the *gun!*'

'Fuck *you*, Krassman!' was the reply. 'I ain't risking no capital-punishment rap just to save *your* fat ass!'

Boris and Lazlo had immediately begun trying to film the sensational fracas, shooting with hand-held Arries while perched on pinnacles and turrets, or crouched in wall niches which used to accommodate great oil lamps and torches. Tony and Dave were also in one of the niches—but they weren't shooting, they were smoking pot and observing the scene.

'Beautiful,' Dave kept murmuring, nodding his head and beaming, '*beautiful.*'

Les Harrison, meanwhile, was in the midst of the action, behaving like a maniac. Fancying himself something of a karate expert, he was leaping about, attempting to deliver deadly chops and kicks all around him, to friend and foe alike—but his coordination had been so undone, to say nothing of his head, by the big M, that he consistently missed his target, and simply went flying about, more often than not doing certain injury to himself.

Lynx Letterman, acting half on hunch and half on cunning, had abandoned the rumble in its earliest stages, but did have the savvy to do so under the guise of 'getting Debbie and Helen Vrobel out of here!'

As for editor Philip Fraser, he was acquitting himself decently enough, in a straightfoward Marquis of Queensberry manner, when suddenly his eye caught a series of very familiar blue-striped film cans being lugged through the crowd.

'Oh my God,' he said, 'they've got the negative!'

The word ran through the film company like a lighted fuse. '*They've got the negative!*'

This served to rally them terrifically, with even Boris, Laz, and Tony joining the struggle, but the odds were hopeless. Just as Tony was going down under a torrent of blows, his glance chanced on Dave, still sitting where he had left him. 'You little cocksucker,' he yelled, 'get your ass down here and help us!'

But Dave only nodded and smiled beatifically, 'Everything's cool, baby,' and he pointed, in the distance, over their heads, where, lo and behold, there appeared a vast procession, like Caesar's legions, banners aloft, colors flying, 'FREE KIM AGNEW!' 'OEDIPUS SUCKS!' etc.

Thus, the balance of power had abruptly changed once more, as Sid saw all too clearly, when the fighting slowed to a stop. 'Okay, you ass-hole,' he shouted at the Cardinal, 'you're *finished!* These guys are with *us!*'

The Card appeared confounded indeed and muttered something to a man with a lean and hungry look nearby— his head-honcho, as it were—who, in turn, frowned his angry consternation, and spoke in rapid Italian to a young, bearded acolyte beside him; the latter nodded tersely and doffed his priestly raiment, leaving him in snug jockey shorts and T-shirt, whereupon they conferred again before the young man abruptly departed.

Sid, feeling no pain now, had watched this odd skit with curious bemusement—until he suddenly realized what was afoot. 'Look out!' he shouted, as he saw the young man emerge from his own group, and cautiously slip into the ranks of the unsuspecting Hippies, where he immediately seized a placard ('NIXON LIVES!?!'), and smashed it over the head of one of the rival Crazies—thereby instigating a full-scale fratricidal riot.

'No, no,' Sid kept crying, 'he's one of *them!*'

Tony had also seen it, and joined to sound the alarm: '*Provocateur! Provocateur!*'

But it was to no avail and, as the fighting grew heavier, the blue-striped film cans were obscured from view, and Sid slumped to the floor with a heavy heart indeed.

2

'Well,' Boris was saying, over one last drink on the veranda at the Imperial, 'at least now we know it *can* be done.'

'Ha,' Tone laughed bitterly, 'that's some fucking consolation.'

'We'll get our film back,' said Sid, toneless.

'Forget it,' said Boris, 'there are plenty of other things to do. I mean, we *did* it, that's the important thing—now, let's do something that *hasn't* been done.'

Tony nodded understanding—at the same time shaking his head, unable to accept it. 'I don't know,' he said wistfully, 'I really would have dug seeing the Dave and Debbie thing—' he broke off, laughed, as at himself. Then he sighed, and added, almost sadly: 'No, they had to destroy it—it would have put too many people out of work.'

'I been over it a hundred times,' said Sid, possessed by total morbidity since their loss. 'He practically *told* me what they done with the film. He said to me: "*You* did it to Eichmann!" So I ask myself, "Did what?" *Kidnap*, right? Eichmann was *kidnapped* and taken to *Israel!* Right? Okay, so where were *those* guys from? *Rome*, that's where! And that's where they got the film right now! Jeez,' he shook his head sadly, 'I still can't get over it—those guys being from *Rome*, and to do something so . . . *tricky*, and then that whole *provocateur* bit . . . well, that's pretty *sneaky* . . . and there I was all along thinking about Rome as being some- place where everything was on the up and up . . . and where guys like *Saint Peter* . . . *Saint Paul*, guys like that, come from—am I right, Tone?'

'Right, Sid,' said Tone, having a drink. 'Not to mention the late great Nick Machiavelli.'

'Yeah?' said Sid, with only sullen interest, 'who is that?'

'Oh . . .' Tony shrugged, 'one of the boys. Right, B.?'

Boris nodded. 'Yep,' and he looked over with a sad and weary smile. 'Just like the rest of us . . . right, Tone?'

'Right, B.' And Tone even toasted it.

New Protocol Mystery at Vatican

By JAMES H. MILLER
Special to *The New York Gazette*

VATICAN CITY, Dec. 13—In recent weeks, a number of *"privileged visitors"* to the Vatican—i.e., persons granted official access to, among other things, the balustrade overlooking the celebrated "inner-court"—have reported observing processions moving both toward and from the lower vault (*sanctum sanctorum*), also known as "Saint Anthony's Vault." A surprising number of such reports have originated with persons who are recognized authorities on Vatican protocol and processional observances, and who say that these "processions" do not correspond to any previously known or existing practices, as officially prescribed (in accordance with the *Dictus Regus Omnium*, etc.). None have felt it within their prerogative to speculate as to the meaning or purpose of these "processions" and they are unable to add much, if anything, of objective value to their descriptions of them. Having observed the phenomenon from a distance, little or nothing can be deduced from the demeanor of the processionals themselves—moving slowly, almost contemplatively, faces shadowed by their ceremonial hoods, expressions shrouded in a somber obscurity, pierced only on occasion by the glitter of their eyes.

WRAP

Bestselling Transatlantic Fiction in Panther Books

All-action Fiction from Panther

THE IPCRESS FILE	Len Deighton	35p	☐
AN EXPENSIVE PLACE TO DIE	Len Deighton	35p	☐
DECLARATIONS OF WAR	Len Deighton	35p	☐
A GAME FOR HEROES	James Graham*	35p	☐
THE WRATH OF GOD	James Graham*	40p	☐
THE KHUFRA RUN	James Graham*	35p	☐
THE SCARLATTI INHERITANCE	Robert Ludlum	40p	☐
THE OSTERMAN WEEKEND	Robert Ludlum	40p	☐
THE BERIA PAPERS	Alan Williams†	40p	☐
THE TALE OF THE LAZY DOG	Alan Williams†	35p	☐
THE PURITY LEAGUE	Alan Williams†	35p	☐
SNAKE WATER	Alan Williams†	35p	☐
LONG RUN SOUTH	Alan Williams†	30p	☐
BARBOUZE	Alan Williams†	30p	☐
FIGURES IN A LANDSCAPE	Barry England	40p	☐
THE TOUR	David Ely	40p	☐
THEIR MAN IN THE WHITE HOUSE	Tom Ardies	35p	☐
THIS SUITCASE IS GOING TO EXPLODE	Tom Ardies	35p	☐
COLD WAR IN A COUNTRY GARDEN	Lindsay Gutteridge	30p	☐
LORD TYGER	Philip José Farmer	50p	☐

*The author who 'makes Alistair Maclean look like a beginner' (*Sunday Express*)

†'The natural successor to Ian Fleming' (*Books & Bookmen*)

Bestselling British Fiction in Panther Books

GIRL, 20	Kingsley Amis	40p	☐
I WANT IT NOW	Kingsley Amis	35p	☐
THE GREEN MAN	Kingsley Amis	30p	☐
THE EXPERIMENT	Patrick Skene Catling	40p	☐
FREDDY HILL	Patrick Skene Catling	35p	☐
THE CATALOGUE	Patrick Skene Catling	35p	☐
THE SURROGATE	Patrick Skene Catling	45p	☐
THE EXTERMINATOR	Patrick Skene Catling	30p	☐
THE DECLINE OF THE WEST	David Caute	60p	☐
GEORGY GIRL	Margaret Forster	25p	☐
THE FRENCH LIEUTENANT'S WOMAN			
	John Fowles	50p	☐
MY FATHER IN HIS DIZZERBELL	Douglas Hayes	35p	☐
THE SHY YOUNG MAN	Douglas Hayes	40p	☐
THE WAR OF '39	Douglas Hayes	30p	☐
TOMORROW THE APRICOTS	Douglas Hayes	35p	☐
A PLAYER'S HIDE	Douglas Hayes	35p	☐
THE GOLDEN NOTEBOOK	Doris Lessing	90p	☐
BRIEFING FOR A DESCENT INTO HELL			
	Doris Lessing	40p	☐
A MAN AND TWO WOMEN	Doris Lessing	40p	☐
THE HABIT OF LOVING	Doris Lessing	50p	☐
FIVE	Doris Lessing	60p	☐
WINTER IN JULY	Doris Lessing	50p	☐
THE BLACK MADONNA	Doris Lessing	50p	☐

*All these books are available at your local bookshop or newsagent; or can be
ordered direct from the publisher. Just tick the titles you want and fill in the
form below.*

Name...

Address ....

....

Write to Panther Cash Sales, P.O. Box 11, Falmouth, Cornwall TR10 9EN
Please enclose remittance to the value of the cover price plus 10p postage
and packing for one book, 5p for each additional copy.
*Granada Publishing reserve the right to show new retail prices on covers,
which may differ from those previously advertised in the text or elsewhere.*